A MEDITERRANEAN MYSTERY

A MEDITERRANEAN MYSTERY

FRED E. WYNNE

WILDSIDE PRESS

TO
ANNIE E. JOHNSON
A tribute to old and lasting friendship

Originally published in 1923.
Published by Wildside Press LLC.
wildsidepress.com

INTRODUCTION

JOHN BETANCOURT

When I ran across *A Mediterranean Mystery*, the author—Fred E. Wynne—was completely unknown to me. Since I enjoy researching obscure authors, I immediately set about trying to discover who he was and what else he had written. Normal online sources proved to have little information. I turned up a second book, *Digby's Miracle*, from 1924: same rough time period, same byline, probably the same author. But it sounds like a mainstream book. Plus there were a bunch of medical articles with the same byline, as well as a letter about healthcare in a medical journal. And, of course, a spate of still-living people, who of course are highly unlikely to be the same person!

One bibliographic listing offered a birth date of 1870, but no death date. So I went to the Fictionmags website, which covers short story publications in magazines, and luckily they had a tad more information:

Wynne, [Dr.] Fred(erick) E(dward) (1870-1930)
Born in Kilkenny, Ireland; Medical Officer of Health, and Professor of Public Health, in Sheffield, and Honorary Pathologist at Royal Infirmary, Wigan.

So, that explains the medical articles and lack of other mystery novels—clearly he wrote a little fiction for his own amusement, while maintaining his day job as a doctor. Alas, he died at age 59, so he wasn't able to continue his fiction writing post-retirement. He did publish a handful of stories for British magazines, though, most of which appear to be mysteries. I will have to investigate them as well.

Enjoy Dr. Wynne's one foray into novel-length mystery writing.

CHAPTER 1

IN WHICH I ORDER CHAMPAGNE

I HATE the sight of those terra-cotta envelopes that telegrams come in. They have often announced ill news to me, and even in the absence of ill news they bear with them an atmosphere of emergency, suggestions of sudden action, which is always detestable to me.

Bates stood by while I read the ugly puce form which announced, had I known it, the opening of the curious chapter in my otherwise quiet life which I am now trying to recall and to record in its incredible details.

Incredible I mean from my then point of view, for a life and circumstances more remote from adventure than mine were then, it would be hard to imagine.

"There is no reply," I said to Bates, who stood awaiting instructions. "It's Mr. Edmund coming for a few nights. Tell Mrs. Rattray he will be here for dinner, and see that a room is ready."

"Yes, sir. And if he comes without luggage again?"

A little pang of a kind of jealousy shot through me.

It was two years since I or Bates had seen this ne'er-do-weel brother of mine, a year since I had even heard from him, and yet the circumstances of his coming without luggage was fresh in this man's mind, there was a lightening of his countenance at the mention of his name, and I knew well that my dinner would be one of unwonted luxury.

"He can wear some of my evening things, and give him pyjamas, and—one of your own razors, Bates."

I will not have other people using my razors or my fountain pen.

Edmund had always been an anxiety and an expense to me. He was now the only incalculable element left in my ordered life. But Bates seemed to be waiting for something, and it was as though a gleam of Edmund's endearing eyes, the crisp curl above his forehead, the flash of his teeth between merrily curved lips, were faintly reflected from the expectant look in Bates's face.

"Oh, and, Bates, you can bring up a bottle of the '47 port, and decant it carefully."

"Yes, sir. Anything else from the cellar?"

"No," I said. "I suppose there's whisky and claret in the dining-room."

"Very well, sir," said Bates reproachfully as he closed the door.

"No," I thought. "I'm hanged if I'm going to have champagne up. He'd only expect it every night, and he hasn't even written for a year. Now of course he's only coming for more money."

Then I rang the bell and Bates returned with suspicious alacrity. "You'd better bring up a bottle of the '93 Pommery," I said.

It was one of those delightful days in March when there is real daylight in the late afternoon, with a white gleam in the sky, and a wind keen enough to make possible the indoor joys of winter.

The aspect of my study in my Sussex vicarage was extraordinarily peaceful to me. When I looked over the top of my book, as I often did, I looked into the bright friendly eyes of a fire of mingled coal and drift-wood. When I turned my face half round to the left, as I also often did, I looked across the familiar, discreet harmonies of my room, to a long French window which framed a view of my lawn whose grass was now smooth-ing and renewing itself after the winter ruffling, of the red footpath and the border already gilt with crocuses; of stately trees beyond my frontier, their bare branches showing the faint pubescence of early spring. Among these trees were the red tiled roofs of the village, and beyond it the Channel, eye-grey today under the silver sky, and covered with rushing "white horses" whipped up by the steady East wind.

There was one long banner of smoke on the horizon, and a few miles from shore the brown sails of a couple of trawlers going close-hauled to windward with the flood-tide under them.

All this peacefulness and beauty was, I say, particularly grateful to me. It was like a gentle accompaniment to the book which I was reading with no less attention on account of this consciousness of my surroundings.

I had attended a clerical meeting in the morning and had, I suppose unwisely, said what I really thought about some of the topics under discus-sion.

Now I was re-reading with especial interest the chapter on "Persecu-tion" in Lecky's *Rise and Influence of Rationalism in Europe*. Only a few hours before I had seen among my colleagues the faces of the persecutor and the heresy-hunter, and I was undoubtedly heretical. It was difficult to reflect that if all this had happened but a short time ago, say in the time of my own great-great-grandfather, these same men would have rejoiced to see my live body roasted; that even now, given the power and the custom, the spirit of Calvin and Torquemada was not dead, that it still lit the eyes of living men who could believe in "Exclusive Salvation."

After the fret, the prejudice, and the spluttering of modern theological controversy there was healing for my soul in the calm intellectual austerity of Lecky.

Such were my preoccupations then. The academic interests of a scholarly, well-to-do, bachelor parson of forty-five with a hobby for homing pigeons.

I had just looked at the clock and realised with another glow of satisfaction that my afternoon tea was almost due, when my man Bates came in with this disturbing telegram.

This Edmund who was about to burst again into the quiet routine of my life was my only brother, now practically my only relative, and some fifteen years younger than myself. At the time of his first appearance in the world I was old enough to regard the news of his arrival as an indiscretion on the part of my parents. My father was a younger son of our old and once-distinguished Irish family. He was one of those soldiers who are always doing the hard rough work of the Empire and seeing the other men in the comfortable positions getting the "Honours and Rewards." I was born in India, and thanks to my mother's moderate fortune had been sent home in childhood to receive an expensive and perfectly respectable education.

At the time of Edmund's birth my father was at home, railing at the Indian Government and the War Office, earning, I fear, the reputation of a bore with a grievance in the Service Clubs, and certainly blasting any prospects of a further career he might have had, by his frank and perfectly just criticism of important persons.

I was at Wellington, destined for Sandhurst and the Army, for in spite of my father's atrocious experiences it never occurred to either of us that the world held any other career for me.

Looking back I don't think I really had any desire to be a soldier or knew at all what was implied in it. It just seemed inevitable, and I suppose I had up to then as much part in shaping my destinies as most people. I suppose that is how the ranks of the pawn-broking, cheese-mongering, grave-digging, and other apparently undesirable callings are kept filled.

But I knew enough to resent quite definitely the halving of my patrimony with this younger brother, concerning whose intrusion I had been in no way consulted.

I bitterly resented also the continued illness of my mother after this event.

During the greater part of my short life, which then seemed so long, she had been but a memory of infancy, repainted during one long summer when she had been home, and then her gracious, lovely presence had utterly outshone even the ideal of memory.

I had for her a boy's romantic devotion, and her death when the child was a year old and I almost a man, overwhelmed me with the force of a man's passionate grief abrading the exquisitely tender sensorium of a child.

And then the baby Edmund began to grow like her. From the first his eyes and mouth were hers. As he learned to speak he spoke with her voice, and innumerable little gestures reminded me of her. This was my first solace; and my early, selfish, boyish resentment died down and warmed into something else, transmuted by grief into the second great attachment of my adolescence.

Nothing could quite kill this, and I suppose that is why, at forty-five, I ordered the champagne for him.

Edmund was of course intended for the Navy, and as he grew older it seemed as if this were Nature's arrangement as well as the family's. There was no mere acquiescence in this case, as in mine.

But all these family dispositions were shattered just about the time I should have entered Sandhurst.

The whole of my mother's property consisted of her interest in certain estates in the Straits Settlements, and by some mysterious fluctuation of trade these suddenly became almost valueless. Relying on the stability of this property my father had invested the whole of his patrimony in an annuity, so that the family might live with more dignity during his and her lifetime.

With this we still could make ends meet, and even overlap, while he lived. But at his death there would be only a pittance for Edmund and myself. It would be utterly impossible for either of us to maintain the family tradition in the Services.

For a youth in my position it was considered that there was only one respectable alternative—the Church.

It was agreed by everyone, including myself, that I had not sufficient brains for the Bar. We were that simple kind of folk that really believe that a high order of intellect is necessary for success at the Bar. I am told that this carefully fostered superstition is not yet quite dead. I was accordingly entered at one of the less expensive colleges at Oxford, where I followed all the fashions, social, mental and moral; acquired the usual affectations; had my mind rendered as far as possible inaccessible to ideas; and otherwise enjoyed the advantages of what is called a "University Education."

It was the fashion then for superior persons to be patronisingly enthusiastic about what they called the "Working Man." I accordingly obtained a curacy in an extremely unpleasant industrial district, and entered Holy Orders without so much as suspecting that I had a mind or a character of my own.

From the "Working Man" I learned a little about the technique of pigeon flying and breeding. This information has been invaluable to me ever since. It has provided me with one of the principal interests in my life, and even a little very precious distinction, when one of my birds came home fourth in a great cross-channel event. I also learned that the "Working Man" has no use whatever for gentlemanly young curates from Oxford, or their quaint little fistful of prejudices. I had the good sense to get out of his way as soon as I could and begin my education.

In the meantime Edmund had developed on rather startling lines. Two preparatory schools had refused to keep him after a single term. The first on the grounds that he had "corrupted the entire establishment," the second because he was "destitute of the moral faculty." My father said the case was much more serious, that "he had not the instincts of a gentleman."

My father thrashed him well and hard. When this was over Edmund said, "I'm afraid, daddy, this hurts you much more than it does me."

Then my father consulted a doctor who said that "a certain insensibility to pain was a frequent accompaniment of the criminal diathesis." He recommended a low diet and bromides. Edmund promptly broke out in spots. Thus he got his way, which was to enter the mercantile marine, as the Navy was debarred by circumstance.

This was grievous to my father's old-fashioned prejudices, but anything was better than living with an insoluble problem with whom everyone fell in love.

The reports received from the training ship went far to reconcile him. These invariably described Edmund as "obedient and keen."

I am always glad to reflect that my poor father's anxiety and perplexity about this well-beloved child were thus allayed before he very unexpectedly died, and Edmund and I were left alone as regards relatives.

For of our cousins of the senior branch in Ireland we knew hardly anything. They wrote kindly and respectfully about my father, but did not offer to come to the funeral.

Shortly after this Edmund went to sea as a gentleman apprentice. He was away some five months and returned "in irons." I learned that he had broached cargo in order to obtain extra rum for his mess. He explained to me that "everybody was in it, and a fellow couldn't stand out. I should have been horribly ragged if I had, and it would have been a damned unsporting thing to do. We drew lots for who was to get the stuff, and of course it fell to me. Just the damned family luck. I didn't want the beastly stuff myself, for the simple reason that I don't drink rum—anything else you like, but not rum. It makes your breath smell beastly."

I was convinced that his tale was true and felt that on the whole he had behaved well.

Of course one could not expect the magistrate to take the same view. This old gentleman enjoyed himself tremendously with such an unusual text to preach about. However, when he had worked off the last of his platitudes, he announced that he had decided to give Edmund the benefit of the First Offender's Act. He said he was influenced largely by the fact of the punishment already undergone by the prisoner through his having come home "in irons." I believe the poor old thing imagined that this expression involved actual fetters.

As a matter of fact Edmund's colleagues and the cook had combined to ensure his having a fairly comfortable time. He said himself "they didn't even get ratty about my having no work."

So Edmund left the Court not without a stain on his character, and saddled with certain responsibilities as to reporting to the police which he described in terms so blasphemous that even to hear him made me feel unfrocked, like Stevenson's maiden lady when she overheard the Jongleurs' repartee.

Of course Edmund's indentures were cancelled, and the problem of his future became to me a very anxious one.

It did not at all worry Edmund. He regarded the world as his oyster.

Shortly before this catastrophe I had been presented to a small "living" in Warwickshire by one of our distant and grandiose relatives who had the iniquitous right of advowson. I took Edmund down there in order that we might "discuss the situation."

My parlour-maid at once fell in love with him, and he trod on one of the best pigeons in my modest loft.

I pointed out that our joint income, including my stipend, was likely to be less than £400 a year.

Edmund said that seemed a good lot for two unmarried blokes.

As his own share was less than £50, I thought this was cool.

"But you can't stop on here indefinitely doing nothing."

"No," he agreed, "not indefinitely. I think there's just time for a cigarette before dinner."

It was impossible to get him to talk seriously about the future. When I tried I was always whirled away on the wings of his stories of places he had seen and men he had met. He talked so vividly and had so fully the artist trick of setting a character before one, in the round and alive in a sentence, that I once suggested writing as a possible career. His whole being radiated scorn.

"Quill-driving be damned," he said. "Even if I knew how to do it, I'm not the sort of man. I'm the sort of man, at least I shall lead the sort of life, for other people to write about."

I was actually, without consulting him, humbling myself to try a jerk at the strings of the "Family Influence" on his behalf, when he disappeared.

After three days he wrote:

"DEAR OLD MAN,—I'm back to the sea, so no need to worry. I've got just the chance I wanted, a first-rate sailing-ship wanting another deck-hand. I made a lucky purchase of a very drunken old sailor-man's papers. No questions were asked as they were short of hands, and I soon convinced them I knew my job. Naturally I have dropped the family name *pro tem.* and won't be sporting our coat-of-arms at present. I've sent a line to Scotland Yard to tell them I've got a nice opening in the haberdashery line in the Midlands, and so won't be looking them up for a bit. I'll send you a name and address to write to as soon as there is any chance of knowing a port of call in advance. Tell Louisa not to fret too much, and I'll try to bring you home a nice parrot instead of the pigeon I damaged. This time I'm going to be a real good, sensible boy, and get on and all the rest of it. Honestly, dry land seems to burn the soles of my feet after a few days.

"Very many thanks to you for all you've done. This is bound to be a long trip, and though I mayn't see you again for a year or two, you may be sure of my real honest love. I shall make a bee line for your place whenever I do come home."

This parting was a wrench to me, and my home seemed very dull and miserable for a time. I had had my second sentimental tragedy, for I had loved, and for a short time had been happy in my love. It had all ended in disillusion and suffering for me, and again Edmund had been my solace. Until he had gone I did not know how much I was dependent on him.

Nevertheless I had again the feeling that he had behaved well. The incident of the papers purchased from the drunken sailor troubled my conscience a little, but I really scarcely knew what was involved in this, or to what extent it might have been a fair bargain. I trusted Edmund not to have done anything mean, and his sailing under a false name was to me nothing but the breach of a social convention. I had come to look upon most conventions as things made for the guidance of fools, to be disregarded by sensible men as soon as they became inconvenient.

I know it may be argued that this theory of mine is exactly that of the criminal. It is; but the criminal is only a fool with some independence of judgment—an exception.

The majority of fools walk between the clipped hedges. The wise minority wanders in safety and at large, being careful that the fools do not witness their excursions. We have our own boundaries which we do not transgress.

In the meantime the deaths of two of our Irish cousins from diphtheria had placed me quite near succession to the entailed portion of the family estate, but the present incumbent being a young vigorous man about to marry an heiress, I had never regarded the possibility of my inheriting.

It was only a few months after Edmund's departure that this youth went fishing in waders when he should have been in bed, and died very suddenly of appendicitis. I was amazed and rather horrified to find myself an Irish landlord.

I resigned my living and went over to Ireland, but neither the place nor the prospect of that life attracted me. I did not understand it, and felt a stranger and usurper. Everything was in the hands of a most capable firm of land-agents in Dublin.

There was a revenue that to me represented great wealth.

The place, though very large, could easily be let for the fishing and shooting. I deliberately ran away, and became that accursed thing—an absentee landlord. I salved my conscience by insisting on a policy of foolish generosity to my tenants and found myself equally abused by the Press of all parties in Ireland.

After some rather distracted wanderings I settled down in the Sussex vicarage in which this chapter opens. My researches in Byzantine history which shared my energies with pigeon flying had attracted a little attention from some of the learned, and thus I had met the Bishop at the Athenæum. He was patron of my present living, and as no clergyman in his diocese could afford the upkeep of the large and beautiful vicarage to which a stipend of £200 a year was attached, he gladly offered it to me and I as gladly accepted it.

I had no qualms of conscience, since I was going to give the Church more than I received from her in the way of money; I liked the work of a country parson, and believed I could be helpful to a few fellow human beings. As to doctrine, that came within my category of conventions. I had acted in good faith at the time I took my ordination vows, and if I thought I had grown wiser since, there was no need to make a fuss about it. I wanted no one to believe or disbelieve as I did, but I did want to encourage people to behave well. I had many of my father's old-fashioned prejudices, and honestly believed it to be a good thing that the Church as well as the Army should be officered as far as possible by gentlemen.

Thus the years passed very placidly for me. I and my house were in the capable charge of Bates and Mrs. Rattray, my housekeeper and cook, one of the best and wisest women I have ever met. Other servants came and went at her discretion, but my household affairs seemed always to run on ball-bearings, and Bates tempered for me the tyranny of the gardener and the coachman.

I acquired four different reputations.

As the breeder of "Amaryllis" who came home fourth in the great cross-channel race already mentioned, my name was familiar in every colliery and public-house in the north of England.

Among a select circle of the learned I was known as a conscientious and critical student of an obscure period of history.

In my parish I was generally esteemed as a kindly and generous priest and friend.

But by my clerical colleagues I was distrusted. If I was only suspected of heresy, I was positively known to be a trimmer in the vital matter of Eastward Position! When I officiated in other people's churches I always adopted the position and methods to which the congregation were accustomed. Thus both parties united in calling me "Mr. Facing-both-ways," and a certain very earnest Evangelical once said quite rude things about "Laodiceans."

This buzzing in my ears was almost my only worry, as Edmund was my only anxiety.

His first ship was burned in the Canton River, and he was landed penniless. He got a cable sent to me by the British Consul. Instead of sending what he asked for I cabled £250 and an urgent message to return.

I waited in vain for his arrival, eager to share with him all the comfort that had come into my life. Instead I got a letter in reply to one I had written on chance of his start being delayed. He congratulated me on my good fortune: had gone up country and invested two hundred of my good pounds in some wild-goose land speculation. All that was wanted to make the money bring forth an hundredfold was another thousand.

It was curious to me that I resented the loss of this £250 much more than I should have done when I was a poor man. I knew that this was the effect of possessing money on ordinary men, but I suppose no man expects to find himself reacting after the manner of his kind.

I was angry and sent another £50 and a peremptory message. Then I was sorry. I could see Edmund cashing the draft and shying from the insult like a young horse from the unexpected. I would have given the thousand to have him back.

But would not the thousand have kept him there until he lost it in its turn?

I heard no more and settled back as comfortably as possible into my groove. But for the first time I felt Edmund had not behaved well, a film formed on the surface of my warm love for him, and I knew there was anger towards myself in his heart.

Nearly two years passed during which he wrote three times when he wanted money—paltry sums which I loathed sending, but I could not trust him with a larger amount, though God knows I was willing to share my all with him, if he would only spend it and live on it.

Then he had come, announced by wire from Southampton.

He came in his fo'c'sle kit, with three sovereigns and some shillings which he called his "savings." But he brought the promised parrot in a gilded cage, and a costly offering of Chinese silk for Louisa, who had long ago vanished into the limbo which awaits parlour vestals disapproved of by Mrs. Rattray.

I admit I was a little nervous about the effect of his arrival and appearance on the arbiters of my household, but in twenty-four hours they were all his slaves. He talked to Bates as to a fellow man without any spurious bridging of the fixed gulf, and presented him with a strange exotic pipe. The Chinese silks destined for Louisa he gave to Mrs. Rattray, and I overheard him telling the entranced lady that he had brought them home for her in gratitude for her care of myself, about which he said I wrote so constantly. Thus I was made as it were accessory to his falsehoods and a partaker in the benefit of them.

Most amazing of all I found him plucking fruit I would not have dared to touch while he told sea-tales to the completely subjugated gardener.

To me he was delightful as ever. There was all his boyish affection, but that film was there, and I was aware of the spell he exercised as something to be resisted in his own interest. We never spoke of my refusal to send the thousand, but the memory of it was there between us.

He was then only twenty-three, but his aspect and manner of a fully equipped man of the world, of vigour and competence to subdue circumstances to his will, made him seem older. It justified a certain humorous treatment of myself as a kind of "dear old thing." I had to brace myself to keep my head.

It was not until the third evening that I fairly got the talk on to his own affairs and prospects.

I unfolded a scheme I had for settling him in the family estate as my representative. I explained my own coward flight and my desire, that notwithstanding that, the name should not lapse.

"In any case," I argued, "your son, if you ever have one, will inherit. I shall not marry."

"Everybody thinks that," he objected.

"We won't discuss it," I said, "but in my case there are reasons why you may take it as definite."

He looked up and saw at once that this was final.

"I'm sorry," he said, "very sorry, old man. But even for the sake of a possible Davoren of the next generation, I can't accept your offer."

"Why?"

"To begin with it's too generous."

"It's my desire—for my own sake."

"In any case I'm not the man for the job. I couldn't do it any more than you could yourself. Fancy me a country gentleman! M.F.H. I suppose, and I can't even ride! I should start comic and become pathetic. I'm only a sort of ticket o' leave man still, and they'd want to make me a magistrate!"

I disagreed with him, but saw that argument was useless and abandoned this favourite project with regret.

"Have you any plan yourself?" I asked.

"Well, you see, it's the old story. Dry land burns my feet."

"But you can't go on always—before the mast."

"No. I can take my master's certificate."

This sounded pleasantly practical to me, and I was surprised and gratified to learn that he had mastered the theoretical side of navigation and could, as he said, "pass the old Board of Trade exams, with one hand tied behind him."

I encouraged the notion and told him I had no doubt of getting the old trouble with the police cancelled by some of my influential friends on the grounds of lapse of time, youthful indiscretion and subsequent good behaviour.

He laughed at the last clause in a way that made me anxious.

"Well," he said, "they know nothing about me over here."

"Then you can go to sea in your own name and in a decent capacity."

"Yes," he drawled satirically, "as Third Officer on a P. & O. I suppose, showing ladies round the ship, putting on a boiled shirt and company manners for dinner. No. I'm afraid I should be no better at that than the squire business."

"But there must be a start of some sort."

"Not that sort. You people who stop at home see life as if it was half a dozen sets of railway lines, and a man must run on one or the other. It isn't like that at all. If a man just dives in as he would into the sea, he can swim, he can live. There's always something to eat. Making money is only the stake on the game, but the game is played for its own sake. All the duffers are losers, and if you're not a duffer you win. Then you can come out of it and be as respectable as you like. You will at least have your own memories to live on."

"It's a bit vague," I said, deliberately unmoved by his eloquence.

"To be precise, then, my game is going to be trade. When I've got my master's certificate I mean to be master and part owner of a little trading brigantine out East. I've studied the thing and I know the business. It's the life I like and understand, and there's pots of money in it when you know the ropes, and the right people. I'm not talking any story-book rot. There are commodities out there that you can trade best in in small boats. Little cargoes of high value. Things people know nothing about at home."

"It all means capital, doesn't it?"

"Oh, of course one must have some capital, very little to start. To people in the know it's a first-rate investment."

I said no more, and Edmund knew I meant to refuse to find the money for him. I can understand better now how exasperating I must have seemed. A country parson wrapping himself in a cloak of ignorance and taking it for superior wisdom!

However, he kept his temper perfectly, but this little root of bitterness between us grew and swelled.

He stopped with me during the weeks it took to obtain his certificate and satisfy the legal authorities of his having purged his early offence. Then he signed on as second officer on board an East-bound tramp. Beyond his necessary expenses and £50, for which he insisted on giving me an IOU, he would take nothing from me.

I know nothing of his Odyssey during the next two years, except that he told me that through friends in Hong-Kong he had secured a small interest in a trading venture and had both made and lost money. But he came home as poor as he went, though fuller than ever of confidence. As gay hearted at twenty-five as he had been at eighteen and delightful as ever to look upon.

I had good news for him. During his absence there had been an opportunity of realising the remnant of my mother's estate, and acting under a Power of Attorney I had from him I had sold out on his behalf as well as my own.

There was thus a sum of nearly £2,000 awaiting Edmund. Had I known why the property came to have a value at all, and held on until the "Rubber Boom" developed, it would have been nearer £10,000. As it was, others made this money. But to do Edmund justice, he never reproached me with this.

He went back to the East with his fortune, his high spirits, and his confidence.

He wrote twice at long intervals, each time wanting money. He explained that this was for necessary current expenses, not for speculation; that his capital was practically intact but locked up in trade. Freights and markets had gone against him every time, but it was only a matter of holding on. He was bound to win out all right.

I seemed to see a wistful eye and a trembling lip in the letters, and I hated the thought of Edmund beaten. I think I wanted him to prove me wrong to myself. And yet the sending of the money was oddly annoying, though I neither missed it nor grudged it. It somehow thickened that film on our affections.

Thus as I have said for over a year I had heard nothing until this telegram arrived.

I trust I have explained my reluctance to order the champagne, and my final capitulation to Bates's reproachful eye.

CHAPTER 2

THE BRANDY HOLE

EDMUND'S appearance on arrival was a surprise.

Instead of the fo'c'sle kit, or the uniform of a needy officer of the mercantile marine, which had disfigured his previous appearances, he came arrayed in blue serge. He wore a suit designed by a tailor with a soul for his art, somehow suggesting an association with the sea in lines that everywhere emphasised the grace and strength of his figure, while conforming to the strictest tradition of Savile Row. Everything about him was in keeping. His luggage, that great index of a man's prosperity, was of the solidest and richest leather, not too new, and with the exquisite surface and the rich tone that leather acquires under the hands of a first-rate servant.

I had never seen Edmund like this. His air of distinction disconcerted me. It made me proud of him, but shy also. This was such a new, strange Edmund. And yet just the same in his warm affection.

His presence blew away all the mists of distrust and resentment as though they were a miasma of my own creation, the remembrance of which shamed me to a feeling of meanness. I felt paltry in my own eyes.

I remembered what he had said of life, and felt myself an empty wagon on a side-track.

A queer shudder of apprehension went down my spine at the thought that he had but to couple me to his motive force and I would be a helpless thing to be dragged behind him.

Then I bethought me I had got the metaphor wrong. I would be on a track no longer, but in tow to him on the high seas of life—a thing terrifying to a middle-aged parson who had long ago found a backwater and bobbed at anchor in it. All these ideas, unformulated, passed through my mind in the fuss of his arrival and our greetings.

At dinner he made merry over the pretentiousness of the wine.

"Confess, now, you would not have had champagne up for a poor devil of a deck-hand!"

"I wouldn't have had it in any case. It was Bates insisted."

"Pardon me, sir," said Bates.

Bates had so got into the habit of talking to me during my usual solitary meals, that he committed the unpardonable indiscretion in a servant of having ears and a voice. It was plain he did not regard Edmund as "company."

"Well you didn't actually say anything," I admitted in justice to him.

Edmund laughed, evidently a little triumphant at the devotion of Bates. He insisted on his bringing another glass and pledging him.

Informal as the occasion was, Bates was a little self-conscious at this.

"My best respects, sir," he said as he lifted the glass.

I watched Edmund, wondering what was the new expression in his face that somehow dissatisfied me.

His experiences, whatever they were, had made little change in him. His charm was undiminished, perhaps increased. But there was some change that would have eluded anyone less intimate than myself.

"A portrait painter would catch it," I thought, seeking for the word to clarify my impression.

As he nodded over his glass to Bates, it came to me.

"Surrender!" I almost spoke it.

What could he have surrendered? Something that had been precious I was certain.

All our talk was of trivial things at home as though by mutual avoidance of any discussion of his adventures; we were dominated by the fencing shyness that comes over men, however intimate, when a discussion of importance is inevitable between them.

There was a silence as we tasted the first glass of the precious port, I wondering if he would say that it had passed its prime.

Then, as though from beneath the table, came a sound, to me familiar and somehow pleasant in its way, but puzzling, even disconcerting to strangers: the distant, muffled ring of iron upon iron. It was the unmistakable thud of a blacksmith's hammer on soft red iron followed by the clear taps on the cold resonant anvil, repeated in regular rhythm.

"What the deuce is that?" asked Edmund, listening.

"They're working late at the smithy."

"Is there a new smithy?"

"As a matter of fact it's a very old one. But, of course, it was closed when you were here before. It's been going about a year now. I've got quite accustomed to the sound. In fact it's company sometimes."

"But the old smithy was right down near the beach?"

"It's there still, but it's not 400 yards in a straight line from here. Our hearing the sound is because it is built over an old passage or tunnel which used to open into the cellar under this room. It is said to connect with an opening in the cliff over the beach. It's a relic of the old smuggling days. We are rather proud of it."

"I should say it looks a bit fishy for some of your reverend predecessors."

"Fortunately for the credit of the Church this was not always the vicarage. I believe it was the Dower-house of the Manor, and very likely some dear old dowagers eked out their jointures by a little 'free-trading.' Shall we have coffee in the study?"

"Wait a bit," said Edmund, "I'm rather fascinated by this noise. I suppose you have explored the passage?"

"No. I've opened the old door in the cellar and gone down the steps leading into it. But I hate underground places. I fear I suffer from what the doctors call claustro-phobia."

"Is that cob-webs?"

"Well, mental cob-webs I suppose! Anyhow, smugglers' passages are a bit out of my line. But I have found the opening in the cliff, at least I think so. It's cunningly hidden from the front by a mass of chalk. I was led to it by what I suppose was the smugglers' old track. One of my birds landed exhausted on the cliff after a cross-channel flight, and I had to rescue him."

"Well, I should have been right down that passage and out at the other end if I'd been you. Any objection to my exploring it tomorrow with Bates?"

"None whatever, so long as you bring Bates back undamaged."

"Oh, Bates!" he said laughing, "It doesn't matter about me."

"Not so much, old man. You've made me get used to doing without you. But without Bates I should be as a pelican in the wilderness. Come on, if you've finished your wine, for I must hear your story, and what you have been doing."

My diary contains a very complete record of my talk with Edmund on this occasion, and looking back it seems to me that he paid me a great compliment. I see now how perfectly sincere he was. Then I was too absorbed in trifles and pettifogging distrusts to rejoice in what he said at all. I had to precipitate the conversation, and I did it bluntly by asking him why he had left me so long without a letter.

"Don't you understand," he asked me, "that I have come to look on you as the 'friend born for adversity'?"

I told him I didn't quite follow.

He said, "It's hard to explain. Potty little things like money come into it so much. But every time I've written to you I've been in trouble of some sort. You've never given me advice. If it's only been money, you've always forked out. But the point is, you've always been there—just yourself—someone to be responsible to. Damn it, I can't explain. But it's kept me—well—no—I can't say straight, exactly, but reasonably decent. So that I *could* come back and shake your hand, anyhow."

"And you have prospered, after all?"

"Well, I didn't lose everything, but darned nearly. You were right not to trust me about that Far Eastern Trade. I was very young and very cock-sure, and it was some time before I discovered there were too many sharks in those waters. Lord, what a young ass I was! Those Hong-Kong fellows had me weighed up to an ounce. I had a bad time kicking myself, but I managed to pull out my last £200. That annoyed them desperately. I got a little of my own back in some other ways too. But I don't think you'd like that story. It was then I met Welfare."

"Welfare? Who's he? It's rather a jolly name."

"Yes. The name influenced me. He's my partner. Captain Welfare he calls himself. You must meet him."

I saw the look I didn't quite understand become accentuated in Edmund's face.

"I didn't know you had a partner. Partner in what? What is your business? Let's have the tale from the beginning."

"It's too long. We're in the Levant fruit trade. Welfare's a rum old chap. The sort one simply can't explain to people at home. He's always knocked about, mostly at sea. Calls himself Captain, but I don't believe he's ever commanded anything. He knows damn-all about navigation; but he can handle a ship all right.

"He's admitted having been a steward on a liner. He got his start by collecting paper money from passengers—changing it, you know. Always getting hold of paper at a discount and unloading it at some port where it was up a few points. It's extraordinary how paper money values fluctuate with latitude. Welfare had the whole thing worked out so that he was on velvet every time. As he says, it's a nice safe line, but dull. And he didn't like being a steward. The old boy has got his pride, and the tips went against the grain, I fancy. He was in the Pacific for a time and did pretty well with copra.

"Then he thought he was man enough for the Eastern coasting business. When I met him he had just been stung by some merchants in Shanghai. He was taking it badly—oh, rottenly! I found him in an opium shebeen and broke his collar bone getting him on a rickshaw. I got hold of a decent European doctor man. Old Welfare carried on frightfully about his collar bone while he was crazy, but the little doctor got him round all right. He used to come and stick a needle into him and squirt stuff into him—atropine and all sorts of poisons. Old Crippen's stuff he told me he used when Welfare was rowdy. Anyhow, Welfare got all right, only beastly sentimental."

Edmund paused to light another cigar, and I did not interrupt him. I find it is impossible in writing to convey any idea of the casual way in which his narrative dribbled out.

Only that morning one of my old ladies in the parish had been much more impressive about the quality of some dried peas she had bought from our local grocer—a relentless monopolist, but a sidesman and communicant.

To her I knew exactly what to say, how to sympathise. But Edmund made me feel as if I had swallowed a bound volume of *The Boy's Own Paper*.

I waited until his cigar was fairly under way.

"You have not yet told me what you are doing now," I said.

"No. I must come to that. We're all right now. Certainly I did old Welfare a good turn, but he has more than repaid it. We had both been stung, but we found we could put up about £500 between us. He said he had always kept this Levant business up his sleeve, and it was absolutely 'It' for people with a small capital, like us. He had a pal, a Dutchman, who kept a hotel in Alexandria. Well, we went down there. The Dutchman was all right but very cautious. Things hung fire a bit. I had to keep myself and I didn't want to touch my capital. There wasn't much left to touch. Well, the fact is I 'managed' a steam laundry there for three months. Made it pay, too."

"That's good," I said.

"Yes—you should have seen the steam! and the natives blowing water from their mouths on the stuff while it was ironed! Nice clean women's frocks! I couldn't stick it."

"It sounds very unpleasant."

"Oh, it was rotten! Summer weather too. However, the luck turned then and we bought the *Astarte* with the help of the Dutchman. We've paid him off now and she's all our own."

"And what on earth is the *Astarte*?" I asked.

"I thought I had told you. She's our boat of course. A rum-looking thing in these waters. But just what I've always dreamed of. I am master and part owner, and I told you years ago that was what I was setting out to be; only I didn't think it would be in the Mediterranean."

There was a long pause in our talk, I looking at Edmund, thinking of him as he should have been, rising from step to step in the Navy, carrying on the old family tradition of service and duty.

I could not help noticing a restraint in his manner, as though he were making careful selection of the parts of his story he chose to tell me. And there was that look on his face, the look of surrender, a subtle weakening about the mouth and chin; and in his eyes, I fancied, the mere shrewdness of the merchant elbowing out the look of command that had been natural to him.

"Tell me about the *Astarte* and the trade," I said.

"Ah, the little *Astarte* is the best part of the story," said Edmund with a return of enthusiasm. "We got her for an old song and we've made a dandy ship of her. She's a Levantine schooner, Greek really, about 150 tons. Wood, of course, but we have a good new copper bottom on her. She's a bit slow, but stiff as a poker in a breeze, and comfortable as a country pub! And she'll point as near the wind as anything I ever sailed. Rum-looking though, when you're not used to the type. Any amount of free-board sloping up to long high bows and an enormous jib-boom. She carries a flight of head-sails like a skein of geese. She has two big leg-o'-mutton sails, and we can shove a couple of square sails on the foremast when we want to. Oh, she's pretty, I can tell you, and head-room enough for a giraffe in the saloon. You must come for a cruise in her."

"I'd love to. Where is she now?"

"She's in Tilbury at present. Old Welfare's there with her on some business. He looks after the trade mostly. I do the yachting. I tell you, it's just owning a yacht that keeps herself and her owners too!"

"And how do you make all the money?"

"Well—mostly fruit. Welfare's great idea was trading direct with the Arabs on the Egypt and Palestine coast. In the season we load up their dates and figs and melons, and take them and sell almost direct to the consumers. So we are our own middle-men and collar all the profits. Then there are lots of odds and ends in the East. Curios and cheap fabrics, brass ware, Gaza pottery, jewellery. No end of things that would sell like hot cakes in this country. We have collected stacks of things. In fact that's partly what brought us home. And what I'm afraid you won't like is that, following up our direct trading principles, we're going to run a shop of our own. Like those places in Port Said, you know. If you saw the prices those fellows get!"

"But why on earth shouldn't I like it? Especially if it brings you home oftener. Why, my dear fellow, shop-keeping is rapidly passing into the hands of the aristocracy while the bourgeoisie buy up the old estates!"

I was greatly relieved, thinking this was the secret of his slight embarrassment and the look that had puzzled me.

All his story was perfectly plausible to me. Looking back now I do not really see that any country parson, ignorant alike of commerce and of the near East, could be blamed for finding nothing suspicious in it.

"Then you wouldn't mind our business being in Brighton?" he asked. "It's a bit near you. But of course our name won't be over the window. No need for anyone to know you've any association with it at all. Welfare wants to call it 'Oriental Bazaar' or some old stale thing like that. He was wild with me for suggesting 'Fakes Limited.' One reason he wants Brighton is because the *Astarte* could stand in near enough to be seen from the front and send in boat-loads of stuff under the eyes of the populace. Then it's handy for London, and of course the real trade must go through London. But of course the main reason for striking Brighton is that its season is all the year round. It's always full of people with more money than brains."

"I think it's a splendid idea," I said, and I really meant it. "Everything you sell, whatever its price, will be the genuine thing—straight from the East. We associate shop-keeping with the huckstering ideas of a servile class. I've often wanted to prove that shop-keeping, all trade, can be ennobled. But what can a mere shareholder do? What does he know even of the things that are done in his name?"

"Wait a minute, old man. I don't want to give you any impression that we're out for the purification of trade, or anything of the sort. We're out for money—and fun. At least I am. Welfare's out for money."

"Quite," said I, in my new-born enthusiasm. "And it's all the better. I don't want any amateur things. They're all quack things. Edmund, I'd like to be a partner in this. If you want capital, you know I can find it."

To my surprise Edmund looked rather distressed.

"It might seem cheap," I continued, "to offer you money now when you are prospering and probably can get it without difficulty. I mean after I refused to finance you before. But I'm sure you know me better than to think it's only security I have in mind."

"I do, old man," said Edmund, "I know you too well. I know you would give me all the money we want and more. And as a financial proposition I could honestly advise you to do it. But somehow I don't want you to. Money after all is a very secondary thing—when you have got it. Welfare can raise all we want, he says, in the city. *You keep out of it.*"

"But I want to be in it! Can't you imagine a little craving for romance, even at my advanced age? And the Levant! Do you know I correspond in Latin with monasteries there? That I have always promised myself a trip there and have been too lazy to go? Couldn't I go to Scutari in the *Astarte* if I were a partner? And I have a dear friend in Aleppo whom I have never seen. I wonder what a monk's Latin would sound like, spoken? This man I believe started life as an Albanian."

"I don't know," said Edmund. "I never tried talking Latin to an Albanian monk. As a matter of fact I never got beyond 'mensa' myself. I started 'dominus' and switched on to the modern side, just when I arrived at the genitive plural. Of course we could go up the Dardanelles and you could get ashore and explore about. But if it's business, you must talk it over with Welfare. He's coming to Brighton."

"Well, let's have him here."

"You could have him here if you like, of course," said Edmund merrily. "He won't actually deafen you with the crash of falling H's, and he won't get puzzled among the forks on the dinner table. But I've told you—he's not what you and I call a gentleman. And unfortunately he's what they call, I believe, a convinced Nonconformist."

I looked at Edmund, but he was perfectly serious.

To me it was as though I had been told that Odysseus had been a homœopath.

"If he doesn't mind being the guest of the Established Church I expect we'll get on very well. I'm not exactly bigoted on doctrinal points."

"No. But I'm wondering how Bates would stick him?"

"Really, Edmund, I know I spoil Bates, and so do you when you're here, but I have not got the length of allowing him to choose my guests."

"Well, old Welfare will enjoy it. As a matter of fact he'll be enormously flattered. He'll take you for a sort of 'swell,' to use his own language. And he'll be tremendously interested in that underground passage."

"Why?" I queried, in surprise.

If this were a play or a novel I suppose the stage direction would be that "Edmund bit his lip." Of course he didn't do anything of the sort. I don't suppose any sane human being ever did, though I have myself bitten my tongue accidentally. I did however get an impression that Edmund some-how felt he had committed an indiscretion, which I suppose is what the novelists and playwrights mean. He went on a little embarrassed.

"I suppose it's a desire for romance on his part too. He likes poking his nose into anything of that sort. No cob-webs about him! Anyhow, I'll spend a good deal of tomorrow working through that passage and find out if there's anything to show him. We might find hidden treasure in it—The smugglers' hoard! If they left any brandy there it would be worth drinking by now."

I was at a loss to understand his eagerness about this passage, and some instinct made me resent it a little. I put it to myself that I did not want the peace of my home disturbed. I did not want foul air and dust coming up into the house. I preferred to go elsewhere for the details of romance. I knew that these were not my real reasons. But I had always avoided the tunnel without knowing why, and I did not want it disturbed now.

"You will probably find there is no tunnel at all," I said. "It may be just a village tradition."

"But you have seen both ends of it. And how else could the noise come from the forge? Anyhow, I'll know all about it tomorrow."

I brought the conversation back to the more congenial topic of the *Astarte* and my projected cruise.

I had always been a keen yachtsman, and the novelty and the uncon-ventional nature of the trip appealed to me.

There was nothing to prevent my finding a suitable man to take charge of the parish for a few weeks or more. Edmund's attitude was a little discouraging. He was certainly not enthusiastic.

"We must see how you and Welfare get on," he said. "It's close quarters with a man if you don't just hit it with him. It's a queer ship's company, anyhow. All the crew are Arabs. You see their food costs next to nothing; flour and lentils and the milk of a couple of goats, mostly. And they work like niggers for a couple of piastres a day. We have a sort of skipper over them called Jakoub, I don't know any other name for him. He's a magnificent sailor-man, knows all our boat and everybody in it. He rules his men with—well, the Arab equivalent of a rod of iron, acts as interpreter and saves us all bother with natives. In fact he's practically invaluable, and I firmly believe, an ineffable blackguard."

"He doesn't live with you, I presume?"

"Good God, no! He's a native."

"It will be an education to me to meet him."

"Then the Eastern end of the Mediterranean would be too hot for you in summer, and in winter one is liable to get a dusting in the Bay that I'm afraid you wouldn't enjoy; not in a little tub like the *Astarte*."

"Oh, I don't think I'd mind that. Anyhow, I could go overland and pick you up at Marseilles or wherever you are calling."

"Yes. You could do that. I'll tell you what, you'd better try a short cruise first to see how you like it. We could have a look round the Channel Isles. In fact we want to go to Guernsey. We'll talk it over with Welfare."

I went to bed cherishing a hope that Edmund might forget or abandon his proposed exploration of the tunnel. But an inveterate ringing of the anvil during our breakfast, and Edmund's evident attention to it, warned me that such hopes were vain.

He instructed Bates to procure a pick and shovel and a lantern, and demanded what time he would be at liberty to assist him in exploring.

"I could be finished for an hour perhaps about ten o'clock," said Bates, "unless Mr. Davoren wants me for anything special."

"Oh no," I said. "I shall be busy all morning."

I could see the fellow was as keen as a schoolboy on this nonsensical burrowing, and that the quick instinct of a servant had somehow detected that I did not care about it. But I felt it was better to surrender with a good grace.

Presently I watched the two of them disappear down into the cellars with pick and shovel, some gardener's baskets, a stable lamp and an electric torch.

I found a sympathiser in Mrs. Rattray.

"It's likely the two of them will be suffocated with foul air," she said, "and Bates wanting to take the bird-cage with the canary in it, because he read in the papers they took them down after explosions in the mines, when all the poor women would be waiting on the top. 'You'd be the easier spared of the two,' I told him, and the dirt they'll be bringing up on their feet—they're like a pair of children, sir."

"No better indeed, Mrs. Rattray. Perhaps the door mat from the hall?"

I escaped into the study, only to be driven out by the muffled sound of blows and horrid scrapings of the shovel. I retreated to the pigeon-loft.

This kind of thing went on all that day and the next.

Edmund was late for all meals and brought to them an earthy smell. Bates was never available when I wanted him.

Edmund reported the passage as being evidently of great antiquity, and quite roomy. It was only blocked in places, he said, and they had had no difficulty in clearing these so far.

"We are propping the roof where it has fallen in or looks dicky," he said, "otherwise we should have been through by now. I'm sure we'll find the other opening all right because the air's pretty fresh and we've found a lot of bats hanging up. You must come down tomorrow."

"No thanks, the bats have decided me. There is between them and me what Lamb calls an 'imperfect sympathy.'"

"Oh, rot! We'll get rid of them for you."

On the second afternoon they had triumphantly emerged on the cliff over the beach. I met them there and found the opening was the place I had suspected. It was about four feet high and the same width, but a great detached mass of chalk completely hid it from below, or from the sea. The rough path that led up to it seemed to have been hewn out of the face of the cliff, but had been much worn and weathered away so that it was quite an awkward scramble to reach it now, and impossible for children. This may account for the curious fact that none of the present villagers seemed to know its whereabouts, though there was a strong tradition of a "brandy hole" somewhere on the beach.

I was tempted to penetrate a little distance into this end of the tunnel and was surprised at its spaciousness. A few yards from the opening one could stand upright, and it was quite five feet in width. Edmund said it was the same size all the way. In places the chalk face had been plastered, and I strongly suspected that this might be the remains of Saxon work. It was certainly of immemorial age, though it very probably had been adopted and used by the smugglers. There were remains of Saxon masonry in my church of which, as a parish, we were very proud. And I was the more inclined to date the digging of the passage to this remote period because I knew of nothing in the history of the parish in later times to account for it.

Altogether the discovery was much more interesting than I had expected; but I refused to face the bats, so we walked home by the village.

"We must report this to the Archæological Society," I said. "If, as I think, it proves to be Saxon there will be great excitement over it."

"Oh, hang the Archæological Society," said Edmund. "Let's keep it to ourselves for a bit, till I have finished my investigations anyhow."

A sudden vision of streams of hungry and extremely boring archæologists claiming the hospitality of the vicarage quenched my new-born ardour.

"Yes, it's really your show," I agreed. "You can write a paper on it yourself in your own time."

"Thanks. I think I see myself."

At home Edmund found a letter from Captain Welfare dating from the Ship Hotel at Brighton. He had found what he thought suitable premises for the new shop, and wanted Edmund to go over and see them.

"Then you can bring him back here for as long as he likes, and we can talk everything over," I said.

So it was settled.

CHAPTER 3

THE BISHOP PROPOSES A TOAST

EDMUND had gone to Brighton to meet his partner and inspect the "desirable premises" for their proposed curiosity shop.

Captain Welfare was to return with him some time before dinner. I had the day before me and I awaited their coming with a great curiosity as to the personality of this stranger. I was uneasy too, for Edmund was so much committed to him, and seemed to leave his destiny so much in his hands. From all he had told me about him, Captain Welfare did not seem to me the most desirable kind of person to have such a responsibility. He was certainly an adventurer, and hitherto not even a very successful one. And he was admittedly a man of low origin.

However, it was clear that Edmund was born a bohemian and would always be one. There had always been some such in our family, and as I thought of what I knew of their careers I could not deny that they seemed on the whole to have been much more charming people and to have got much more really out of life, than the sober average of the rest of us.

I was certain that Welfare would prove to be vulgar and could only hope he had a sense of honour.

Although I had carefully refrained from any criticism, which I knew would only irritate Edmund, I did in fact rather dislike the idea of the shop, and though my ignorance of commercial matters was fairly complete, it seemed to me unnecessary and unbusinesslike to have brought the *Astarte* all the way from the Eastern Mediterranean for the purpose of establishing and stocking it. I could only suppose it was a case of combining business with pleasure.

I determined to put aside all these worrying preoccupations and return to some literary work that had been interrupted since Edmund's return.

Again I was interrupted, and somewhat fluttered, by the receipt of a telegram.

This was from the bishop to say he was coming over about lunch time and would stay the night if convenient.

Whatever Captain Welfare proved to be I felt he would harmonise ill with the bishop, and my first impulse was to reply with some honourable fiction that would postpone the visit. But even as I cast about in my mind for the suitable subterfuge to commit to the pre-paid form, I bethought me of how seldom my dear bishop got a chance of taking refuge with me for one quiet bachelor evening, of the disappointment it would be to both of us to lose this one. Besides, I reflected, Parminter is a man of the world, much more so than I am, and he has a catholic taste in mankind. Captain Welfare will interest him, whatever he is, and he has always wanted to meet Edmund. Anyhow there would be time enough to explain everything to him.

I wrote "Delighted" on the telegraph form and gave it to Bates.

"It's the Bishop," I said to Bates.

"Yes, sir."

"He will be here for lunch and will stop the night."

"Yes, sir."

"Of course his Lordship will have his usual room. Put Captain Welfare somewhere else."

"Very well, sir."

Having thus made my preparations as a thoughtful host, I found it was impossible to settle down to my monograph on the "Greco-Turkish Alliance of the Sixth Century."

I went out and awaited the bishop amid the sedative influences of my pigeons.

The Right Rev. John Parminter was not only my diocesan, but for some years had been, and thank God still is, my dearest friend. He shared my interest in the Byzantine Empire, and, as I think I have mentioned, it was this which first brought us together.

As a bishop he had less spare money, and far less leisure than I had, to devote to our common hobby. He professed to envy me as an "authority." As a matter of fact I am but a painstaking student. What my few books possess of merit in the way of generalisation, of inference or speculation, they owe entirely to Parminter's inspiration.

He is one of those men born to distinction, who show the fact from schoolboy days. At this time he was in his early fifties, some eight years older than myself, but quite among our younger bishops. He was a young man, and indeed still is, in mind and heart, and even in physique.

But he was already a power and influence in both Church and State, and had managed to avoid the hatred and mistrust of all parties in the Church although he wore the label of none of them.

I believe I alone knew the extent of his heterodoxy. It was indeed my greatest honour to have been chosen as his confidant.

Whenever it was possible, he loved to come to my vicarage for what he called "a night's holiday," and the one mystery of my household was that the bishop kept here, and always wore, an ordinary layman's dinner-jacket and *trousers*!

"This is dreadfully short notice," he said as I met him at the hall-door, "but I know you would have told me if my coming was a nuisance."

"I would. If you could ever be a nuisance, I'm the man to say it. Come along in."

He could not abide any ceremony in my house, and insisted on my calling him "Parminter" when we were alone. Before Bates I addressed him as "bishop" and if anyone else were present I put in all the necessary "My Lords."

"We shall not be alone tonight," I told him as we lit cigarettes in the study.

"Oh. I'm sorry, if it's not rude to say so. Who have you got with you?"

"Edmund."

"Oh, good! I've always missed the wicked brother, and I long to meet him. I do hope he is not reformed or anything disastrous?"

"I hardly know yet. He's quite prosperous this time."

"Ah? Well, perhaps it's ill-gotten gains and quite interesting. I want to hear his adventures from himself."

"So no doubt you will. But I must warn you there is a stranger as well."

The bishop's face fell. "So I suppose I won't be able to wear my 'tea-gown,'" he said.

I tried to explain Captain Welfare, as well as one can explain a man one has never seen.

"I think we may be a most interesting party," said the bishop. "I wish Captain Welfare would turn out to be a pirate in disguise. It would be so refreshing and stimulating. I should love to meet a pirate with a Nonconformist conscience."

During lunch our talk wandered away to the early Byzantine Empire, and I explained my difficulties about that old first Greco-Turkish alliance.

I could see that Parminter was less interested than usual.

"It shows how deep the Balkan question has its roots," he said.

We went for a favourite walk of ours across the Downs.

We crossed ridge after ridge, rounded and smoothed by forgotten oceans, with delicate shades of green and mauve blending under the March sun like the colours on the wing of a moth.

Before us as we walked was the dark distant line that marked the beginning of the Weald, and, turning, we looked back across the grey and silver of the Channel. Far away on our right the sun struck a gleam of white from the cliffs of Beachy Head. An old shepherd and his dog slouched after a slowly moving flock of sheep on their browsing way to Lewes. On the sky-line a string of race-horses walked to their stables after a gallop.

The bishop drew long deep draughts of the keen air, and I could see some of the care fade out of his eyes.

"This is England to me," he said. "So I hope to remember it when my time comes not to see it any more. I hope I shall have earned the right to forget the paved streets under the soot blanket, and those awful rows of red-brick 'property'—not homes, mind you, but someone's property, some vulgar greedy person's 'property,' where children die, and women slave, and their husbands avoid. You have not lived among them as I have, and you don't have to attend 'Housing Conferences.' The cant I have had to listen to during the last few days, from sleek unimaginative chairmen of amateur committees of busybodies, and aldermen from the provinces with weird voices and ghastly accents. All these people with a lust for spouting platitudes and a determination not to look things in the face, with their total failure to get anything done."

"It must be very unpleasant—meeting that sort of people."

"It is. But one must do it. They stand between all right principles and the unconsciously suffering people, who actually vote for them! They represent the Kakistocracy which we have made of our pretended Democracy."

I looked at the bishop.

His lean, humorous face was grave and earnest, his eyes shone with enthusiasm. I saw that he was quite serious.

We walked for some distance homewards in silence.

I have given but an outline of what the bishop said, but it depressed me to know of all these things going on in the great world outside my quiet home, my somewhat paltry life. It made me feel my own littleness and inadequacy. I frankly admitted to myself that I had no moral right to my wealth, that I had shirked the responsibilities it brought with it. But if I had undertaken them I knew that I should only have done harm through my ignorance. I had to content myself with being merely harmless; spending and giving my money decently and judiciously. The bishop had good reason to know that I was always ready to support with money any of his schemes that required it. As a rule I had none of Hamlet's uncomfortable sensation that I was born to reduce dislocations of the Time.

The bishop was quite distressed at a lame attempt of mine to express something of this.

"My dear fellow," he said, "we all have our Fate and our Function. It need not trouble your conscience that yours is somewhat pleasanter than the average. In these days the combination of scholar and gentleman has ceased to man the professions. When we do find one, I think he should be endowed by the State if necessary. When chance endows him, as in your case, we should thank God for it. But I ought not to have burdened you with all these harassing things that afflict us public men. You can't imagine the relief it is to me to have someone to whom I can blurt out all that is in my mind without fear of his being 'scandalised.'"

Our intimacy rendered any polite disclaimer from me unnecessary.

We began to talk about Edmund, and I explained in further detail the projects of the partners.

"How old did you say your brother was?"

"He's about twenty-five now."

"Twenty-five. Well, some men are a long time growing up. Within limits it's the best men that take the longest. I am sure from all you have told me that there's a fine man somewhere inside your brother. But I hope he'll soon get tired of play."

"I suppose it is just play," I assented.

"It's nothing else," said the bishop. "And we can't afford to have well-bred men shirking their job."

"Sometimes I fear Edmund will never be very different. He's a bohemian—a marine bohemian, if such a thing is possible. But there have always been people like him in our family."

"Want of opportunity," the bishop replied with emphasis. "Such men are simply victims of our social system. There is always a job for them, the biggest kind of job. When they find it or make it, they become our greatest men. Very often they miss it through the hide-bound stupidity of our organisation. However, his chance will come, it is sure to come, if he keeps himself fit and ready for it. But I don't like this commercialism."

"He won't take my money, so he has to make it pay."

"Yes, of course. I hope he'll get rich at once and be done with it—or else fail altogether."

"You don't like the idea of the shop?"

"Oh, that's only a detail. The whole thing appears to be petty trade."

"He seems to leave that almost all to his partner."

"Well, I don't think he should. We don't know this Captain Welfare. But anyhow, in spite of all the modern tendency, shop-keeping is not for gentlemen. It's bad for them. The worst fate that can befall a gentleman is to become 'déclassé'."

"I don't see what else we can do with him at present," I protested.

"If he's the kind of man I imagine, they'd take him up at the Colonial Office. I would introduce him to Brocklehurst myself, and he could start as deputy commissioner or something in a place where he would get all the adventure he'd want."

"I should like that, of course. But I can't answer for Edmund. He's like a man in love—with the *Astarte*."

"Oh, we'll give him time to get over that. There's no hurry at his age."

We reached home to find that Edmund and his partner had arrived before us.

We saw them walking on the lawn and went on to meet them. They were deep in conversation and did not hear us approaching on the soft turf, so that we were close to them when they turned and faced us. Edmund was speaking and I caught the words "dry and level from the cellar to the beach."

I remember a feeling of amusement that he should so soon be inflicting his obsession with the underground passage on Captain Welfare, whom I did not associate with antiquarian research. But this was swallowed up in my curiosity as to the personality of that mariner.

Edmund stopped short, naturally surprised at the unexpected presence of the bishop.

My first impression of Welfare was his look of astonishment, almost of fear, at finding himself in so august a presence. For an instant he looked like a man who thought himself trapped. Edmund hastily introduced him to me and he said "Pleased to meet you."

I presented them both to the bishop.

Captain Welfare said "Pleased to meet your Lordship," and kept his bowler hat in his hand as we all strolled back to the house.

It was that terribly uncomfortable hour after six when tea is out of the question, and one does not know what to do with a stranger before dinner.

"Have you had tea?" I asked Edmund.

"No thanks. We only got here ten minutes ago. Bates offered us some, but we didn't want it. I was just showing Welfare the view before it got dark."

"Very charming prospect, sir," said Welfare. "Very eligible place altogether I call it."

"Come in to the study. There's time for a cigarette before we dress."

The moment I said it, it occurred to me that perhaps Captain Welfare did not dress for dinner. I looked apprehensively to Edmund, who understood and nodded reassuringly.

I handed round cigarettes.

"Would you like anything else, Captain Welfare? After your journey? Edmund, I'm sure you want a whisky-and-soda."

"Yes, I think I do," said Edmund ringing the bell.

"No whisky for me, thank you," said Welfare. "Perhaps if you have a sherry and bitters?"

"That's an excellent idea," said the bishop. "You haven't asked me, Davoren, but I think I'll join Captain Welfare in a glass of sherry."

I had always admired Parminter's tact, and now Captain Welfare was manifestly gratified with the sense of having done the right thing under difficult circumstances.

Captain Welfare was kind enough to praise my sherry.

"I hadn't ought to have put any bitters in it," he said. "It puts me in mind of the Green Man at Southampton, a little place near the docks. Naturally you wouldn't know it. But they give you a glass of sherry there——"

He went on with this topic in a kind of meditative way, as if he had forgotten to stop talking.

As there was evidently no necessity to attend to his story, I took the opportunity of examining him more closely.

His short powerful figure was curiously like what I had expected. But his face was quite a surprise to me. Most strange faces are somehow familiar. I suppose they fall into one or other of certain categories of faces we have unconsciously formed in our minds.

This face was extraordinarily large, forming, as it were, the front wall of a massive head which was scarcely raised above his wide shoulders by a thick and very strong neck. I had noticed that while he was standing up. Now as he lay back in his chair the edge of his low collar made a groove in the flesh under his jaw, and his large indented chin almost filled up the opening of his waistcoat.

His complexion was quite colourless. I thought at first it was scarred by small-pox, but the reticulations in his tough skin were finer than those left by that disease. I don't know if I am right about this, but it looked as if no hair grew on this sterile surface. I doubt if any razor could have shaved it. His vertical forehead, short straight nose, wide but well closed mouth and powerful chin were all rather admirable in a slightly grotesque way. He had undoubtedly the look of a man of considerable force and determination. But his large, well-shaped, greenish-brown eyes had a curious dreaminess in them, and something of the wistfulness of those of a small monkey.

I thought as he sat there how impossible it would be from his appearance to determine either his age or his occupation. I could conceive of him as an ecclesiastic, a lawyer, a tailor, or an actor. But nothing about him suggested the mariner. It is a curious fact that in whatever line of life my fancy placed him, I pictured him at the head of it as a cardinal, a Lord Chancellor, or a Scotch comedian. Yet he had been apparently an indifferent success as an adventurer. I thought of the bishop's dictum—"Want of opportunity," and wondered if the *Astarte* was destined to give this man his belated chance?

He was at all events physically hard and well-conditioned, evidently a man accustomed to self-control. As his appearance became gradually more familiar I found something strangely likeable in it.

His conversation so far was evidently a thing of habit, a mechanical process like most people's reading, quite unrelated to any cerebral process behind it. I began to wish that he would stop doing it and let us talk.

Through the vision he had unwittingly called up in my mind of a frowsy bar-parlour with seafaring men on horse-hair seats expectorating and drinking sherry, I heard the bishop apologising to Edmund for his presence.

"I did give your brother a chance of putting me off," he explained; "but he was too kind to do it. We don't often meet, and he knows how I value these little escapes into his delightful bachelordom. Besides, he knew how much I wanted to make your acquaintance."

"It's very kind of you to come in spite of us, my Lord," said Edmund. "I'm afraid we'll be rather in the way of your Byzantine conversation."

"From what your brother has told me, I should say you and Captain Welfare have more of the Byzantine spirit than either of us."

"The worst of me is that I don't even know what the Byzantine spirit is!" Edmund warned him.

"And we can only guess," said the bishop. "But they strove and fought, and they did make an Empire out of the ruins of an older one—even if they didn't make a very good one."

"I'm afraid," said Edmund with a self-conscious smile, "Welfare and I cannot pretend to be empire-builders. We're only business men and sailors."

"Those are two of the essentials. But I don't think it's empire-builders we want. It's empire-repairers."

Edmund waited when the bishop and Captain Welfare went to their rooms.

"Why on earth didn't you put the bishop off?" he asked a little irritably.

"I've just heard Parminter explaining to you. Really it's just as he said."

"That's all very well. But you can see for yourself. Welfare is a very good partner for me to have. He's all right on board ship. But one doesn't exactly want to brandish him in the faces of one's friends."

"I think I shall like him. And if he'll only tell us about himself and his life, I'm sure he'll be interesting."

"Are you going to charge the bishop something extra for seeing him fed?"

"My dear Edmund, when you know Parminter better, you'll be as fond of him as I am. You will understand that his interest in both of us is a really brotherly feeling."

"Well, I wish he'd get it fixed in his head that we're traders, fruit-merchants, out for a profit, and not go gassing about empire-building and cant."

I saw now what was causing Edmund's irritability. It was the consciousness, or at least the fear of becoming *déclassé*.

"It's not cant with Parminter," I said. "He's tremendously keen on meeting men out of the beaten track; men who live in an original way. And yours is an original way. I think he's got an idea that this old country has got to be jerked out of its ruts by original men. Although he's a bishop he has sort of lost faith in respectability."

"By jove, I didn't know a bishop could have so much sense!"

"I'm afraid I haven't expressed it quite right. But you'll understand what I mean when you have seen more of him."

Edmund went upstairs mollified and quite cheerful, and I was able to congratulate myself on having restored the situation. For I was a little nervous about the success of my curiously assorted party.

The bishop came down in full episcopal evening splendour, silk stockings, silver buckles, and purple coat.

"The admirable Bates evidently considered these things necessary," he said, looking down with a sigh. "He left me no alternative."

"Bates has doubtless scented a nonconformist in Captain Welfare. He would be jealous of the dignity of the church in such company."

"For myself," said the bishop, "I would have inclined to any little concession that might soften the dissenter's preconceived idea of the arrogance of the episcopacy. But Bates's instinct is probably right."

"It always is," I said, and then Welfare came in.

His evening raiment was quite correct and good and gave his heavy face an air almost of distinction. His only marked peculiarity was a brilliant red silk handkerchief folded inside his waistcoat, and showing for about an inch above its opening. I thought it quite an effective patch of colour.

The bishop told me afterwards that it was considered quite essential among the numerous class who had recently adopted the evening dress of civilisation as a ceremonial costume.

"In the north of England," he said, "parliamentary candidates have to display this red badge at mayoral receptions and such functions, whatever their political colour may be. I have never heard of anyone wearing a blue one."

Bates's instinct had not been at fault, and it was clear that Captain Welfare was gratified by the bishop's apparel. He seemed at first a little oppressed by the ritual of dinner. Not that there was anything unbecoming to a country vicar about my table.

But when I reflected how much the element of squalor must have entered into his life, how little he must have seen of the routine of a comfortable English home, I understood that my inherited plate and glass, the damask which was Mrs. Rattray's tender care, the arrangement of flowers in which my gardener gratified his pride, the shaded candles, and the quiet, sympathetic ministrations of Bates and a parlour-maid, must all seem unfamiliar, even grandiose, to Captain Welfare. He seemed subdued and impressed, watchful but happy.

Edmund had been telling us of the beauties and the discomforts of the Eastern Mediterranean.

"I suppose," said the bishop, "you will eventually be running quite a fleet of boats as your business extends?"

Edmund looked across to Welfare as though doubtful how to reply.

"No, my Lord," said Welfare. "It wouldn't pay to extend. It's too personal a business. We've only had the *Astarte* a little more than a year, but she's paid for herself, for a new suit of sails, and a new copper bottom. Now it's all profit and I don't mind saying she's making us a big percentage. But another boat without us aboard wouldn't do it. It's knowing the trade and knowing the natives and working your boat yourself. And of course there's side issues to the trade. This Brighton business we're starting is one. I guess we'll make enough to retire on out of the *Astarte*."

"Do you think you'll want to retire?" asked the bishop.

Captain Welfare looked at him with a puzzled expression in his wistful eyes.

"Well," he said, "what's one in business for?"

"Surely not merely to get out of it? It's a dangerous thing to retire, Captain Welfare. I've seen a lot of men in the Services retired under the sixty-three years rule. They've been active, useful, young-seeming men, keenly looking forward to enjoying their pensions. But, when it's come, they've grown old and boring all at once, simply tumbled headlong into old age, and very often they've died in a year or two. You won't want to retire, will you, Davoren?"

"Oh, I should simply knock about in some other part of the sea," said Edmund.

"I don't know how it may look to gentlemen waiting for pensions," Captain Welfare remarked with deliberation. "They're gentlemen all the time. But it's different in business. I don't see how a man can help wanting to make his bit and get out of it. I hope you gentlemen won't think the worse of me when I tell you my father was a man who got his living in his shirt sleeves."

The bishop and I made appreciative noises. Edmund emptied his glass and threw a savage but quite ineffectual look at his partner.

"Yes. He had a dry-salter's business in a small town in Lancashire. He always said he looked forward to putting on his coat for the last time and being a gentleman. He had his eye on a little house in Southport with two bay windows. He never managed it, poor man. It was partly my fault. I never took to the business and didn't give him the help he had a right to expect. I was considered bright at school too, and the lessons were no trouble to me, but I couldn't see any *use* in the things I learned, or in the dry-salting. So I got aboard a ship at Liverpool, as boy. It upset the old man a good deal, but it didn't break his heart. It was kidney-trouble carried him off."

"By the way, I've often wondered what a dry-salter is?" said the bishop.

"Well, I don't rightly know. I'm not sure if anyone does nowadays. I think it's an old-fashioned sort of name. Father sold Epsom salts, and sulphur and things, wholesale to the druggists, but he sold paint and turps and varnish and paraffin and patent medicines. Oh, and soap and candles and brushes. I think a dry-salter can sell pretty well anything he has a mind to."

"Well, of course these things must be distributed," the bishop said. "It's useful necessary work. But I can understand a man not wanting to go on doing it all his life. And yet we're all of us better, and look better, in our shirt sleeves."

Captain Welfare looked sceptically at the bishop, as though he feared he were being mocked. I had a horrible fear that he might attempt some sarcasm about lawn sleeves. But if he thought of it his manners were too good to permit him to utter it.

"What I mean is that there ought to be more in life, for all of us, than merely 'making a living,' and waiting for death in more or less discomfort."

"There's preparing for the next world, my Lord," Welfare said solemnly.

The bishop looked suspicious at once.

"I didn't mean anything of that sort," he said. "I'm afraid I don't understand."

"Well, I suppose a man has a better chance of making his peace with his Creator when he's out of business and—and isn't distracted like."

"No, I don't see that. I cannot anyhow think of the Creator as condescending to be at war with his creature, or conceive of Almighty God deriving any gratification from the worship of people who have nothing else to do."

"Of course it's not for me to argue with your Lordship. I was brought up Chapel, and learned to stick to the Good Old Book."

"Have a walnut, Welfare," said Edmund pushing a dish across to him.

Of course I had known he was hating the conversation, but there had been no chance to intervene. Parminter had an intense curiosity about the religious ideas of laymen, and I knew that to him it would be an irresistible temptation to dredge in the mind of so unfamiliar a specimen as Captain Welfare. I too would have enjoyed it but that I knew Edmund's sensitiveness would revolt at the idea of his partner being regarded as on exhibition. He wanted to be loyal to Welfare, to have him, as it were, accepted, without having his peculiarities emphasised.

On the whole I hoped Edmund's intervention would be successful, and seconded his effort by starting the port on its second journey round the table.

Just then the hollow thud and ring of the hammer on soft iron and anvil was distinctly heard from beneath the floor and diverted the thoughts of us all.

Captain Welfare looked almost startled, and then glanced enquiringly at Edmund.

"Somebody's getting his horse shod out of hours," said the bishop. "The sound seems plainer than ever tonight. Have you heard it before, Captain Welfare?"

"No, my Lord. Mr. Davoren was just telling me something about it when you came up."

"Edmund has been exploring and opening up the fabled passage, which proves to be quite genuine."

"Really? What did you find, Mr. Davoren?"

"Oh, the passage is all right. Bates and I only shifted some rubbish in places and shored up the roof here and there. There's a good sound passage with a vaulted roof right down to the beach."

"And you think it was really a smugglers' passage?"

I explained my theory of its Saxon origin.

"It should be quite an important find. You must have old Smith and some other experts down."

"Some day," I said, "but we're keeping it to ourselves for a bit."

"I see," said the bishop. "Yes. Those antiquarians are a hungry horde, Davoren."

"They would probably dig up the whole of my lawn, and undermine the foundations of the poor old house."

"Quite true. I understand your feelings. I shall keep your secret."

Captain Welfare had watched us thoughtfully during the discussion, and I thought he seemed relieved at my decision.

"Your brother tells me you think of having a cruise in the *Astarte*, sir?" he said abruptly.

"I should like it immensely, some day when I can get away."

"Well, we've some business in Guernsey before we go back East. I thought of making the trip as soon as we've fixed up the Brighton business and put in our manager there. In about a fortnight, I hope."

"You go, Davoren," said the bishop, "you'll be quite in time to see the bulbs at their best. And I've just the man to take your duty. One of my unfortunate out-of-work clergy depending on guineas for Sunday duty. A few weeks here would do him no end of good, and he's perfectly civilised and harmless."

"I reckon that about settles it," said Captain Welfare.

"I only wish I could go too," said the bishop.

Captain Welfare's countenance exhibited a sudden astonishment, which faded into the pain of a hospitable man compelled to withhold an impossible invitation.

"That would be a great honour, my Lord. But I'm afraid—our accommodation——"

"Oh! I'm sure that would be all and more than I desire or deserve. But don't worry. I could no more get away than fly."

Welfare tried to hide his obvious relief in a long sip of his port.

"I don't drink port as a rule," said the bishop, "but you must allow me one glass, Davoren, for a toast—Success to the *Astarte*."

I was astounded at a look of horror in Captain Welfare's face, as if he had witnessed an act of sacrilege.

Edmund gave a cynical laugh as he raised his glass.

"The *Astarte*," said I, as I emptied mine, and rose to return to the study.

CHAPTER 4

I SAIL IN THE ASTARTE

WE all went to bed early that night, but before we went there was a good deal of talk about my holiday on the *Astarte*.

Captain Welfare seemed keen on my going. Edmund kept himself curiously aloof from the conversation.

I had the idea that he wanted to dispose of the business side of the matter first. I was determined to become, if possible, a part owner of the *Astarte*, and all the enterprise associated with her. But it was impossible to discuss actual business until the three of us were alone.

The bishop was innocently emphatic on the subject of my voyage.

He insisted that I wanted a "change," and that the longer I stopped away the better for his starveling protégé, who was to occupy my house, and preach sermons in my absence.

So the subject was bandied about until we came down to details, and I began to realise that I was really going to sail with them.

A fortnight's yachting is no great enterprise; but I had somehow a kind of reluctance. I think this was determined by Edmund's aloofness. He had been, I thought, a little "queer" all the evening, and I had a feeling that he did not want me to start.

But Captain Welfare was pressing in his invitation, and the bishop, in his kindness for me, backed him up.

So before we parted, the rather hazy project had become a definite plan, and I had promised to send the bishop due notice of the date when I should be ready for my locum tenens.

"Remember," he said as he bade good-bye the next morning, "if you're away six months it will be all the better for poor Snape. Much as I shall miss you personally, I give you indefinite leave."

During the next fortnight Captain Welfare and Edmund were much away on business. The furnishing of the shop was completed, and the stock brought down from London.

A young Jew was installed as manager. He was sleek and ingratiating in his manner. I tried my hardest to persuade myself that I liked him, upbraiding myself for insular prejudices.

However, Captain Welfare vouched for his integrity and knowledge of the business. He had been born and bred in the Levant, he said, and was an expert in Oriental bric-à-brac. I was compelled to admit, when I saw our emporium as arrayed by him, that he had much of the artistic instinct of his race.

There was in the small window only a single very beautiful Shiraz rug, which hid the interior of the shop, and formed a background for a couple of brass and copper vases inlaid with hammered silver.

Inside, the polished floor was covered with a few more Shiraz and Khorassan rugs. There was a large screen and some chairs of mesharabieh work. Small electric lights, hidden in imitation mosque lamps of Egyptian brasswork, depending from the ceiling, lit the room with a mysterious glow. In the background a couple of luxurious couches flanked a low table whose top was formed of an immense brass tray. Here Turkish coffee and cigarettes were always ready for visitors, whether purchasing or not. On shelves around the sides, the dim light was reflected in stray gleams from brass and copper-ware and pottery, and faintly lit up silks and embroidery, and a museum of native work, curios, and "anticas" from all the countries of the East.

"It's not in the least like a shop," I said with an involuntary note of relief, as I sipped a cup of excellent though syrupy coffee.

"It's like an Eastern Shop," Edmund explained. "And we're going to run it on Eastern lines, bargaining, coffee, and a bit of rubbish as 'backshish,' and all."

"There is very much money in that, sir," said the Barber's Block, so I had mentally christened our Hebrew manager. He had the delicate beauty of one of those waxen heads on which hair-dressers sometimes exhibit their wigs, and his teeth reminded me of those lovely designs in pearl and coral that one sees displayed in glass cases outside the doors of the humbler kind of dentists.

He had his own atmosphere too, like a perfumed asteroid. He revolted me, and I knew that there was something subtly, disgustingly attractive about him.

"We ask one pound," he continued, "for something we can sell for eight-and-six and have our profit, and very often we get twelve or fifteen shillings, and the customer is more pleased than if we ask eight-and-six, and he pays it. So we give him some little thing, 'backshish,' and almost always he buys something more."

This account of our business methods was extremely disagreeable to me and I remarked:

"I think it's a rotten way of doing business."

"It is always so in the East."

His air of imperturbable finality made me feel merely foolish and fussy. I realised he had dignity in his way.

"He's quite right," Edmund agreed, "we've got to make this a little bit of the East. After all, throwing in the customs is one way of giving people the genuine article. They get a whiff of Cairo along with their purchase, and it's well worth the money."

"Well, I want to be the first customer anyhow. How much is this?" I asked, picking up a little Japanese netsuké in dusky ivory.

"That one I can sell for ten shillings and make a profit. This one I lose if I sell for thirty shillings."

"But I like this one best."

"No, it is not so good. See, it has not the signature of the artist. But it is here on this one."

He pointed out some minute Japanese writing cut in a tiny square.

"Never buy any work of a Japanese artist without the signature. He signs only what is best—perfect."

"All the same," I said, "I'll take this cheap one for luck and because I like it."

He smiled as he gave me the change.

"I would have sold the pair for four guineas," he said.

Edmund laughed.

"I think our friend Iscariot will manage very well for us," he whispered.

He never called him anything else, and Mr. Schultz appeared to have no objection to his nickname.

During this period I learned an extraordinary number of things about some of the practical commercial affairs of life, and I was surprised and somewhat gratified at the energy and capacity displayed by Captain Welfare, and indeed by Edmund too.

It was soon evident that the shop was going to be a paying concern. In the slang of the day "it caught on." I had always had a general idea that shop-keepers made very large sums of money except when they failed altogether, but I never could understand how they did it. It seemed to me that if they sold expensive things their customers were too few, and if they sold cheap things their profits must be too small to afford them a comfortable interest on their capital. I do not understand this yet, except in the case of people like butchers, and publicans, and very large shops that are crowded with people all day.

But when I learned what our "takings," as they called them, amounted to on the first day, my fear was that the whole stock would disappear in a week. But Captain Welfare assured me we could double our sales and carry on till long after the arrival of our next consignment from the East.

I asked him if he was quite satisfied to leave everything in the hands of Mr. Schultz.

"Oh yes. We've given him sufficient interest in the business to keep him straight. We shall take stock twice a year, so he could only swindle us for six months in any case. It will pay him better to be honest. Oh yes! he has plenty of good reasons for playing fair with me. I've done business with him since he was a nipper with bare legs doing conjuring tricks on the foot-walks of Port Said."

"You think he is grateful?"

"No, I don't. He's a low-class Jew. But he'll not run any rigs with me for the present."

I dropped the subject, which was one I did not care to dwell on in any case.

We had come to a general agreement as to the terms on which I was to become a partner, and my lawyer came down to take my instructions and prepare the necessary deed.

Marshall was a personal friend of mine and I never transacted any business except through him, with the exception of the matters that were naturally in the hands of my agents in Ireland.

He had, I knew, a considerable affection for me, and respected my literary work as beseeming a man in my position. But he detested my pigeons, and always disapproved of any suggestions of mine concerning my own property. He had always disapproved too of Edmund, whom he had never met.

"Put him on an allowance and stick to it," he always said.

It was in vain that I explained that Edmund refused an allowance. This only made Marshall snort.

I dreaded intensely telling him of my present proposals.

He listened to my story in absolute silence, which made me more and more nervous as I went on.

His lips stuck out in an unpleasant way which reminded me of the Psalmist's description of those hateful people who used to say "tush" to the godly.

My account of the enterprise began to seem unconvincing even to myself as it had never done before, and the narrative tailed off on a note of apology, which for the life of me I could not keep out of it.

"That's all you know about the business?" he asked.

"Yes. I think so."

"My dear Davoren, you've wasted my time and your own money bringing me down here."

"I'm sorry; but why?"

"You don't want a lawyer, you want a doctor."

"Oh! no thanks. I don't care about doctors while I'm well. They talk shop and smell of iodoform, or whatever they call the stuff."

"You want a mental specialist, what they call an alienist."

"I've always wondered why they call them that?"

"You can look it up in the dictionary. But that's not the point. You must consult one. You're ill."

"Oh? I hadn't noticed it. Bates hasn't said anything about it."

"I presume you have not informed Bates that you propose to embark not only your capital, but your self, on a rickety old Levantine schooner with a crew of cut-throat niggers, a young scapegrace of a brother, and some kind of a sea-captain, about whom you know nothing whatever, except that he has spent his life trying to pick up a precarious living among all sorts of dagoes in the East."

"Edmund is a pretty good judge of a boat, you know, and if she has come here from the Mediterranean she ought to be able to take me to the Channel Islands and back."

Marshall only snorted in the way that I particularly loathed.

"Anyhow," I continued, "my taking a trip for pleasure is no part of the business. It does not come into the agreement. As for the money, you know I should not be ruined by the loss of a couple of thousand pounds, though I don't want to lose it, and I don't believe I shall. I'm doing it to help Edmund."

"Well, I won't draft any such damned agreement!"

"I'm sorry. I shall have to get somebody in Brighton. Who is the best solicitor there?"

"I had better recommend you to the worst, I think. But, seriously, Davoren, are you going on with this?"

"Certainly I am. I've promised."

"Well, in that case I had better protect you to the best of my ability."

I was immensely gratified to find I had won a victory at such a comparatively small cost to my self-respect.

Marshall went to my desk and began to write hurriedly, and very soon "This Indenture Witnessed that Whereas &c." I made a transitory appearance in the document under my proper name and title, being "herein-after known" as something else, as which I should never have recognised myself. I had always a difficulty in understanding this kind of composition, and Marshall's essay was no exception to the rule. But I gathered that the payment to me of five per cent. on my capital was to be a first charge on the assets and profits of the concern, and was to be independent of any agreed share of such profits "if and when accruing."

There was another clause empowering me at any time to have all "ships, vessels, premises, stock-in-trade, books, accounts," and various other things which might or might not be our property, examined, inspected, valued, and various other things done to them, by an accountant to be nominated by me, and who was to make me an account, and do all sorts of other arduous things which would have conveyed nothing whatever to me.

I protested against both these clauses; against the first as showing avarice, and against the second as suggesting suspicion.

"I don't think Captain Welfare would like it," I said.

"I don't expect for a moment that he will," Marshall replied grimly, "but they're going in all the same. That's what I am here for."

I had gained so much of my own way that I did not care to contest the point. Besides, I reflected, I could explain to Edmund that I didn't intend to act on either of them.

When the drafts of the agreement came down for signature, however, Welfare took them quite as a matter of course and assured me he would have insisted on them himself.

I wrote and told Marshall this, but he had conceived an inveterate prejudice against Welfare.

We were now in the beginning of April, with the spring coming in like a flood-tide and all was ready for our start. Mr. Snape was coming to be introduced to the parish, and a boyish feeling of emancipation and excitement was making me feel rather absurd to myself.

I wanted to go with them to Tilbury, so as to have as much sailing as possible, but it appeared that there were objections to this. They agreed that the *Astarte* would want a lot of furbishing up before she was ready to receive a guest.

"I want you to see her at her best," Edmund said.

It was almost the first time he had spoken cordially about my going at all, so I readily gave up the point.

"What about Newhaven? It's the nearest port," I said.

"Oh, Newhaven or Dover would be all right," said Edmund.

"I'll tell you what," said Captain Welfare. "I've been looking at the beach down below here. It's a nice handy cove for landing, and there's soundings enough for the *Astarte* up to within a quarter mile of the shore. Why not let us lie to and take you off right here? We'd save time and harbour dues, and economy's the motto for the *Astarte*."

"That's an A1 idea, Welfare," said Edmund.

It appealed to me too in my new-born spring mood of adventure. I agreed at once.

"And we'll have your kit taken down by the famous tunnel and so make some use of it."

Even my repugnance to the idea of that passage had vanished, and I consented to this arrangement also. It added a touch of mystery to the adventure.

"Talking of that passage," said Captain Welfare, "we'd save railway freight if we brought the rest of the stuff for the shop along with us. If Mr. Davoren wouldn't mind storing it till Schultz can fetch it?"

"Not a bit. It would be all right in the cellar, I suppose?"

"Oh, certainly. The men will carry it up the passage and store it till it can be fetched. It'll save a lot of handling, as Schultz can have it all brought straight to the shop by road."

It all seemed to me a perfectly natural and convenient arrangement, and I remember laughingly stipulating with Edmund that he should drive away the bats before I ventured down the passage.

They left the next day, expecting to be away about a week.

I was to receive a post-card telling me as nearly as possible when the *Astarte* would fetch up.

I was left alone with my locum tenens, Mr. Snape. I fear he found me an uneasy host.

He was a terribly earnest young man, who had made himself ill by overworking and under-feeding in slum parishes.

He was the kind of clergyman who is always described as a "good organiser." In certain circles this is the highest praise that can be bestowed on a clergyman. I never quite understood what it meant, or what these people organised. I always vaguely associated it with having printed tickets for things, and lists of names.

He was very polite and agreeable, and even inclined to be deferential to me, I suppose regarding me as a man of comparative wealth, and possibly impressed by my position as a Justice of the Peace, a position that had been forced upon me, for which I was quite unfitted, and of which I certainly was not proud. I only supposed these were the reasons for his deference, because he had never heard of my historical researches, or of my reputation as a pigeon-fancier.

In spite of this, and without at all intending it, he made me feel that he was shocked.

The modest comfort of my habits shocked his ascetic instinct. He was shocked by my not saying grace before dinner, and bowed his head and crossed himself in silence before he took his soup. I knew this would upset Bates, who is an Evangelical of rather strong views. If I had only thought of it, I would have said some ordinary sort of grace myself, which Bates would not have minded nearly so much.

But it was worse when he began to question me about the "parochial organisation," and discovered that there was no communicants' guild, no G.F.S. (I had to think hard before I could remember what a G.F.S. was), no lads' brigade, no mothers' union—none of the things he thought there ought to be. I had never before realised the utter nakedness of my parish in the paraphernalia of organised soul-saving.

Poor Snape, who was a gentleman, was more embarrassed than myself.

"Is there much debt on the church?" he asked after a pause.

"Not a penny," I said, brightening up, for the moderate debt that I had found I had myself paid off, and I thought our solvency at least was in our favour.

But it was not so. Snape looked more than ever depressed.

"I have always found that a debt is such a stimulus to the laity," he said mournfully. "It unites them in organised efforts."

"Yes, perhaps, in some places, but I'm afraid bazaars and things would never go well in Borrowdean. People would not understand about getting them up, or know what to do with them. They have a great idea of getting value for their money."

"But how do you work your parish, Mr. Davoren? What do you do in it, without any of the usual methods?"

"Oh, I just—potter about. They don't behave badly as a rule, and I try to make them behave better. I'm always here if any of them want to see me, or want me to visit them. I don't think they'd care for a parson strolling into their houses as if he had a right to do so. Then there's the church. Our service is really restful and harmonious. And of course we have a Sunday School."

"Oh, of course."

"Then the publican is a tenant of mine and I insist on his selling honest liquor. I also try to stop fellows drinking too much of it."

"But do you think that the church should countenance the public-house?"

"Oh yes! I think it's most important to have our public-houses decent, respectable, civilised places. I often drop in to make sure all is well."

"I am afraid it would be impossible for me, as an abstainer, to do that," he cried, dissimulating his horror with difficulty.

"Of course. I should not advise you to try. But if I were to become an abstainer, not only should I dislike it very much myself, but nobody would behave any the better for my sacrifice. As it is, some of them do behave better for knowing that I may come in to their public-house for a chat and a glass of beer with them."

I saw that Snape was not only puzzled but pained by the unfamiliarity of my views, so I hastened to change the subject.

"I think a country parson can really do a little good for his flock by just living among them and not putting on side," I said. "One can help in various ways, material and other. I have been able, for instance, by a little timely financing to help a young couple to get married, and so have prevented an otherwise inevitable scandal."

"But that sort of thing would be utterly impossible in a large industrial parish!"

"Of course it would. But this is a small country parish. It would have been impossible for me to do what I have said if I had not had some private means; though of course the young people paid me back by degrees. But isn't it possible that the methods which seem best in the populous parish may not be equally suitable in a little community like this?"

Without really meaning to, I had got the better of him in mere logic. I saw that he was distressed by feeling that my logic, though unanswerable, was wrong. It is a feeling I know well myself and hate.

"I daresay I am only defending my own laziness and incapacity, to myself as well as to you," I continued. "The fact is I don't understand how to run these things. If you like, I shall be delighted if you inaugurate all the organisations you think necessary while I am away. Then perhaps you can teach me to keep them going when I return, if they seem to work well."

"I'm afraid the time is too short," he said regretfully.

"Well then, stop on as long as necessary—on the same terms, of course."

His look of gratitude was very affecting. Yet I regretted my hospitality; for though he commanded my respect, he bored me terribly. I was not uneasy about his organisation, being confident that not even Paul and Apollos could stimulate my Sussex parishioners to a "combined effort."

"I must ask the bishop about it," Snape said.

"Do," I said, cravenly sure that Parminter would rescue me from the full consequences of my impulse.

This was our only long conversation during the impatient days while I waited for Edmund's post-card.

A note came at last to say they were starting. I was to begin looking out for them on the afternoon following the day I received it. The time of their arrival of course depended on wind and tide. I had somehow forgotten to allow for this uncertainty in my anticipation, and now it added to my impatience.

Bates packed up my things wistfully. He had pleaded hard to be taken, and I should have been glad to have him in many ways. But it appeared there was no possible accommodation for him on the *Astarte*. Besides, I had no one else to leave in charge of the pigeons and Snape.

Bates had the imagination and sympathy which make the best kind of servant, and he conceived of me as something utterly helpless in his absence.

I shook off Snape as soon as I could after lunch, and went up on the Downs where I could get a wide view of the Channel.

There was a fresh topsail breeze from the east, a fair wind for the *Astarte*. I knew it had held steady for forty-eight hours. It was not unreasonable to expect that she would come up to time or ahead of it.

I had an unreasoning desire to see her for which I could not account. But I had a feeling that something was going to intervene to prevent my sailing. When the idea had first been broached, it had been but a matter of a trip to me. Now it had somehow assumed an unwarranted importance. My desire for the start filled me with senseless apprehensiveness. I was like a schoolboy dreading rain on his holiday.

I could not account for this mood in myself; it made me uneasy, and intensely intolerant of any society—especially Snape's.

There was a warm April sun glowing on the Downs, and glistening on the loose flints that everywhere pushed their way up through the chalk, and lay about among the short grass of the sheep-pastures. The Channel was a crisp blue under a shining sky, and the air was full of the infinitely soothing sound of the distant calling of sheep.

Peace came over me as I lay watching for the expected sail, wondering what exotic form it would take, trying to picture the long bowsprit and the head-sails "like a skein of geese" that I had been told of.

But the afternoon wore on and no sail came in sight, none at least that could be the *Astarte*.

The wind grew cold as the sun dipped to its setting, and I rose with a little shiver to go home, calm but disillusioned.

"No sign of Mr. Edmund?" I asked deceitfully of Bates.

"No, sir."

I felt that the moment had passed, that he would not now come at all, and that I should not set sail in the *Astarte*.

But I did not want Bates to know I had been watching for her all afternoon.

The sky had clouded over, and it was dark in my study when I heard Edmund's voice outside.

I went out and met him coming from the passage that led to the kitchen and cellars. He must have come up the tunnel.

"Hullo," he said. "Sorry I'm late. We were delayed starting and miscalculated the tide a bit. We expected to get the ebb sooner, however it will be making nicely now. How are you? How do you do, Mr. Snape?"

"Is the *Astarte* here?" I asked.

"Of course she is. We're not mooring her, just keeping her lying-to till we get the stuff—the stock I mean—ashore and take you off. Are you quite ready?"

"Can't you stop and dine?"

"Oh, just some soup and a snack, but we mustn't be long. Just while the other boat comes ashore and we off-load her. Let's get in to your fire. It's cold on the water."

We went into the study and I switched on the lights. The rosy comfort of my room struck me with a kind of pang as I thought of leaving.

"Thank you, Bates, just what I wanted," said Edmund as Bates brought in a tray with decanter and syphon.

He drank with a little shudder as though of cold, though he did not look cold, but ill at ease.

Snape shuddered too as he watched him.

I knew that seeing a man drink a whisky-and-soda, unsanctified even by the presence of a meal, gave him a feeling of being in some unhallowed presence, and filled him with a desire to protest that was choked down only by his shyness.

"Get some dinner in at once, Bates," I said, "anything that's ready."

"Got all your traps ready?"

"Yes. All strapped and waiting. I had almost given you up."

After a hasty meal we walked down by the road to the beach. Snape came with us, smiling vacuously as though he thought we were doing something comic, but couldn't see the joke.

"The niggers can bring your kit down when they have stowed away the goods," Edmund said.

It would be long before the moon, nearing its last quarter, rose. The only light was from a pale border of sky in the west under the straight edge of the great cloud mass that had overspread the firmament.

It had rained a little, and the roofs of cottages and loose stones on the beach gleamed feebly in the dark.

The sea broke dully on the shore, each wave drawing away from the shingle with a regretful sound. A dark blotch on the edge with two motionless figures beside it was the dinghy.

As my eyes grew accustomed to the faint light I could make out a dim nucleus of blackness against the dull pewter of the sea. This was all we could see of the *Astarte*. She looked a long way off in the gloom.

Presently Edmund said, "There comes the boat."

I could see nothing, but very soon I heard the double-knock of oars in rowlocks. Then a moving blackness became visible with pale flashes from the blades of the oars.

The boat was much nearer than I had judged, for a few strokes brought her to the shore.

Immediately a harsh guttural gabbling broke out among the crew, which was at once checked by a gruff order from someone in the stern-sheets.

Edmund hurried down to the boat, as her crew hauled the bow a few yards up on the beach.

Snape and I followed him more slowly. We seemed to be forgotten in the silent bustle that was taking place.

I could just make out the lines of an able, roomy ship's boat, and I was a good deal surprised at the amount of cargo she had brought ashore. Case after case was being handed out and stacked on the beach. They looked like good-sized packing-cases, and the men handled them as though they were fairly heavy.

However, the crew of six had them out in about a minute, and then each man shouldered a case with surprising dexterity and they started in a group stumbling up the beach under their loads.

In the darkness I could just make out that some of the men had loose Turkish trousers and some wore the long robe or galabieh of the Arab. Their faces were invisible in the dusk, except for glints of white from eyes and teeth, and most of them seemed to have a white handkerchief or turban bound round their heads.

Edmund and the man who had been in the stern-sheets were talking aside in low tones, and now they guided the laden men to the rough path in the cliff leading to the tunnel.

Snape and I followed, fascinated by this strange, impossible invasion of our quiet Sussex cove.

"It is quite like the old days of the smugglers!" giggled Snape.

It irritated me to feel that he had no sense of the real eerie strangeness and mystery of the scene, and I wished I were alone.

I heard Edmund's voice, almost unrecognisable in the harsh gutturals of Arabic, giving directions, as I guessed, about getting up the path. Then someone slipped and I heard the quick swish of a whip, the thud of its lash on flesh, and a growl like that of a wounded beast.

I drew in my breath with a little gasp and a throb of the heart, wondering if Edmund had struck the blow.

It seemed a horrible and hideous thing to me then.

The two men who had been with the dinghy now passed us also bearing loads, and three of the first party came back for others. Edmund and the rest had evidently gone on up the tunnel to my cellar.

It was strange to me to think of these wild-looking creatures even in the cellar of my peaceful home, and I wondered what Bates would think of them. I sincerely hoped that Mrs. Rattray would keep out of their way.

I knew how utterly she would disapprove of them, and feared I should sink in her estimation by such an association.

And Mrs. Rattray's good opinion was very precious to me.

In an incredibly short time all the cases had disappeared and the men were back with my luggage.

Bates came to see me off, bringing some things he had thought of at the last moment as likely to add to my comfort.

"Is everything all right, Bates?"

"Yes, sir. Everything stowed away quite right."

"What do you think of the crew?"

"Well, sir, I didn't see much of them. But I hope you'll keep your things locked up."

"You think they're thieves?"

"Well, I believe those sort of low-class foreigners mostly are, sir."

As we were getting into the boat Snape asked which I thought would be the best evening for the G.F.S.?

"I don't know," I said firmly, "ask Miss Gregson at the post-office."

I don't know what put Miss Gregson into my head, but as the Arabs rowed us through the night with a strange grunt at each stroke, I felt the Girls' Friendly Society was very remote.

Edmund remained silent, and it seemed to me there had been an air of silence and speed about the whole proceeding that was puzzling. I regretted it because it took away from my feeling of holiday exhilaration.

"You had quite a big cargo," I said.

"Must keep up the stock, you know."

"Of course. I didn't know you had so much in reserve. How quickly these fellows handled it. They're very smart."

"They've got to be smart when Jakoub is around," said Edmund grimly.

I guessed that the silent native who sat with us in the stern was Jakoub, and remembered Edmund's description of him.

I hoped it had been he who had used the whip.

"Here we are," said Edmund, as the *Astarte* suddenly became distinct and closer to us.

Someone fixed the port light in its bracket. There was no other light on deck, but a glow came through the sky-lights covering the saloon, and shone upwards along the tall pointed mainsail.

The boat was brought alongside, a short ladder slung from the side and, as I put my foot on it, a hand grasped mine and Captain Welfare said, "Welcome to the *Astarte*, sir."

I thanked him and came aboard, followed by Edmund and the crew. At the same time the dinghy came alongside and was made fast.

There was a gruff order "Esta'ad," followed by other words in Arabic which had the curious effect of fierceness to which the language lends itself. There was a rattle as sheets were hauled down and belayed and, with the two boats still in tow, the *Astarte* was on the wind and gathering way.

My heart leaped to the glorious sensation.

"We're off!" I exclaimed in surprise.

"Yes. We don't want to miss any of this tide," said Captain Welfare. "But it's no good standing here in the cold and dark. Come down to the saloon and have a look at your cabin. Get those boats aboard, Jakoub."

CHAPTER 5

WHAT THE LITTLE STEAMER BROUGHT

IT was clearly impossible for me to make the real acquaintance of the *Astarte* that night and, as it was certainly raw and cold on deck in the dark, I gladly followed Captain Welfare down the companion to the saloon.

Here I found a most unexpected scene of comfort and civilisation. Most of my limited experience of yachting had been gained in small boats, and I had foolishly modelled my anticipation of the *Astarte* on my recollections of these. So I was surprised at the width and spaciousness I found.

A powerful lamp deeply shaded in red and suspended from the skylight lit up the table, which was laid for some sort of late evening meal. There were deep-red tulips in vases, and a pleasant gleam of silver and cut glass on the white cloth. The chairs, of course, were of the marine type, fixed in the floor with revolving seats.

Over the lockers along each side were deep luxurious seats, upholstered in dull red morocco, and over these, between the wide port-holes, each panel was filled with a pictorial tile of Delft ware, with a singularly clean and restful decorative effect of blues and browns. The further bulkhead on either side of the narrow door leading for'ard was filled with bookcases. A soft Persian carpet and the curving sides of the ship, the cunning shelves and cupboards that occupied odd corners, all combined to produce that air of cosiness that can be found nowhere in such perfection as in a ship's cabin.

Captain Welfare was openly delighted by my praises of all these arrangements. There was something comical though pathetic in his anxiety for my approval. In fact I began to fear that his apologetic attitude would become a little wearisome if he persisted in it.

Thus he apologised for the leather upholstering and entered into a long explanation of the reasons for the absence of velvet. It was in vain that I assured him with the utmost sincerity that I greatly preferred leather. He simply did not listen. It was evident that he himself considered that red velvet cushions would have done me more honour, and really deplored their absence. My protestations he regarded as mere politeness, and he was concerned only in his own explanations. In the same spirit he kept apologising for the absence of many things which I should have loathed had they been there.

My cabin had been newly furnished throughout, and I found something very touching in the almost ladylike care which had been spent upon it.

I had for some time realised that, as Edmund had said he would, Captain Welfare regarded me as a "swell"; and simply because I was quite unconscious of being anything of the sort, he had conceived a queer kind of devotion to me.

Like the great majority of mankind, both Welfare and Edmund were pleasantest when acting as host. Especially Edmund, because his pride in the ship was gratified by my real pleasure in it, and he was of course free from that well-meant but fussy solicitude that is so common in hosts and so very wearing for the guest.

After our early and hurried meal the supper on board was most acceptable.

The *Astarte* was footing pleasantly before the fair wind with very little motion, and as we chatted in the warm light of the saloon I felt that my holiday was going to be a great success.

"When do you expect to reach Guernsey?" I asked.

"If this breeze holds we shall be there the morning after tomorrow at latest," said Captain Welfare. "But we can't count on it this time of year. It may fall calm any minute. Then it will be a matter of luck with the tides and what bits of wind we can catch."

"I'm in no hurry," I said with a sense of luxurious freedom, "I rather hope we shall be delayed."

"Well, we'll be a few days in Guernsey anyhow, and then I want to go on to Jersey. I hope that will be quite convenient to you, Mr. Davoren?"

"I shall be delighted. If you call at Alderney and Sark and all the rest of them, it will be all right to me!"

"I've heard from my correspondent in Jersey," said Captain Welfare with a little grandiloquence, "of a bit of cargo there we might as well bring back. It will help to pay our expenses."

"That's delightful. The touch of business takes away all the sense of futility one usually has on a yacht."

"Yes," said Edmund, "going to look at places and photograph them simply because everyone else has labelled them pretty, or picturesque, or interesting or something. That kind of yachtsman is only an expensive kind of tripper after all."

"I've had good times on a yacht too, I must admit," I said with a retrospective sigh.

"And I never have," said Edmund with sudden bitterness. "I've had to watch other people, ladies and asses in white flannels, floating into a harbour on some millionaire cheesemonger's 1000-tonner, while I've stood, black to the eyes, watching the dagoes coal ship, or punching niggers on some bit of a trading scow. It's simply a case of 'sour grapes' with me, old man!"

He ended with a laugh that grated on me. It was a cynical laugh, very unlike the Edmund of old, and yet, I felt, typical of much that I had noticed in his bearing since he had been home this time. I did not like to think of him having been driven to envy mere prosperous, idle people; and I was sure there was something deeper in his resentment than common jealousy of idleness and wealth. The bishop's words came back to me with painful force—"There is nothing worse for a gentleman than to be *déclassé*." And with this there recurred my old wonder, what it was that Edmund had "surrendered"?

"I don't think you need envy anybody while you're on the *Astarte*," I said quietly.

"Oh! I haven't a word to say against the *Astarte*," Edmund admitted.

Captain Welfare leaned back with a sigh of relief. He had watched Edmund anxiously during his momentary discontent. Indeed I had noticed that he often seemed uneasy when Edmund expressed any dissatisfaction, as though some restraint were needed to keep him in the partnership. I attributed this merely to the want of steadfastness I knew so well in Edmund.

"Of course," he said, as if in explanation, "we've not always been on the *Astarte*. We had some rough times before we got her, as you know, sir. But if things go as well as they're doing for another three years, you'll be able to have your own yacht, Mr. Edmund, and bother no more about cargoes."

"I shan't want it then. Once I'm independent of trade, I shall want to stick to it."

This was of course unintelligible to Captain Welfare, with his ideal of "retiring"; but I understood perfectly. I said to myself, "The bishop was right. Edmund must have some service to perform as soon as possible."

A tremendous sleepiness came upon me, and early as it was I said good-night and turned in.

I was on deck betimes next morning and found the sun well up in a clear blue April morning sky. The *Astarte* was foaming along very gaily with free sheets, two big square sails set on her foremast and all her headsails drawing. There was a fair amount of following sea from which she lifted her short counter with exhilarating buoyancy.

She struck me as bigger and more of a ship than I had expected. The bulwarks round the afterdeck were nearly breast high, as she had a great deal of free-board for her size. There was a kind of short waist amidships, covering the hold, and a small deck over the fo'c'sle. Her slightly raking masts and leg-o'-mutton sails looked a tremendous height from the deck, and the whole boat seemed to taper away to the great sloping bowsprit with its flight of jibs. I thought what a weird-looking craft she must be from outside. But I realised that her lines, though strange, must be beautiful.

Her decks were holystoned and scrubbed to the whiteness of paper, and the thin lines of caulking between the planks had the polish of jet. The inside of the bulwarks and other parts were newly painted in green and white, and the mahogany and brass of the sky-lights, the wheel and binnacle, all shone with the lustre of well-tended furniture.

Two or three of the crew were busy about the deck.

Their bare legs, shining like brown silk stockings, their bright, exotic costumes, and dark faces with teeth flashing as they grinned and chattered at their work, gave me a queer feeling of having been transported in my sleep to the unknown East.

One of them was a thin, delicate creature with a skin of the colour and polish of black-lead—a Soudanese as I afterwards learned.

The wheel was a little abaft of the saloon companion. It was in charge of a tall, gracefully built Arab in a handsome blue linen galabieh. As we were practically before the wind there was little strain on the wheel, which he handled delicately and instinctively with one hand. The soft fez at the back of his head was bound with the green of a descendant of the Prophet. His lean brown face had an essential air of aristocracy and command in its repose. Only his accipitrine eyes seemed alert, intent on everything from the horizon to the details of the work of the man nearest to him. He reminded me irresistibly of a half-tamed falcon on a perch.

I guessed this must be Jakoub, who had sat next us in the boat, but whom I could not be said to have seen, and to whom I had not yet spoken.

"Sa'ida Effendi," he said gravely as I approached him. He made his dignified salaam, touching his forehead, lips and breast with a gesture that surprised me, for it was so like the Christian ceremony of crossing one's self.

"Good morning," I said; "do you speak English?"

"I speak all the languages. They are alike to me."

"You are—er—Jakoub?"

I knew no other name for him, but I was honestly afraid of being unduly familiar in addressing him by his—whatever the Mohammedan equivalent of a Christian name may be.

"I am your Excellency's servant—Jakoub," he replied.

He seemed to wait for me to continue the conversation if I wanted to; but would evidently be quite unembarrassed if no more were said. I uttered the usual futility about the morning.

"It is, sir, ver' beautiful," he replied. "Your English sea can be sometimes beautiful, but it is not so often."

He politely offered me the wheel, asking if I would like to steer. I took it from him. Being better used to a tiller, I did not at first find my touch, and allowed a following sea to break square on our counter. A heavy dash of spray wetted us both, but Jakoub only smiled politely at my vexation.

It was then that I began to hate him. His manner was polite, in fact obsequious, but from the beginning of our acquaintance I felt that he regarded me as a sort of joke, as something utterly negligible. In the covert insolence of his handsome face I thought I read too that were I ever in his way he would see me thrown overboard as if I were a rat.

I wondered at Edmund's easy-going toleration of such a man.

This was, however, my only disagreeable impression on board the *Astarte* and, as I had no occasion to see the man, it soon passed from my mind as I fell into the mood of the cheerfully passing hours aboard ship.

The weather kept fine, and the breeze held throughout the day and the night.

Intent on picking up a little colloquial Arabic, I spent a good deal of time talking to the Arab who acted as waiter and servant in the saloon. Although I had never before heard the language spoken, I had in the course of my researches gained some little acquaintance with the terrors of Arabic grammar, and even some vocabulary, which I now found I pronounced all wrong.

It was a relief to find that the extraordinary complexities of the language, as written by scholars, disappeared from the tongue as spoken, and I hoped it would not be impossible to compass a passable imitation of their weird gutturals and deep chest tones.

Hassan, as our servant was called, professed to be astonished at my proficiency, and I was encouraged by finding that I could soon pick out some words and phrases in listening to the jabber of the Arab crew.

Edmund was often able to help me in points I could not well explain to Hassan, although he averred he only knew enough of the language "to curse the niggers in."

To Captain Welfare my progress was miraculous. He said that to have been able to speak and understand the language would once have been worth a thousand pounds to him, but he had been told it was derived from camel-talk, and had not believed it was possible for a Christian to learn it.

He had all the ignorant Englishman's feeling that there is something undignified in using any language spoken by what he calls generically "natives," which is curiously mingled with profound respect for anyone else who can do it.

It was on our second morning out that I found Captain Welfare on deck before me.

"That's Alderney," he said, pointing to a long low coast-line just visible on our port bow.

"Already?" I asked. "We seem hardly to have started."

"I'm glad it's not been tedious, sir. But we're a good way from Guernsey yet. The wind's inclined to south a bit though, and if it goes a few more points we'll get our square sails set again. Then if it holds we'll be there or thereabouts tonight or tomorrow morning."

"Well, I'm in no hurry to get there, as I said."

"That's maybe just as well. You never know your luck at sea in a sailing boat."

By midday I was watching the sea break over the famous Casquets, which looked like the jaw of a dog in the water. We went down to luncheon, and were just having our coffee after the meal when the saloon door opened and Jakoub came in.

This was an unwarranted intrusion, for Jakoub had neither the status of a guest nor a servant, and etiquette is necessarily rigid at sea. I saw Welfare flush angrily and look at him with astonishment in his round bright eyes.

"What the devil——?" began Edmund.

Jakoub looked at him quite impassively and said a few words in Arabic which I did not understand.

I saw Edmund look startled.

"Get away on deck and I'll follow you in a minute," he said.

Jakoub gravely salaamed and left, carefully closing the door.

"What's the matter?" asked Welfare.

"I'm just going to see. Nothing much, I expect," Edmund replied, but I thought there was a note of anxiety in his voice.

"Infernal cheek of him walking in here, whatever it is," grumbled Welfare.

"Yes, of course," Edmund agreed. "He should have given his message to Hassan."

I was enjoying the situation, taking the cowardly pleasure that one does when a man one dislikes incurs the blame of people one suspects of supporting him. I had felt I was in a minority in my resentment of Jakoub, and now I tasted the craven joy of having others on my side.

"Excuse me," said Edmund as he finished his coffee, and he went on deck.

"I hope there's nothing wrong?" I said to Welfare.

"Oh, there can't be anything *wrong* exactly. A bit of a scrap among some of the crew, I daresay."

In spite of his words he looked uneasy as he lit a cigarette.

"Don't let me keep you if you want to go up," I said.

"Perhaps I might as well have a look." He followed Edmund and I was left alone.

There were no unusual sounds, nor any sign of alteration in the weather. I felt that if it was only some matter of the ship's discipline they would prefer me to remain below.

I drank another cup of coffee, but then curiosity overcame my scruples and I went on deck.

A little dirty steamer had come up to within a quarter of a mile of us, one of those tiny nondescript things that knock about near harbours with a bit of deck for'ard and a funnel right in the stern making a vast amount of black smoke. Someone on her deck was handing down a string of signal-flags as I came up, and I noticed that our course was altered so as to bring us right down to her. There was nothing else to be seen save the spouts of foam over the Casquets, now far astern.

Captain Welfare, Edmund and Jakoub were leaning on the port bulwarks, watching the little vessel and then Edmund came past me to take the wheel from one of the Arabs.

"What's up?" I asked.

"It's a letter from the people in Guernsey—I don't know what they want."

The wheel was put over a few spokes, the crew paid out some of the main and fore-sheets, and the *Astarte* went foaming down widely to leeward of the steamer.

I heard the "cling-cling" of the steamer's engine signal, and her noisy propeller stopped.

Then our wheel was put hard over, the big booms came aboard with a swing, and the *Astarte* came into the wind with a tremendous flapping of her head-sails. Her way took her within a few yards of the steamer, and as the helm was put over again she slid slowly along her lee.

A man on the dirty little bridge gave us a hail and swung out a small packet attached to a light line which was neatly caught by Jakoub.

"All right?" he hailed in English.

"All right."

The steamer's skipper rang his engines on again, the *Astarte* gathered her way, and the two boats parted with a wave of the hand from the man on the bridge.

I saw Captain Welfare cut the canvas wrappings from the packet that had been thrown aboard. He took a letter out, opened it, and glanced at it swiftly.

Then it seemed to me that he looked across the deck at myself with an expression of regretful perplexity on his great heavy face.

It occurred to me that this was how he would look if he had to announce to me that someone very dear to me were dead.

But at the same time I knew I was the one member of the party who could not be affected by the news, whatever it might be.

Still holding his letter in both hands and glancing at it, Captain Welfare walked across to Edmund and spoke to him.

Edmund nodded, called Jakoub, and handed over the wheel to him. Then they both disappeared down the companion.

I set down all these details as minutely as I can remember them, because it is from them that I have since had to piece together in my mind all that was happening during this time when I had no clue to their meaning.

I had no mind to speak to Jakoub, and stood leaning over the bulwark watching the lessening smudge of black smoke that represented the little steamer.

Edmund had left us sailing with free sheets on our course to Guernsey, so I was surprised on looking up to see the crew getting in sheets, while Jakoub put us on a course close-hauled to windward.

I surprised a look in Jakoub's face as though he were waiting for some sign of uneasiness on my part. His face was more than usually insolent, I thought, so I merely looked up along the leech of the sail till the tremor died from it as the *Astarte* settled to her new work. Then I returned to my former posture and waited ten minutes by my watch before I went below.

The saloon was empty, but I heard voices from Welfare's cabin, which had room for a good-sized table in it, and served as a kind of office and chart-room.

I lay down on one of our delightfully comfortable locker couches with a novel I had been trying to get interested in. The steady motion of the boat and the soft diffused light that came down from the skylight were very soothing.

The book was one that Captain Welfare regarded as a masterpiece of literature. He would not be satisfied until I had read and praised it. I was conscientiously trying to do the former, and intended afterwards to praise it without consulting my conscience. It was one of those novels that people write again and again, like the pictures that turn up season after season at the Academy—"Nymphs Bathing," "Autumn's Fiery Finger," and the like. I forget whether this book was about Cavaliers and Roundheads, or the French Revolution. But very soon I began to be interested in the patterns made by the spaces between the printed words; they seemed to run in wavy lines down the page, and soon the book had lost all power to bore me. Presently I heard the cabin-door open, and Edmund and Welfare came out, speaking in low tones.

"You'll have to tell him," Edmund was saying.

"But what am I to say?"

"Stick to what we arranged. You must chalk it all down to Jakoub."

I perceived from their voices that they thought I was asleep, and though their conversation had conveyed no meaning to me, I did not want to over-hear more. I coughed and sat up.

"I hope we have not disturbed you?" Welfare asked, looking, I thought, a little guilty.

"Not at all. But I'm afraid I have dozed a little over this most interest-ing book. It's the sea air, and the motion."

"Quite so, quite so," said Captain Welfare solemnly.

Edmund said nothing and went on deck.

Captain Welfare sat down facing me in one of the revolving chairs on the opposite side of the table.

His eyes looked distressful in the midst of his great cicatrix of a face, and I noticed perspiration on his forehead and upper lip.

"I hope there's nothing wrong?" I said.

"Well, we've had some rather upsetting news. Nothing wrong exactly, but upsetting. It alters our plans a bit. I was just going to tell you. Me and Mr. Edmund have been talking things over a bit."

His big right hand was pinching up creases in the table-cloth and set-ting it all crooked in a maddening way.

"Well?" I said interrogatively.

"I don't often drink between meals, Mr. Davoren, but I think I'll have a brandy and soda if you don't mind."

"Of course," I said, as he touched the gong on the table and gave his instructions to Hassan.

"Perhaps you'll join me?" he asked hopefully.

I elected to have some whisky, so as to put him a little more at his ease, for he was perturbed to an extent that was quite distressing.

I anticipated nothing but some trouble, possibly some loss, in connec-tion with the business, and was chiefly anxious to know whether Jakoub had been authorised to alter our course.

Captain Welfare swallowed about half of his brandy and soda and mopped his forehead, still regarding me with a look of perplexity and dis-tress.

"Yes," he said, as though continuing a conversation. "Yes. We'll have to give Guernsey a miss."

"Oh! Are you going straight to Jersey, then?"

In the back of my mind I knew that the course we were on was taking us away from the one island as fast as from the other; but I had not thought it out, and felt there must be some way of accounting for the manœuvre.

"No. I'm afraid we'll have to give Jersey a miss too. In fact, we'll have to cut out the islands altogether this trip."

"Really? That's very disappointing. Are we going straight back?"

"Oh no. No, we'll not go back for a bit."

"Well, where on earth *are* we going, Captain Welfare?"

Captain Welfare slowly finished his drink and looked as if he were pondering the advisability of taking another. He finally put his glass down a little tremulously.

"The fact is—you saw this message come aboard?"

"Yes."

"Well, it seems we're wanted out East at once, very urgent. There's nothing for it but to make all sail and get there."

"Out East?"

"The Mediterranean, you know—the old beat."

"But that will take weeks!"

"We should do it in a month with luck, if the weather holds."

"And where are you going to put me off?"

"We were just talking about that, me and Mr. Edmund. You wouldn't think well of making the trip with us, I suppose?"

"That's quite out of the question. I only arranged to be away for two or three weeks."

"It will be a bit warm out there, of course, but not bad really, especially at sea, and the worst of the Khamsins—that's the hot winds, you know—will be over."

"But, Captain Welfare, I don't care about the climate there, for I'm not going. It's impossible. I must ask you to call at Guernsey or somewhere and put me off. Then I could get back to Southampton. I shall be very sorry to leave the boat, but there's nothing else for it."

"It's the time, Mr. Davoren. It might mean missing our markets. We can't afford to take any chances."

"I don't profess to know much about trade——"

"You don't, sir. You don't know anything about it. That's what makes it so hard to explain."

"All the same, I don't see how a delay of twenty-four hours or less in a month's voyage is going to make such a vital difference as all that."

"That's just it, Mr. Davoren. You don't see it. You can't."

"No, and therefore I demand to be landed at Guernsey. After all, I'm a partner."

"To be sure, sir. Nobody questions your right. But we—well, the fact is we can't call at Guernsey. It's not only missing our market—but we should lose Jakoub."

"Jakoub? That would be no great loss, in my opinion. But what has he got to do with it?"

"I'm afraid Jakoub hasn't a very good record. We knew that, of course, when we took him on. I think Mr. Edmund told you?"

"He did. And my own impression is that he's the biggest scoundrel unhung."

"I wouldn't be a bit surprised. But he's extraordinarily useful to us just at present. I don't know what we should do without him. Then they would want us to give evidence, and you don't know what the Egyptian courts are for delay—and worse things."

"But what is it all about? For the Lord's sake, man, tell me straight what's happened."

"I was just going to. It seems he's wanted by the Egyptian police, and they have traced him on to the *Astarte*, and have warrants out for him all over the place. They might put the ship under arrest, and that would simply ruin us. We've got to get him back to Egypt, sir. We can get rid of him there, and we cannot get rid of him any nearer home."

There was an air of finality in his tone which warned me I must try to preserve my dignity, even if bereft of my liberty.

"I think this is a matter that ought to be discussed between all three of us," I said. "Do you mind if I send Hassan to ask my brother to join us?"

"Not at all. I'll go myself," said Welfare with an air of intense relief.

For the time being the thought uppermost in my mind was the anxiety of Bates and Mrs. Rattray at my absence. I had not been long enough away, nor far enough, for the home foreground to recede.

Edmund came in, looking, to my surprise, more cheerful and jollier than he had done for a long time.

"Well," he said, "I suppose Welfare's broken it to you? Ah! I see you've been drinking to the cruise! I'll join you. Hassan, get another glass. I'm really jolly glad, old man, you're coming. You will simply love the Mediterranean."

"It seems to me," I said, with a sincere attempt at austerity, "that I am being taken to the Mediterranean against my will, in order to help a criminal to elude justice."

"Only temporarily," said Edmund; "nothing could keep Jakoub from the gallows in the long run."

"This kind of thing may be all very well for you. But in my position——"

"I know. It wouldn't be considered good form in a clergyman. But I assure you nothing will ever come of it—at home. We're not going 'East of Suez, where there ain't no ten commandments,' but to Egypt and the Levant, where there are so many commandments that nobody can remember them all, or bother very much. Besides, you've no responsibility in the matter, anyhow."

"You forget I'm part owner of this boat."

"We'll make that all right. We'll sign a declaration that you have been shanghaied and brought along under protest. You'll sign, Welfare?"

"Certainly, if Mr. Davoren thinks it necessary."

"I don't want anything of the sort. But you must see it is impossible for me to be so long away from the parish."

"Why, we heard the bishop telling you to stop away as long as you liked; and it will be a godsend for that poor fellow Snape."

"Oh! he won't object, I know. But Bates and Mrs. Rattray will be frantic with anxiety—and all my letters unanswered!"

"We don't suppose it's convenient; but on the other hand there's the chance of making a clear two thousand. Welfare and I can't afford to risk losing that."

"Two thousand pounds? I wish you had let me go back to Guernsey in the boat that brought the message."

"I never thought of that," said Captain Welfare.

"Naturally. We didn't know what the message was. It wouldn't have done, anyhow. No, it's far better as it is. The only thing now is to have as good a time as we can. So here's luck!"

"And I hope you won't feel as if any constraint was put on you, sir," said Captain Welfare with profound solemnity.

Edmund and I both laughed, and in the laugh was my capitulation.

"I can't feel that, Captain Welfare, as long as you do nothing to prevent me swimming home!"

Captain Welfare held out his hand, and took mine gravely.

"Mr. Davoren," he said, "I wouldn't have had this happen for a great deal. I don't know how to thank you for taking it as you do, sir; it's a great relief."

"That's all right," said Edmund; "and now we'll drink prosperity to the trip, and may nothing cheat the gallows of Jakoub."

CHAPTER 6

A PLAN TO SAVE JAKOUB

AS I have said, I used to keep a careful diary as long as my life contained nothing eventful to record.

As soon as things began to happen to me I naturally ceased to record them. I was too busy experiencing them.

The diary habit, I think, presupposes a certain placidity, both of mind and circumstance.

The days that followed each other now on board the *Astarte* were placid enough, but the habit was broken, and I have only a rather confused memory of the long journey.

The wind held from the north and nor'-west, steady and moderate, with bright skies, and the *Astarte*, with the big square sails set, marched steadily over the waters.

One night, as Edmund and I were on the deck before turning in, a great light flashed on our port bow. There was a slight haze, and we could see the great white beam move round across sea and sky like the hand of a vast clock until it struck the *Astarte*, and seemed to pause for an instant searching and almost blinding us ere it moved away again on its night-long quest.

"That's Ushant," said Edmund. "We'll soon be in the Bay now."

For days and nights we were borne along on great following seas that seemed to fling us from one to another. Running before it we felt nothing of the wind that hummed continually in the shrouds, and it was as though we were swept down the current of a mighty river.

Each day Edmund marked our position on the chart, and declared happily that we had beaten all records for a vessel of our size.

Home and all my little anxieties about it vanished from my mind. Even the existence of Jakoub ceased to trouble me.

I lived absorbed in the splendour of our motion and in the rising and setting of the sun.

Then the sea became smoother, though the good wind held, as the land came out to meet us.

For whole days, it seems, I watched the dry, greenish-brown foothills of the Portuguese coast, with white farms and villages embedded in the valleys, and the fantastic outline of the higher land behind them.

We passed fleets of sardine-fishers in boats that seemed to be absurdly small to be so far from land, and for a whole day we were among a school of dolphins that raced and played around us.

Until I had seen those creatures I always thought a flock of swifts, screaming round the roofs in the evening, were the highest expression in nature of speed and delirious joy in life. But now I long to be a dolphin when I die. As they tore past us in groups and couples on the surface of the water, now leaping clear, now diving deep in a common impulse, one expected to hear great shouts of laughter from them in their play. Yet I was told there are men who shoot them and leave a useless, bloody carcass wallowing in their vessel's wake.

One evening it fell almost calm, with a deep-red sunset touching the sea to flashes of rose among its blue, and lighting the coast with a purple and orange glow.

One of the Arabs in the fo'c'sle was singing, or rather chanting, in a high-pitched tenor, and at the end of each sentence his hearers chimed in with a deep chorus of "Kham leila, kha-am yome?" ("How many nights, how many days?")

There was a strange mysterious melody in the monotonous chant which was afterwards to become so familiar. It fixed the whole strange sunset landscape like a dream picture in my mind.

Jakoub came out cursing them. The weird Oriental music ceased, and hatred of Jakoub sprouted anew in my heart.

During all this time we were a cheery, cordial party in the cabin. Edmund seemed to be continually in high spirits as we got farther south and the *Astarte* continued her record-breaking, and every day I found Captain Welfare more likeable as I got to know him better. He had quite stopped apologising to me for things, and had become used to treating me as a man of like passions with himself. He was very interested in the bishop, not having, as he said, met one before.

One day he asked me in strict confidence if I thought his Lordship was really a God-fearing man. I naturally found this a delicate question, and one very difficult to answer.

"I should be very sorry to misrepresent him," I replied cautiously, "but I should take him to be a man who feels he has no need to fear God. After all, why should he?"

Captain Welfare looked at me with as much horror as though I had said something blasphemous.

"No need to fear God!" he replied. "Well, I don't know!"

I saw that if fear, craven fear of a petulant and unreasonable Deity were deleted from his religion, there would be nothing left.

For Welfare was a very simple, literal-minded man. He was one of those who meant "fearing God" when he said it. The words did not convey to him their usual meaning of being bored on Sunday; a commoner and, after all, a much less harmful form of superstition.

I was glad he was shocked, because Ju-ju worship makes me angry, and, unlike the bishop, I am not much interested in the theological ideas of primitive people. I never could see that these ideas had any influence on their conduct. So I was relieved to feel that Captain Welfare would probably not want me to talk about religion any more.

In the intervals between eating and sleeping—the main concerns of a passenger on board ship—I made very material progress in Arabic as expounded by Hassan, and, spending thus a good deal of time in the saloon, I noticed that Captain Welfare was very busy in his cabin. He seemed to spend hours a day writing in a number of large strongly-bound commercial books of the type I was accustomed to think of as "ledgers."

One day he came to me with an air of great satisfaction on his large countenance, as though he were going to give me an unexpected treat.

"I've been thinking, sir," he said, "that now as you're a partner you ought to have a thorough overhaul of the books. So I've got 'em all up to date and summarised, and ready for your inspection, whenever you feel inclined to take an hour or two at them."

"I'm afraid it would not be the slightest use," I said, determined to take a firm stand at the beginning. A great disappointment clouded his expression, and I thought of the hours I had seen him spending over his lamentable occupation.

"You see," I continued, as kindly as I could, "I should not understand them. To me your volumes are simply what Charles Lamb called 'books that are no books.' I have sometimes tried to read the balance-sheets published by charities to which I am a subscriber, and I always find that everything that would normally be regarded as an asset is placed on the debit side of the account; while debts and other liabilities are on the credit side, as if they were something to be proud of. I have tried, but I cannot understand this. There is either some perversity in the business mind, or some blind spot in mine, which prevents our ever coming together, as it were. I have definitely abandoned all idea of trying to grasp what seems to me to be rather absurdly called 'book-keeping.'"

Captain Welfare tried several times to interrupt this long speech; but I was determined to make my position perfectly clear at the start and would not let him.

He looked very disappointed.

"I know what you mean," he said. "I don't mind admitting that sometimes those fancy ways of accounting lays me over myself. But I've got my own method—perfectly clear and—and straightfor'ard. You'll soon pick it up. Just let me show you the 'profit and loss' account."

He looked so pathetic, so like a child when one has not time to take an interest in his toy, that I yielded with a sigh and went into his cabin.

He had a great array of large folios. I admired the binding and the smooth thick paper. I praised the neatness of his handwriting and figures, and particularly admired the diagonal lines which he had ruled in red ink across half-blank pages. These guided the eye down to the words "Total" or "Brought forward," followed by certain pounds, shillings, and pence.

I told him that I had never been able to rule a line with a pen without the ink forming little pools along the ruler, which made blots when you removed it.

I asked him to show me how to do it properly.

But it was no mere manual dexterity of which Captain Welfare was proud. I had to tell him regretfully that his figures conveyed almost nothing to me, although I admitted that they appeared to be based on something more like a rational system than the usual products of professional accountancy.

"Besides," I said, as a cheering thought struck me, "if I want to I can get an accountant to go through all these books and report on them. I might be able to understand his report."

"I don't know," said Welfare doubtfully, "but what I could explain these books better to you than what I could to one of them professional gentlemen. You see, they want things shown by their own method, which ain't applicable to our business, as you say yourself. And they want vouchers which you can't get in our business."

"Vouchers? Oh no, of course not!"

Whatever vouchers might be, I felt I should greatly dislike them.

"I'm glad you feel yourself we hadn't ought to produce vouchers. How can you get a receipt from a native what can't write his own language, let alone any proper one?"

"No, that's obvious," I agreed.

"Well, I just wanted you as a partner to feel you had access to everything, and to know you were perfectly satisfied. Now this," he added, turning up a page in a smaller book, "this is an idea of my own. Just to show you we are running everything on sound business lines. This is the Depreciation Account on the *Astarte*."

"Oh!" I said, trying hard to make the monosyllable sound intelligent and interested.

"Yes; every year we write so much off her value. In a few years' time she'll be depreciated away to nothing."

"Oh! I hope not," I said in alarm at the idea of a few gaunt ribs representing all that was left of the good ship.

"Hope not?" asked Welfare. "But don't you see that every penny we make out of her then will be pure bunce?"

"Is that what they call 'scrap price'?" I asked.

I saw at once that I had said the wrong thing.

"Scrap price? Why, we're not going to sell her!"

"Oh no. Of course not. Yes, of course, it's a splendid idea. I don't quite see where the extra money comes from. Wouldn't it pay better to keep her in repair?"

"Well, I don't know! Of course, we keep her in repair."

"That's all right then. I didn't quite follow."

"The point is, she stands at nothing in the books."

"I see; and sticks at nothing on the sea, eh?"

I laughed at my own pleasantry, and was surprised to see a look of quick suspicion and annoyance on Captain Welfare's usually genial face.

"Nothing in the way of weather, I mean."

Captain Welfare closed his books in silence and put them back on their shelf.

"Well, so long as you're satisfied," he said.

"Oh, I'm perfectly satisfied."

"And the books is there for your inspection whenever you've a mind."

"Thank you. But I'm afraid you'll have to look upon me practically as a sleeping partner."

"Perhaps it will be as well."

I had lost count of the lapse of time under the strange nepenthe-like influence that a sailing-ship at sea possesses. If I thought at all of Bates and Mrs. Rattray, of Snape or the bishop, of parish, or pigeons, or the Byzantine Empire, it was as of dead friends remembered, and dim interests of the past.

The thought of anxiety on the part of people at home no longer worried me. I had no worries. I had hardly even anticipation. The *Astarte* had become my planet, bearing all I knew of humanity. The ocean had become space, through which my planet ever moved, and measurements of time had ceased to matter, as though we were already in Eternity. I was content to lean for hours on the bulwark looking down at the stream of bubbles for ever forming on the ship's side, begotten of the sea by the ship's motion, falling behind us, spinning for a moment on the surface, and expiring in their myriads, countless and insignificant as human lives.

Then one day the horizon was decorated by the delicate white edges of the still snow-covered Sierras of Spain. I do not know for how many days I watched their delicate aerial loveliness. We came nearer the land, and someone pointed out Trafalgar Bay. But even that one magic word was powerless to move me from the trance that had got possession of my soul.

We passed through the Straits at night, and I awoke in the Mediterranean.

We kept near the southern shore, passing under the savage precipices and gullies of Ceuta. The Rock of Gibraltar I saw only in the distance, standing pointed like a helmet. The wind, still northerly, was now on our beam, and there was less of it, so that our progress, though still steady, was slower than it had been.

For days and days it seemed we hugged the African coast, sometimes so close that we could see the stones and sand on the shingly beach below barren rocky foothills. For the most part the land seemed utterly uninhabited, but occasionally we passed a greener tract, where there were sparse crops and stunted bushes, occasionally a flat-roofed hovel among them, and through Captain Welfare's telescope I could make out goats and children moving.

It was strange to me to think of the lives of human beings there.

On other days the land would recede quite out of sight as we passed deep bays, and again we passed islets of rock, precipitous and fantastic in form and colour.

So desolate were these places, it seemed as if ours must be the first eyes to see them, impossible to realise that for ages men had known them, charted, mapped and measured them.

The only human incident I can recall in all this time is that Edmund and Welfare quarrelled one night over their game of piquet, and did not speak to each other until after dinner the following evening, when they resumed their play, and each politely insisted that the other had been right. That is one of the beauties of piquet. It can only be rightly conducted in an atmosphere of eighteenth-century courtliness. It is a game for ladies and gentlemen, and soon, alas! will be played no more. I was surprised to find that Welfare played it, and could as soon have pictured him walking a minuet.

I was still dreamily content, and had ceased to have even any curiosity as to our destination; but as we drew nearer to the coast of Egypt I noticed a new preoccupation in Edmund and Welfare. They made long and intimate studies of the chart, and several times I saw them in conversation with Jakoub.

I began to awake with pain to the renewed sense of the responsibilities and anxieties of life. I had forgotten Jakoub, and to remember his existence again brought back to me all the doubt and fear of the future which is the real tragedy of mankind.

I had seen the splendour of the Mediterranean sky, the pageantry of dawn and sunset, of moonrise and the evening star, as they might have appeared to the first man; but now all was tarnished again by human associations. I had to put on life again as one might don a hair-shirt. And I shrank from it.

Edmund began to hold aloof again, and some instinct warned me that Welfare was seeking in his clumsy mind for the easiest way of making some difficult proposition.

I began almost unconsciously to arm myself against him. So I was on the alert when he said to me one afternoon with an elaborate attempt to speak unconcernedly, "You'd like to see something of the desert while you're out here, I suppose?"

"I should have liked to see Egypt, of course," I replied, pre-warned, "but I can't now. I shall simply have to send a cable and get the first boat for Marseilles."

"To be sure. I know you must be getting home. I shall be very sorry when you leave us, sir."

"Thank you. I shall be quite as sorry to go. It's been a delightful trip. I feel as if I had been dreaming. But I've woken up to reality now, and I must make up my mind to a certain amount of awkwardness after being so long away and sending no word. I must get home and put things straight."

"That is so. I quite understand. I was thinking you would actually save time, and see a bit of the country into the bargain, if you landed near the western frontier and went on overland to Alexandria."

"Is that possible?"

"Quite easy. It would be hot in the desert, of course."

"I don't think I should mind the heat."

"It would be about a day and a half's camel ride from the place I'm thinking of to the railway, and then only a few hours to Alexandria. It would take us longer by sea, even if the wind holds, and it's falling lighter. We'll soon only have the morning and evening breeze to count on."

I found the idea of a camel ride across the desert rather attractive. It would be an adventure, another instalment of the utterly unexpected, a fitting end to this extraordinary voyage.

"You wouldn't, of course, be seeing the Pyramids, or the temples that everybody goes to see, but of course you can visit them any time," Captain Welfare continued, as though impartially weighing the advantages of his own suggestion, "and I don't fancy many tourists get to see the western desert."

"I should like it," I said. "It would be intensely interesting. But how on earth am I to get a camel and a guide? I don't suppose one can whistle for them like a taxi?"

"No; it's a pretty lonesome part. But Jakoub will manage all that."

"Jakoub?" I asked with instant suspicion.

"Yes; Jakoub has got to go that way."

"Then he can go alone," I said with sudden emphasis. "I will not go with him."

"No? I'm afraid that settles it then. It's a pity too, for I think you would have found it interesting."

Captain Welfare walked away as though the subject were closed. If for any reason he wanted me to go with Jakoub, this was the cleverest thing I had known him do; for he left me longing to discuss the matter. Indeed, I came to the conclusion that he could not want me to go, for it was difficult to credit him with so much subtlety.

I resumed the question myself at dinner, anxious to know if Edmund had been consulted before the proposal was made to me. Edmund made no attempt to conceal the fact that it was their joint idea.

"I don't think," he said, "that Welfare has made it quite clear to you why we want you to go."

"I understood that it was to be a sort of pleasure trip for me in charge of this malefactor of yours."

"As a matter of fact, I think you would find the journey interesting, though fatiguing. But that is not the point."

"My point is that I have no wish to be murdered in a howling wilderness by a man of whom I utterly disapprove."

"Jakoub may be a murderer for all I know," Edmund admitted. "I am sure he would become one if it suited his convenience. But you must know that neither Welfare nor I would suggest your going if there was the slightest chance of his murdering you!"

Of course, I did know this perfectly well; but with the babyish perversity that sometimes afflicts quite sensible people, I felt compelled to go on being offended. I was making myself ridiculous, and I knew it, and nothing feeds anger in one's heart like that. But having once adopted a pose, even a pose one dislikes or is tired of, it requires immense strength of mind to abandon it.

I have known the happiness of families wrecked by this fatuous adhesion to a worn-out, discredited and detested pose.

"I don't see," I said, "what is to prevent his murdering me if he wants to. I'm sure he dislikes me as much as I do him."

"Very likely. But under the circumstances you will be necessary to his own safety. Jakoub has sense enough to control his dislikes."

"And in what way am I to protect him?"

"You'll be part of his disguise. He'll go as your dragoman. It's the only way to get him safely into Alexandria, and we must have him there for a few days to negotiate this sale."

"Why can't you go yourself, or Captain Welfare?"

"I'm wanted to navigate the ship. Welfare couldn't manage the business, because he can't talk the lingo. And Jakoub must be got off the ship before they come and look for him."

"And why should I help the brute to escape? I don't want him to escape!"

"Mr. Davoren," said Welfare very solemnly, "Jakoub is a wrong 'un, I admit. A dead wrong 'un. I've never disguised my opinion about that. I don't know what the charges against him may be—not all of them. But I know this, however bad you may think him, if you saw the convict prison at Tourah you wouldn't want to help get him there. If you saw the poor devils there working in chains in the quarries under the desert sun, you'd know that no man is bad enough for it. I tell you, sir, if a convict's friends have any money when he's sent there, they try to bribe a sentry to shoot him. It's all they can do. Men have prayed their judges to hang them, sooner than be sent there."

This appeal of Captain Welfare's impressed me, but I only said, "All the same, I don't see why I should help him to escape the law. It's a very unpleasant, a very risky, a very wrong thing for a man in my position to do."

"But," said Edmund, "you don't know anything against him really except what we've told you—our suspicions."

"You forget that you mentioned warrants for his arrest."

"Aye. We did mention that," said Welfare; "it's a pity, but we had to."

"Captain Welfare, am I to understand that you decide beforehand how much of the truth I am to be told?"

"Oh, dear no, sir. You've been told practically everything. I only meant that if we had kept it quiet about the warrants you'd maybe have been easier in your mind."

"There's no need for us to start disliking each other," Edmund remarked judicially; "the situation is simply this. Jakoub must go. If you don't like to go with him he must go alone. In that case he risks his own liberty and our profit. If you choose, you can save both. I quite admit it's asking a good deal of you. But what you do not know is Egypt and the ways of the Egyptian police and their courts. Jakoub probably does not deserve justice, but he certainly won't get it from them. He would probably get off scot free simply because he really is a rogue. In the meantime, I don't see why he should not be serving us."

"It seems to me that I am now being asked to go practically on behalf of the firm. That is a very different thing from having a sort of pleasure trip arranged for my benefit."

I spoke thus in loyalty to my pose, of which I was getting sicker every moment. I had made up my mind to go, since I had learned that Jakoub had good reasons for letting me continue to live, and that handing him over to Egyptian justice was apparently patronising a kind of lottery, in which he might draw a ticket entitling him to be tortured to death, or a different-coloured one letting him go free. I wanted to see him decently but quite certainly hanged.

"I'm afraid I'm to blame," said Captain Welfare. "I hadn't ought to have put it to you as I did. I was going on to explain how you might give us all a leg-up, all of us as a firm I mean, but if you remember, sir, you rayther cut me short about Jakoub."

This was a very unnecessary remark of Captain Welfare's. It merely emphasised the personal side of my present attitude, which I was now anxious to abandon. Edmund's delicate tact evidently recognised this.

"I am certainly asking you to go on behalf of the firm," he said. "We must have someone we can trust in charge of Jakoub, whom we cannot trust. And at present there simply isn't anyone else but you."

This, of course, settled it, and I had very soon graciously promised to go.

On looking back it seems to me that in every one of these transactions I allowed myself to become as it were committed, without knowing the details, or anything of the possible objections. When these became obvious it was too late for me to withdraw.

I was, in fact, dragged at the heels of Edmund's fate. That is the only excuse I can offer to those who, knowing the sequel, will judge that I require one.

For myself I require no excuse, for I was not conscious of wrong-doing. But then, I have already tried to explain to the reader something of those terms of pleasant familiarity on which I and my conscience dwelt together. I am sure it should be a function of any true religion to promote this cheery co-partnership, and that if it were only commoner there would be far more agreeable people in the world. I always take at their word those who go about calling themselves "miserable sinners," and I notice this always seems to disconcert them.

We had been for some time out of sight of land, as the coast of Tripoli had fallen away from us into the great Bay of Sidra, but now, on the morning after our discussion, I saw for the first time the edge of the great Libyan Desert.

We still carried a breeze with us, but inland of us the sea lay becalmed, so smooth it seemed to be some viscous sea like that imagined by the Ancient Mariner, while the miraged atmosphere above it was fluid. The remotest part of this shimmering fluid was threaded by a thin line of broken points of yellow light, like fragments of the moon.

That was the distant coast, the margin of the great desert.

CHAPTER 7

I MOUNT A CAMEL

BY the next morning the coast was more distinct and we were still approaching it. But our progress was now very slow, and we could depend only on the land breeze of early morning and the sea-breeze of the evening.

The heat of the day was tremendous, or seemed so to me even under the awnings which were rigged fore and aft and kept constantly wet. Metalwork on deck became too hot to touch, and even the painted wooden bulwarks burned through one's sleeves when leaned upon.

The Arabs worked unwillingly, dropping down and sleeping in any patch of shade that presented itself, and I constantly heard the horrid swish of Jakoub's whip as he woke them. I spent the long intolerable days dripping in a hammock chair on deck, feverishly watching the sweep of the sun across the sky and calculating the hours to be endured before he would again become red and harmless in the healing vapours of the western horizon, and the sea-breeze would surprise me again with its chilliness. Or I gazed with aching eyes at the palpitating sand of the coast, wondering if it would be possible for me to live and move on it at all?

Edmund and Welfare had the acquired eastern habit of sleeping during the hot hours, and spent most of the time in their cabins, when they were not required on deck.

At that blessed hour before sunset, however, we met on deck, and Hassan brought up ingeniously cooled drinks for the party.

It was on one of these occasions that I expressed my fears as to the heat of the desert journey.

"It won't be as bad as this, really," Edmund said. "We'll land you in the evening when Jakoub has got the camels together and loaded. You'll travel through the night and make for a place where you can spend the day under shelter. Then it will be only one trek of a few hours to the nearest station on the railway. I've never been on that Western Railway, but I'm afraid they're fairly rotten old carriages. If you get a day-train it will be beastly hot and dusty. Five or six hours will get you into Alexandria."

"That certainly does not sound alarming."

I had a twinge of something like disappointment at the idea of my adventure dwindling to such modest dimensions. Once it was over, I should have liked to tell people at the Athenæum and other comfortable places at home about "the long trek on camel-back across the burning sands."

I would have welcomed quite a considerable degree of real discomfort as a basis for exaggeration within the limits proper to a clergyman.

"I shouldn't mind trying a part of the journey in the daytime," I said.

"Perhaps not," said Captain Welfare. "But the natives won't allow their camels to work in the heat."

"I thought a camel could stand any amount of heat!"

"Not them. They're the softest beasts that walk. They drop in their tracks in the heat, and if it's cold at night they have to be rugged up better than a horse."

"There is more rot believed by people at home about camels," said Edmund, "than about any beast of the field. What do you suppose is a camel's load?"

"I confess my ideas are very vague. I couldn't tell you to a ton."

They both laughed.

"I think it's the natural history books that are given as Sunday school prizes that are responsible for the average Englishman's ideas about camels. Their proper load for regular work is 300 lbs. Of course they can take more for a short time. The natives overload them badly themselves, but they won't let us when we hire them. You bet they watch that. And he's got to be watered every second day to keep his condition—not about once a week as people imagine. As his pace is two-and-a-half miles an hour, a horse can really get just as far between drinks. All the same he's a most invaluable beast. We could do nothing without him on the desert. Oh, you'll get to like them all right when you're used to them."

As a matter of fact, now that the time was getting so near, I began to have qualms of uneasiness at the idea of riding on one of these uncouth beasts.

I like riding my own familiar cob, but am somewhat nervous of mounting even a strange horse, and to me a camel had never been anything but an object placed for my amusement and instruction in the Zoological Garden. There he had always amused and instructed me from the other side of a tall and impregnable iron fence.

I knew of course that trippers in Egypt always got photographed mounted on a camel with the Sphinx and a Pyramid in the background, as if all their tripping in Egypt were done on camel-back, and they had not in fact gone from Cairo to Ghizeh in an electric tramcar. But I now reflected that these were doubtless special camels kept for the purpose, broken, as it were, to trippers—heart-broken no doubt!

But to have to mount and control the ordinary camel of Arab commerce, picked up by Jakoub on a wild and inaccessible part of the desert, I felt, might be a very different proposition, and one making a heavy demand on the courage of a middle-aged and naturally timid vicar.

"I hope," I said, "I shall be able to ride the beast all right."

"Oh! you'll manage that easily," Edmund said. "They're perfectly quiet. We'll show you how to mount, and after he gets up, you have only to sit there and oscillate."

It sounded quite simple, and yet there were vague misgivings left in my heart.

"How many camels are we taking?" I asked.

"Well, we've roughly 2,000 lbs. of stuff. That will take six baggage camels. Four could do it for such a short journey, but the natives are sure to insist on our hiring six. Then there'll be a riding camel for you and one for Jakoub."

"By the way, what is this merchandise I am shepherding?" I asked.

"We'll have to explain all that," said Edmund, cutting in as Welfare rubbed his great chin thoughtfully. "We've got to give you a lot of rather elaborate directions. I suppose we might as well do it now as later."

"Yes," added Captain Welfare, "the whole thing is a rather delicate business. If it's not worked right we'd spoil our own market, and you see we can't let Jakoub know too much."

"I'm very glad to hear that," I said.

"You must not tell him anything," said Welfare, "though he has to hand the stuff over to our agent, and even that has to be done quietly. The stuff is—well, it's a kind of chemical. It's one of the rare earths used in making incandescent gas-mantles. There's hardly any of it in Egypt and there's tremendous competition to get it. That's why if it was known as we'd brought in such a big lot as 2,000 lbs. the price would go flop, and we'd lose a lot of money."

"I see." This really did seem to me an obvious and easily comprehensible proposition.

"And so," said Edmund, taking up the argument, "we want you to take it into Alexandria as curios, and specimens and things you have collected in the desert. That is if you're asked any questions, which you probably won't be."

I could feel their eyes upon me as I took in their suggestion that I should become a party to what certainly seemed to me a transaction very near akin to fraud. I was amused to feel that they both expected me to be much more shocked than in fact I was.

As long as I was satisfied that nobody was going to be injured or defrauded, the mere "verbal inexactitude" was to me only a harmless breach of one of those conventions which, as I have already explained, I regard as maintained for the guidance of persons of inferior intellect.

This attitude of mind may seem rather shocking to some quite intelligent people. I suppose it represents the effect on me of my theological training.

"Don't you think," I asked after a rather pregnant pause, "that my position would be a somewhat uncomfortable one if it were discovered that my desert collections consisted entirely of rare earth for incandescent mantles?"

"It would," Edmund admitted, "but there's not the slightest risk of that happening. Do you think I would ask you to do it if there were?"

"Honestly, Edmund, it is becoming difficult for me to estimate the limits of your possible requests."

Edmund smiled gaily, with a look of relief, but Captain Welfare still watched me, leaning forward with his hairy hands on his knees and an expression of anxious solicitude in his large pathetic eyes.

"If you like, sir," he suggested, "we could easily put in a layer of shells, and fossils, and native ornaments; things a clergyman *would* pick up on the desert."

"No, thank you," I said snappishly.

"There's not the remotest fear of anyone wanting to examine the cases, or asking any questions, as long as they're under your charge. I merely suggested you should yourself say they were your collections, or whatever you like to call them, when putting them on the railway. I've worked it all out. Now, listen, we put you ashore at a quiet spot on Egyptian territory. If the stuff were dutiable, that would of course be smuggling. Certainly if we landed at Alexandria the Customs people would examine it, and we have told you why we don't want it known that we have brought the stuff into Egypt. The camel-men won't bother, as long as they're paid about double the proper price for their camels, and at the station, for a hundred piastres backshish, you will have both station-master and guard ready to shine your boots with their tongues.

"At Alexandria you will go straight to Van Ermengen's hotel. He knows all about the consignment, and Jakoub will follow you with the cases as soon as he is able to get a vehicle to put them in. Then you will hand them over to our agent in Alexandria, who will call for them with a note signed by us, which you will have posted yourself in Alexandria. Then you will have finished with the business, and Jakoub will get back to us if he can, and go to the devil if he can't."

As thus stated by Edmund, the proposition seemed to me quite a harmless *ruse de guerre*. I was suspicious of all commercial methods, and nothing would have induced me for instance to co-operate in anything like the trading habits of our grocer, who was nevertheless, as I have already mentioned, one of the most eminent members of my Sunday congregation. But I saw nothing in this transaction to which anyone could object who kept his conscience in reasonable subjection, and I said so frankly.

Captain Welfare's tension immediately relaxed. He leaned back in his chair with a sigh and wiped his forehead and upper lip with his handkerchief. As the evening was now cool, and no amount of heat ever seemed able to make Captain Welfare perspire, this was a sure indication that he had been in a condition of considerable mental agitation. He drew a long breath and I saw at once that he was under the necessity of making a speech. This happened to him sometimes, just as other men get periodical attacks of asthma or gall-stones.

"Mr. Davoren, sir," he began, after clearing his throat in the most approved oratorical style, "I think this is the third time as we've had to put before you a proposition that must have seemed distasteful to you. A proposition you might have been justified in refusing without examination, if so be you had been a man as is not prepared to look into things and do the square thing, and the kind thing, and the generous thing——"

"Oh, stow it, Welfare!" said Edmund.

But Captain Welfare was not to be stopped now, any more than a body of stampeded mules. He ignored Edmund, who stretched out his legs, shut his eyes, and pretended to go to sleep.

"I want to put it on record, sir, as I appreciate—as *we* appreciate the handsome way you have met us on these occasions. You've acted as a gentleman, sir, because you are a gentleman, and as a man because—well—because you *are* a man."

There was a prolonged groan from Edmund.

"I wish to thank you, sir, for the spirit in which you have met all our suggestions."

I felt extremely embarrassed.

The *Astarte* lay becalmed and almost motionless between the still glowing desert shore and the vast disc of the sun, now falling through a mass of slate-coloured vapour to his setting. In all this golden and purple immensity there was no living thing in sight outside the ship, which was suspended like a fragment of dust in a sunbeam. The only human sound was Captain Welfare's egregious clap-trap.

He was talking away exactly as if he were moving a vote of thanks to the chairman of a board of guardians or a town council, or proposing a toast at an Oddfellows' supper. He was in that state of orgasm which oratory of this type always produces in the lower middle-class Englishman.

This habit is ridiculous enough, even among its normal surroundings of stuffy rooms, half-cleared tables, and black-coated pork-butchers and pawnbrokers. But here, poised in the silence where sea and sky and desert met, where Nature seemed to have unveiled her immensity in a sacramental moment, Captain Welfare ceased to be absurd.

Edmund and I both felt him as something almost obscene—a sacrilege.

I managed to murmur, "Thank you," when he finished, and I was indeed thankful for silence when it came.

But grateful as the silence was, it seemed necessary to say something, if only to prevent the discovery by Welfare that he had not the sympathy of his audience, and so the development among us of embarrassment and discomfort.

I asked him how long he thought it would be before we reached the landing-place.

"We're close to it now," he said, "not above thirty miles or so, but of course we're at the mercy of the wind and the current."

"The current?" I asked. "I thought there was practically no tide in the Mediterranean."

"No, there's no tide to speak of. But coastal currents? My word! You pick up a point ashore, and see how we're drifting now."

Distant as the coast was, I could see that we were indeed slipping slowly back on the way we had come.

"The worst of these currents is that you can't reckon on them like the tide. They're wind-driven, or caused by heat, I suppose, but when you're ashore don't you go bathing on this coast without you know where you are. There's often a four-knot current inshore that would sweep any man away, and often does. But if we get a breeze tonight, we ought to land you tomorrow."

As he spoke the last limb of the sun sank below the horizon, lighting it for a moment with the mysterious green flash that is sometimes seen in these waters, and is said to be due to its rays shining through and illuminating the water at the edge of the sea.

At the same time the sea, which had looked like a bath of mercury, suddenly blackened to northward of us, and the *Astarte's* booms swung out to starboard with the cheery rattle of sheets running through the blocks. The ship leaned over with a little thrill as of a happy awakening, the ripple began to play again at her bow, and we were under way once more.

"That's better," said Captain Welfare, rising from his chair. "Would you like to see just where we are on the chart?"

I thanked him, and we all three went below to his cabin.

A section of an Admiralty chart was pinned out as usual, with the *Astarte's* position from day to day marked on it in pencil.

Captain Welfare put a broad forefinger close to the last mark.

"That's where we are now," he said, "as near as we can tell from sound-ings. As you see yourself, there's no land-marks anyone could pick up here-abouts. Those figures show you it's all shoal water between us and the land, until we get here."

He indicated a place a little farther east along the coast, where there was a small bay or indentation.

"Here you see there's water enough for the *Astarte* up to within a few yards of the beach, and there's some tall sandhills and a bit of an old ruined sheikh's tomb that we can pick up even at night with this moon."

"Yes; but are there any human beings or camels there?"

Edmund laughed. "I think," he said, "you still suspect us of some ill do-ings. Do you really think we are going to maroon you on a waterless desert with a single cut-throat for companion?"

"Don't be an ass, Edmund; but if you know anything about the busi-ness, tell me how we're going to get camels here?"

"From the Arabs," said Captain Welfare; "there's a tribe of them al-ways in camp at this time of year a little inland of where we're going to land you. At least so Jakoub says, and he knows the district. They'll be getting in their barley crop now. They do some camel breeding here too. Jakoub says he is sure to find them here, because the calves will be still too young to go on trek. You'll see now, Mr. Davoren, how we're bound to depend on Jakoub in a business like this is."

"I suppose it would be impossible," I suggested, "to find an Arab with Jakoub's knowledge, who was not also a scoundrel?"

"I don't believe," said Welfare solemnly, "that such a man exists. A straight man couldn't know all Jakoub knows."

This remark silenced me. I had so often myself observed this inverse ratio between knowledge and virtue.

At dinner that evening I was somewhat oppressed by the feeling that it was probably my last night on the *Astarte*. We had been such good friends on board. The little cabin had come to look so familiar and so homelike to me; the whole experience had been so strange and withal so delightful to me, that I could not but feel saddened at the thought of leaving it all. In-stinctively I shrank a little from the unknown and solitary experiences that awaited me in a strange land.

I knew too that I would be missed, if only because three are much bet-ter company than two—where men are concerned at all events. Without conceit I knew I should be missed in a much deeper sense than that. I am one of those insignificant but cornerless people who make a good third in such close quarters as ours were, and I was conscious that Edmund and Captain Welfare liked each other the better for my presence.

Captain Welfare openly expressed his regret at my impending departure, and it required some skilled manœuvring on the part of Edmund and myself to head him away from another speech.

"By the way," I said, "you have forgotten to tell me what your plans are after you leave me, and when we are to meet again?"

"Oh! we'll pick you up in Alexandria in a few days," said Edmund. "We'll see you off home, unless you make up your mind to continue the cruise."

"I wish that were possible," I said regretfully; "but it isn't."

"When we put you ashore, sir," said Captain Welfare, "we'll get out to sea as best we can, and get in the regular track of boats bound to Alexandria. If the police are on the look-out for Jakoub, they'll board us either there or when we're signalled at the harbour. I only wish you knew as much about the Gyppie police as we do, and could enjoy the laugh same as we will."

There was an unusual vindictiveness in Captain Welfare's tone that made me wonder for a moment what were the experiences that had so prejudiced him against this branch of the public service.

But this was not a time for uncharitable thoughts, and I put this one aside.

"By the way," Edmund said, "we'll have to look you out some clothes. I presume you didn't bring any tropical kit?"

"No," I told him; "Bates fixed me up with these blue serge things and several pairs of white flannel trousers, most of which I am afraid I have soiled. He has also included a complete clerical rig-out, without which he never allows me to travel."

"Good!" said Edmund. "You have got some dog-collars then? Bates is a pearl of great price. That is the only thing that was worrying me."

"He has packed some clerical collars and a stock, if that's what you mean."

"What on earth is a stock?" Edmund asked.

"It is the black silk thing below what you call a dog-collar. The two combined are the symbol of the Apostolic Succession. A stud, or a button-hole in front, is a split—the stigma of Schism. It is commonly associated with a white tie, an arrogant assumption of individual blamelessness only possible in a heretic."

"Well now, that's something I never understood before," said Captain Welfare. "You mean a church parson isn't better than another man, or don't reckon to be, outside of his official position? Out of his uniform, eh?"

"I don't know that I meant all that," I said, rather taken aback by this literal interpretation of my frivolous talk. "I'm not much of a theologian, but I think what you say is something very like the Anglican idea."

"Well, I like it," he said; "I've known preachers at home as has worn the biggest kind of white ties, and it's some of their ways as has stuck in my gizzard and made me the back-slider I am. Mr. Davoren, when I get ashore, I'd like to join your church. I'd take it kindly if you'd baptise me, sir."

I said I should be delighted. I did not see what else I could say under the circumstances, although I have a rooted objection to proselytes of every description.

"The question is," said Edmund impatiently, "whether Welfare's drill kit or mine would fit you best? We've both got plenty of clean spare suits, and I can rig you up with a pith helmet. I was only worried about the collar. You won't want one in the desert; but it's rather important you should turn up in Alexandria in clerical kit."

"I can manage that all right," I said indifferently. "I suppose my own clothes would be too warm?"

"Much too warm. You couldn't stand them."

Edmund spoke decisively and I sighed, for I dislike wearing clothes that have not been made for me. Edmund is two inches taller than me, and of late I have shown distinct signs of what my father used to call "the elderly spread." On the other hand Captain Welfare, though about my own height, is immensely larger in all his other dimensions.

There is however, fortunately, a remarkable flexibility about men's clothes, and I was able to pick out a couple of suits which I could wear with comfort and without loss of self-respect. Indeed I can say more than that. So persistent is human vanity that I found myself admiring my own appearance in the clean white drill. It gave me, I thought, a look of youth and distinction to which I imagined I had long since renounced all claims.

Edmund caught me in front of the mirror deciding on the most becoming tilt of the pith helmet. This persistence of the peacock in one's nature is very disturbing.

I was woken very early in the morning by a rattle which shook the whole ship. I started up and realised that it was the anchor chain running out. My long journey in the *Astarte* was at an end.

I went straight on deck, and saw the desert close to me for the first time.

The sun had not yet risen, but the dawn was foretold by a lilac glow in the east where Venus still shone illustrious as a morning star.

The *Astarte* was at anchor in a little cove, evidently the one I had been shown on the chart, for on my left I could see in the twilight the tall sand-hills mentioned by Welfare. They were strangely carved by the wind to sharp, delicately curved edges with a surpassing beauty of line. Beside them on a lower level rose the little rounded dome of the sheikh's tomb, over which leaned a single tall, crooked date palm. Away to the right of this the sand stretched to the horizon in wave after wave, yellow and silver in the faint light, with violet shadows between the vast undulations, and a few black patches of camel-scrub here and there.

The wind had almost gone. It ruffled the sea outside to a dark grey, but around us in the little bay the water lay silent, polished and opalescent under the growing dawn.

The dinghy was already being rowed ashore, and I recognised Jakoub's back, sitting crouched like a bird of prey in the stern-sheets.

The crew were busy getting the sails off the ship and stowing them. They worked quickly and in a strange uncanny silence.

Edmund and Captain Welfare were both on deck, already dressed. They stood together watching the crew, and speaking almost in whispers with an unwonted look of anxiety on their faces. Captain Welfare kept searching the shore with his telescope.

Very soon I saw the morning star fade out in a red glare that filled the east, and then the sun came up, climbing swiftly from the horizon. For a moment the desert sparkled with the lustre of jewellery; then the effect passed, and its surface settled into the burning yellow and white of the common light of day.

But the smooth shallow sea of the desert's margin turned from the pearly opalescence of the dawn to a glory of blue such as I had never imagined. It was not the blue of the sea or sky, but the incredible blue of a butterfly's wing. It brought to my mind childhood's dream-pictures of the glory of the river that flows round the Throne of God, and my heart ached with the splendour of it.

The sun came as a tyrant. It seemed to take but a few moments before he was clear of the vapour of the horizon, and the heat of the day had begun.

I went below to my cabin. I dressed myself, and sorrowfully bestowed what I needed for my journey in a hold-all.

The hot day seemed intolerably long. I lay on deck trying in vain to read. Their manifest anxiety kept Edmund and Welfare in an irritable silence.

The cases I was to take with me were brought on deck. They were roped and sealed, and the word "Anticas" was painted on the outside in large black letters, with some Arabic characters below which I took to be a translation of this lie.

The boat was lowered and they were stowed in it with my hold-all and all brought ashore and laid on the beach. There was nothing more to do, and by four o'clock our nervous tension was becoming almost unbearable when the sandy sky-line was broken by the tall silhouette of a camel, with a man mounted on it, advancing majestically towards us.

Captain Welfare had a long look at him through the glass.

"Thank God!" he said. "It's Jakoub all right. The others must be following him."

Jakoub put his camel into a trot and came rapidly down to the beach. I watched with anticipatory dread the process of making the camel kneel, or as it seemed to me, fold itself up. Jakoub sprang lightly off and tied the animal's nose-rope round one of its knees to secure it. The camel stretched its long neck along the ground and began nosing in the sand for something eatable.

Jakoub came out in the dinghy and was aboard in a few minutes.

Captain Welfare met him, and coming aft announced, with a look of relief, that the baggage camels and one for me were only a mile or so behind Jakoub.

"We're lucky," he said, "for I think there is a land breeze coming up, and the sooner we're out of this the better. I only hope for your sake, Mr. Davoren, it isn't a 'khamsin.' I'd be sorry if you made the acquaintance of the desert in a sand-storm."

I went below to finish my packing. Hassan showed me with pride the hamper of provisions and wines he had provided for the journey, together with two great water-jars.

When I came back on deck, rather self-conscious in my white suit and helmet, I saw the camels crouching on the beach, and heard with dread their deep guttural grumblings and threatenings as their loads were roped on to them.

But what surprised me most of all was the sudden appearance among us of a stranger. This was a young clean-shaved Egyptian of the middle class, dressed in a suit of drab linen with a tarboosh on his head.

Edmund laughed as he came up to us with an obsequious salaam.

"Let me introduce you to your dragoman," he said.

Then as the man looked up with a smile of insufferable insolence, I saw that it was Jakoub!

He was not merely disguised by clothes; it was the total change of the consummate artist. It seemed that he *was* another man. He had deliberately revealed himself by his smile, and when that faded from his face, it was impossible even to think of him as Jakoub, utterly impossible to recognise him.

Edmund drew me aside.

"You're not in the least likely to want this," he said, "but you never know. You had better have it in case——"

He gave me a revolver, which I had unwillingly to put in my pocket. It seemed an enormous size and weight, and I always have a feeling that these things go off of themselves. Still, when I thought of Jakoub, I was glad to have it.

"Here's another dozen rounds," said Edmund, "you can give me the lot back in Alexandria."

The crew were already busy making sail under Welfare's directions.

I said good-bye to him with great regret. Edmund came ashore with me in the dinghy.

I looked back and said, "Do you know this is the first time I have seen the *Astarte* from outside?"

"So it is," said Edmund. "Well, she's pretty, isn't she?"

She looked very beautiful lying there, "Idle as a painted ship upon a painted ocean," her lines aspiring to the tall pointed bows and the noble length of her bowsprit, her tall pointed sails drooping gracefully to their own reflection in the water.

"I am very, very sorry to leave her," I said.

"I hope," said Edmund gravely, "that whatever happens you'll always keep a kindly feeling for her in your heart."

Edmund led me up to my camel. The brute slewed its head round and eyed us with a supercilious and malevolent expression that reminded me of Jakoub. It kept its mouth open, ready to protest against whatever was done to it, showing a great bunch of teeth in its lower jaw. As we approached it made a noise as if it were gargling its throat.

"All you've to do," said Edmund, "is to nip on to the saddle quickly and hang on to this wooden upright. He'll start getting up the minute you're on and that throws you about a bit, but once he's on his feet you'll be all right and quite comfortable. Cross your feet over his left shoulder, and hold on to the upright at first till you're used to the motion. Keep him in a sort of half trot if you can, it's less tiring than walking. But he'll follow Jakoub's beast anyhow."

"What am I to do if he runs away?"

"He won't do that. He'll keep in the string all right."

I watched Jakoub mount, and with a great effort of will-power followed his example.

I stretched one leg over the brute and was pulling myself into my seat to an accompaniment of appalling growls, when an earthquake seemed to take place. I was flung forward, then backwards and forwards again, and shot up skywards at the same time, but remained safe on the bundle of mats they called a saddle. I found myself at a dizzy height with the camel's greyish white neck stretched out a long way below me, and a single slender rope in my hand to guide him with.

However, the brute stood quiet. He was now silent and showed no disposition to do untoward things.

"Well done," Edmund called up to me; "you'll be all right now."

"I'm all right," I said, "unless he turns round and chews my feet."

"He's a tame beast. Don't be uneasy. Good-bye."

He reached up and I managed to catch his hand.

"Good luck," he said.

"Good-bye."

As he went back to the dinghy, I could hear the click of the *Astarte's* windlass getting up the anchor. Our string of camels moved off across the sandhills, and I felt nervous, insecure, and very lonely.

CHAPTER 8

WE ARE CAUGHT IN A KHAMSIN

AS I got used to the apparent insecurity of my position and the rocking motion which the camel's gait imposes on one, I began to find something soothing in the slow but dignified progression. The vast monotony of the desert had a hypnotic effect, and I was even anxious lest I might fall asleep and slip from my lofty perch.

The heat was most oppressive, and I noticed a new quality in the slight wind. It was from the south, a quarter it had not blown from before, and it came in puffs like a breath from the opened door of a furnace; a dry fierce heat that burned one's cheek and made the eyes smart. In the full glare of the afternoon sun, the desert was disappointing in its monotony. I had read novels full of "word-painting" and gush about the "mystery and wonder" of the desert. I had seen it in a moment of iridescent loveliness at dawn. But now there was neither mystery nor beauty: it was just sand, sand and loose stones, stretching everywhere in billows to the ring of the horizon. The ridges of sand hid nothing but other ridges, and hollows full of sand. I found I hated it.

Away to the south, in the wind's eye, the horizon was darkened by a strange haze, yellowish brown, rising slowly higher in the sky, a queer, unnatural, threatening cloud.

There were three Arab boys who trudged along beside the baggage camels, occasionally addressing what sounded like insults to them. I thought they looked uneasily from time to time at the southern sky, and tried to hurry the unwilling camels.

The hot wind blew every moment stronger and more steadily, and now it blew up a cloud of dust and sand from the shuffling feet of the camels.

Jakoub rode on ahead with a mounted Arab, whom I took to be the owner, or at least the hirer of the camels.

We were travelling about east-sou'-east, our route making an acute angle with the coast. After about an hour's going, the desert rose to a stony ridge where there was an outcrop of some pale fossiliferous rock which lay in flat slabs like an artificial pavement. Turning to look back from the summit of this ridge I found I could see the sea again. It was ruffled and grey. Darker "cat's-paws" flew over it here and there, and already the waves were beginning to curl and show white gleams of foam.

The *Astarte* was visible near the sky-line, standing out to sea with a free sheet. My heart yearned after her, as I thought of the familiar cosy saloon and the friendly faces I had left.

Jakoub halted his camel and waited till I came up. He salaamed respectfully, perfect in his part of dragoman, and rode side by side with me.

"It will be a bad night, effendi," he said. "It is a khamsin."

"Well, I suppose we must grin and bear it."

I spoke boldly, though I quailed at the word khamsin; I had heard so much of this dreaded wind.

"As long as the camels will travel," he said. "But the sky looks as if it will be a very bad sand-storm."

"How far is it to this place we are going to?"

"If the camels go well, we might do it in six hours, in five hours from now. But it will be difficult to find the place in a sand-storm."

"What is this ruin? Another Sheikh's tomb?"

"No, no. This very great ruin. How do you call a mosque of the ancients?"

"A temple?"

"That is it. It is the Temple of Osiris. Very grand ruin. There is plenty shelter there for all, camels and all."

"Is there any shelter nearer?"

"We could go back where I fetch the camels from. About two hours now."

"How long will this storm last?"

"It is a khamsin; it may last three days."

"Then we must go on and find the temple if we can."

"It is as your Excellency wishes."

I had almost forgotten it was Jakoub speaking through the mouth of this pleasant respectful servant, but now he added with a touch of the familiarity I loathed, "If anyone is looking for Jakoub he will not find him in a khamsin."

I ignored this remark.

"And they will not find what the camels are loaded with," he said with his most insolent sneer.

I could have chastised him with scorpions, but I maintained silence, and only looked my disapproval. I knew silence was more dignified than any speech to such a man; besides, I had no doubt at the time that he was trying to find out from me what the packing-cases contained.

But there was in his smile a suggestion that we shared some vile secret; a suggestion which gave me nausea of the soul.

He trotted forward and rejoined his companion, and at once I heard an order shouted to the foot-boys, who began belabouring their camels, and the whole procession moved forward at a mended pace.

I ventured to guide my camel a little to the right so as to bring it to windward of the baggage camels and out of the dust their feet stirred up. I was gratified to find the animal obedient, even obsequious.

Then the wind suddenly grew stronger. I cannot say it freshened, for it came as a hot blast that burned and threatened. The surface of the desert seemed to slide away from the camel's feet, as the loose sand shifts away with a receding wave in shallow water. It made me giddy to look down at it. The air became dark, opaque with the sand blown up from a thousand miles of red-hot desert.

The particles of sand drove and pricked my skin. Sand filled my eyes and nostrils and stuck to the streaming surface of my sweating face and hands. I had to keep close to the baggage animals. I had a horror of losing touch with them, in this new strange opacity.

I knew that if I found myself alone I should go mad with horror. I felt the beast under me tremble with some similar terror, and for the first time there was sympathy between us.

The scorching wind hummed in my ears with a strange thin sound, mingled with the hiss of the moving sand. It made my helmet a maddening incumbrance, and set loose parts of my clothes and the corners of the rugs I sat on flapping.

The flying sand was all around us now, and sky and sun were blotted out. I knew that the sun was near its setting and dreaded to think of the darkness of night added to this new terrifying darkness.

A blank misery of fear settled down upon me, and I cursed the wretchedness of my discomfort.

It seemed impossible that I should be here, perched unfamiliarly on the back of a camel, unprotected and wretched amid the unknown dangers of this horror of the sand. The thought of my home came to me, of Bates and Mrs. Rattray! What had brought me here?

The darkness became denser and denser and I felt that the sun had set. But it's going brought no coolness. The burning wind seemed now to parch my lungs. My camel was pressed up to the baggage animals, its nose almost touching the tail of the beast before it. It evidently shared my dread of finding itself alone.

Much as I hated Jakoub it was a relief when he again joined me.

"You all raight, effendi?" he asked.

"All right," I said. I would not expose my craven fear to him. I could have found it in my heart to bless him when he handed me a bottle of tepid water. As a rule I hate drinking out of a bottle. I have seldom done it, I have not got the knack. The motion of the camel did not make it easier, and some of the precious water ran over my chin and down my neck. Nevertheless that was the most precious drink of all my lifetime.

"Shall we be able to find the way?" I asked.

"Oh yes, we will find it. The camels know," said Jakoub, "but we must not halt. It might be impossible to make them start again."

"I don't want to halt."

"Good. The effendi is very strong, what you call 'very hard,' is it not? There will be times when we will be able to see a little with the moon, when the sand will not be so thick in the air to blind us. So, we will find the temple and rest."

The man's confidence encouraged me and I could not but admire it in face of the wrath of Nature.

Every joint of me ached with the ungainly motion of my mount, and my skin was become as sodden paper. A stream of tears cut channels in the dust that plastered my face. Sometimes the darkness lightened a little, and a greenish light filtered through the sand from the invisible moon, reminding me of the faint light that comes down through the water in glazed tanks of a darkened aquarium.

I could now just see the pale hindquarters of the beast in front of me, and the long neck and head of my own solemnly bowing as it went.

I do not know how long this torment lasted, for I lost all count of time. My only fear was lest the camels should stop in their march, and I counted every painful step a gain.

I had reached the stage of half-conscious misery when suddenly the wind seemed to cease blowing. There were harsh guttural shouts from the Arab boys, and the camels stopped. Then I felt rather than saw the loom of a vast building beside me on my right.

An Arab boy came and took the head-rope from my hand, and dragging at it he made a noise as though he was clearing his throat of all the colds that ever afflicted humanity. Again I was flung backwards and forwards as my camel folded itself up and came to rest on the ground. I slid off too weak in the knees even to get out of the range of its teeth. But the poor beast made no assault on me, and I felt that it had carried me faithfully and well and was grateful.

I saw a match struck, and Jakoub came up with a lantern. My heart faintly warmed to him.

"All raight, effendi?" he asked again.

"All right," I said. "You have done well to find this place on such a night, Jakoub."

"The camels have the wisdom that Allah has bestowed," he answered quite simply and humbly.

I came nearer liking him then than at any moment of our short intercourse. But I distrusted him profoundly all the same, and the pressure of Edmund's revolver against my hip was a kind of comfort to me.

"This way, effendi," he said, making a kind of servile sweep with his lantern.

I followed him into what I took at first to be a cave. But there was a hot draught and sand blowing through it, and the swinging light of Jakoub's lantern lit up great blocks of stone that must have been placed there by human agency. I don't know why, but I followed him more willingly when I realised that I was among the work of human hands, however many thousand years they had been dead, than I would have followed into some crevice that represented a mere process of Nature. My feeling about Jakoub demanded human allies, however remote in time.

I realised that this was some gateway or entrance in the vast building that had saved us from the sand-storm.

Jakoub turned sharply to the left, and I followed him through a narrow entrance where I had to stoop among enormous blocks of stone.

I found myself in a moderate-sized chamber. As far as I could see by the feeble light it was built entirely of stone. Some of the stone was blackened as though by fire. There was another opening in the great stone-work that looked like the beginning of a narrow staircase. But I was too tired for exploration. The floor was soft sand, and there was no wind blowing here.

I sat down thankfully and began scooping dust out of my eyes.

Two of the Arab boys who had walked by the baggage camels came in with rugs and mats, and the hamper packed by Hassan.

Jakoub gave them directions in their own language, and all these people busied themselves about providing for my comfort.

I asked myself why I hated Jakoub, and how I knew that he despised me. I did not know these Arab boys at all. If among them they had decided to put me to death, they would have an easy task. They might have done it before I could even have pointed my revolver at them.

Jakoub skilfully made a kind of couch for me with the rugs, and opened the hamper. Hassan had packed enough to keep me for a week, so there was no need to economise. I did not know what provisions Jakoub or the Arabs might have. After all he had so far served me well. I offered him some meat and bread, which he gratefully accepted.

"I suppose," I said, "you do not drink wine, Jakoub?"

"I keep the fast of Ramadan, Excellency," he said, "but for the rest of the year——" He ended with a shrug and a smile which seemed to suggest his belief in the tenderness of Allah towards human nature which could not always live up to the exacting standard of the Prophet.

"The wind has burned the roots of my tongue and the sand grates in the gateway of my lungs," he added apologetically, as he drank off the tumbler of Burgundy I handed him.

The wine revived him and I realised that he too had been suffering from the exhaustion of our terrible ride, but had waited on me before refreshing himself.

I finished my strange picnic alone in this dim vault of some old forgotten worship; then lying down on the outspread rug, I slept profoundly in the sand.

When I awoke a faint daylight was trickling in through a kind of irregular hole or tunnel in the titanic masonry that surrounded me. A distant humming of the wind recalled to my mind the horrors of the storm outside, and I knew it had not abated. During the night, sand had drifted even into this chamber of mine. I was covered with it as I lay, and I noticed it piled up like snow against the farther wall.

But someone, Jakoub I knew it must be, had left a canvas bucket of water beside me, and I was able to have the wash my soul was craving for.

The faint light made me think that it was dawn, although the heat even here was oppressive, but looking at my watch I found it was twelve o'clock! I had slept for ten hours. At first I could hardly move my aching limbs.

But the healing touch of the water restored me. My parched skin seemed to absorb it, and my courage, such as it was, became restored. I began to take a kind of pleasure in the sense of adventure, and thought with pride of the story I should have for the other old fogies at the Athenæum!

If I had had a companion I should have been happy, but it was lonely work as it was.

I made a table of my hamper, and breakfasted heartily on lukewarm ham and the remains of the bottle of wine I had broached over-night.

Then I began to explore my surroundings.

I went down the short narrow passage leading from the chamber, and found that it opened into what looked at first like a tunnel through which the wind and the sand still raved. This tunnel I found was really a gateway piercing a vast wall, in the thickness of which my chamber was built. I turned to the right retracing our steps of the night before and came out into the day, which I found was darkened by the sand-storm. I huddled under the lee of the great wall, and I could see the camels were still lying there in a row, placidly chewing the cud with a queer sideways movement of their jaws. The nearest turned its head and looked at me with a sneer of ineffable contempt.

I went back and found that opposite to the passage which led to my chamber was another similar opening.

Listening I heard the deep fierce tones of Arabic talk and a man laughing. I guessed there must be another chamber there where Jakoub and the Arabs had taken refuge. I felt I would be glad of even Jakoub's society, but shyness prevented my seeking him, shyness and nothing else!

I returned to my chamber, intent on exploring the staircase or passage I had seen leading from it.

The opening led, as I thought, to remains of a broken staircase, roughly spiral, in the thickness of the great wall. Many of the steps were broken away, and I was soon in darkness. I came back, shuddering, for Jakoub's lantern which he had left with me, and stiff and sore and frightened as I was, I clambered up and up and came at last out into the rushing, blinding storm again, on the top of the vast wall of the Temple.

It was broken into irregular masses of enormous masonry, and must originally have been some twenty feet in width. The tunnel piercing the bottom of the wall was forty feet in length, and I guessed I must be about sixty feet above the ground. But the storm drove me down before I could form any estimate of its length, or discover how much of the building existed. I could see nothing through the driving sand.

I came back to my chamber, which had already begun to seem home-like to me, and Jakoub was there waiting for me.

I was glad to see him. I think I would have been glad of the company of an orang-utan, if adequately chained, for I was finding out what a horrible thing solitude can be although it was not twenty-four hours since I had parted with Edmund and Welfare.

Jakoub greeted me with his invariable "all raight?" and I grunted at him for reply. I felt I had a reputation as an English gentleman to maintain.

"We cannot start the camels today, effendi," he went on, "the sand is still very bad."

"We didn't reckon to travel today," I reminded him. "What about to-night?"

He shrugged his shoulders in his disgustingly expressive way.

"No good, effendi. The camels would not put their heads—I mean what you call—face it. It may blow all tomorrow again, or it might stop tonight."

"Well, we've got to wait for it then, and not worry," I answered irritably. "How are you and the other fellows off for food?"

"We have enough to eat. The others like the Excellency's white bread if there is any to spare. The wine made paradise of my stomach."

I gave him a loaf of bread and a bottle of wine.

"What about water?" I asked.

"There is here a very good well. All the water bottles I have filled. The camels have drunk when they did not expect. They give thanks. But the sand drives even here and there is today and tonight. If the effendi likes and will come five minutes through the storm I can show him better shelter. Very good place, no wind, no sand, very cool place."

I was used now to the place I was in, and averse from changing it until I started back to civilisation. I was profoundly distrustful of Jakoub, and I did not like the idea of going out again into that stinging storm.

But the man offered me better quarters. I had no good reason for refusing to try them. I was determined not to seem to fear him, and my wretched shyness prevented me from discussing the matter and questioning him as any sensible man would have done.

"Very well," I said, "go on."

He led me out again and we trod the ankle-deep sand past where the camels lay. They were of course unloaded and looked very contented and supercilious.

We reached the limit of the great wall, and I could just see that it was only one part of a vast building; we were at an angle where another wall met it. But the driving sand hid all the mysteries of the structure. Jakoub led me away from the Temple, and down the slope of a ridge on which it seemed to be built. I had to keep my head down for protection from the moving sand, but even so I could see that I was stumbling over masses of broken, worthless pottery. I passed fragments of marble pillars and fractured capitals lying in the sand. My feet slid on the loose sand covering a portion of tessellated pavement.

There had been Greek artists here, and I knew that, as I suspected, I was among the ruins of some old Ptolemaic pleasaunce and place of worship.

Jakoub stopped.

"Down here, effendi," he called through the wind, pointing to a hole that the moving sand had silted up but could not fill.

I hesitated. It was like being invited to go down a rabbit-burrow. Jakoub disappeared down the hole, and his lean, brown, beautiful hand alone was left inviting me to follow.

I took his hand and went down after him. It was impossible to hesitate, alone there in that blinding hurricane. I slid down through sand, and sand followed my clumsy descent like an avalanche. Then I found my feet on rock. I felt my way down a rough descent, with Jakoub's loathed assistance, and I found myself on level solid ground in total darkness.

Jakoub had brought his lantern and lit it at once.

At first I could see nothing but his hated face, smiling into mine.

"All raight here, effendi," he said, and behind him I saw all the packing-cases the camels had carried.

Although I had seen the camels were relieved of their loads, I had never thought of how the things might be bestowed. I had thought of nothing but my own discomfort, and had accepted all Jakoub's efforts to lessen it. He and his Arabs must have worked hard to get all this merchandise down here, while I slept. I recognised that he did not despise me without some reason.

Of course Edmund or Welfare would have seen the stuff bestowed before anything else. I had shown myself a mere passenger.

Jakoub saw me looking at the packing-cases.

"They would be hard to find here, like Jakoub," he said.

I took the lantern from him, and began to examine the cave, for such I took it to be.

I found myself in a large rectangular chamber hewn out of the solid rock that here closely underlay the desert sand.

At one end of it I found a grave-like excavation about three feet deep and six feet long. I saw the remains of an earthenware pipe leading into it, and turned away with an involuntary shudder.

In the opposite wall there was a narrow pointed opening. I had to stoop to go through it, and found myself in a circular chamber. There were low seats, or sedilia, carved in the rock all around, and over each seat a square niche cut in the rock. In the centre were the broken remains of a slab of rock which could only have been an altar.

I did not know what hateful rites had been celebrated on it, but everything told me I was in a place of ancient secret worship. I recalled a smattering recollection of Mithraic superstition with its blood-bath. That was probably the meaning of the grave-like place with its conduit. Here men had hidden themselves from the light of day 2,000 years ago, and here a man lost now would never be recovered.

Jakoub smiled in my face. I put my hand on the revolver. If this were a trap he had led me into, I swore to myself that he should die in it too.

"No sand comes here," he said. "The effendi will be cool while we wait."

It was evident that the man was still considering only my comfort. My fears of him were nothing but the cowardice of jangled nerves.

The two Arab boys joined us, bearing my rugs and hamper, some extra candles, and a copy of *The Contemporary Review* with an article of my own in it; the sort of encumbrance that clings so long to civilised man. And under Jakoub's directions they proceeded to make a kind of couch for me, where I should be able to spend the hours before us in comparative comfort.

Then they left me. I began to read my own article in the review, but I found that matters that had once seemed intensely interesting and important had become profoundly boring, and I slept.

I suppose it was exhaustion, but I slept most of that afternoon. I fed again and went to sleep again. So I spent those hours amid circumstances that from a distance would have seemed the most enthralling. But I had examined this weird subterranean chamber. Its bare rock faces had nothing more to tell my ignorance. I had not the knowledge or experience to interpret the history that might be graven on them.

I slept again lightly, and not for very long. Consciousness returned in the form of uneasiness. I was in utter darkness, but awake and alert. I was in no uncertainty as to my whereabouts or the recent events that had brought me there. I was not even quite sure that I had slept.

I knew I had but to stretch out my hand to find a box of matches and light my candle, but I found I could not make the effort. Fear kept my hand immobilised. I can say honestly that it was no mere superstitious dread of my surroundings. I was perfectly conscious of my unseen environment of hewn rock beneath the remote desert. I was untroubled by any thought of possible horrors enacted there in the distant past. Yet I was afraid, afraid of some human presence that I knew was there, invisible and unfelt, unheard, yet palpable in the darkness and silence which surrounded me. I lay there conscious that my face was distorted by fear, waiting, longing for something, anything that would stimulate any normal human sense. I think I could have welcomed the thrust of a dagger if it had ended that horrible suspense in the darkness of the old subterranean church of a forgotten religion.

Something moved near me and the spell was broken. I was aware of myself sitting up, my blanket thrown aside, my left arm doubled across my face by some defensive instinct.

"Who is that?" said a voice that must have been mine.

Without knowing what I did, my right hand went out and found the matches beside me. The box rattled faintly as I grasped it, and before it rattled again, before I could move it towards my left hand, my hand was seized and held in a soft firm grip.

I fell backwards again incapable of effort. "No light, effendi. Make no sound. There is danger."

It was Jakoub's voice, whispering.

I dreaded and feared the man, yet I knew his whisper was not that of my murderer. I felt that for the time at all events we were allies against some unknown danger threatening us both.

"What is it?" I asked, whispering like him. "Let go my hand."

"You will make no light, if my hand leaves your hand?"

"No; not till you tell me. Why are you here?"

The delicate firm pressure of his hand was removed, and I was again out of touch with the universe. But I was relieved. All those visceral disturbances which attend pure fright began to adjust themselves. The pumping of my heart ceased to be palpable, the rhythm of my breathing was restored, and I was conscious that I was no longer making queer faces in the dark. These are but normal reactions to stimuli, labelled "cowardice" by the insensitive. I am as little inclined to apologise for them as for hunger or sea-sickness. They passed, and reflection returned to aid my will.

"Why have you come, Jakoub?" I asked of the darkness. It was strange to speak, not knowing in which direction to send my voice, nor whether my hearer was close to me or far away.

"I must remain here with you, effendi. Those who seek me have come. They too shelter from the storm. They seek also this that we have brought with us. But Allah is merciful, and I remembered to put it here where they will not find it."

From the sound of Jakoub's whisper I could tell that his usual imperturbability had gone. There was fear in every syllable he uttered. Fear is said to be contagious, yet I took heart. "Those who sought him" must be the police. I knew, of course, that he was a hunted man. But I had nothing to fear from the police, and as yet I had no reason to suppose that they were concerned with our merchandise. They would, of course, examine it if they found it, and that, as Welfare had so carefully explained, would spoil the market for our "rare earths for incandescent mantles."

I felt that I had nothing to lose by their discovering Jakoub. I shrank from the thought of sharing with him a long vigil in this subterranean darkness, and his arrest would rescue me from this.

Even if I wanted to, however, I could make no move to compass his arrest. At present he was in a sense my protector, at least my ally. The least suspicious move on my part would convert him into a deadly and ruthless foe, and I remembered how he had instantly found my hand as though he saw in the darkness, while I was blind and helpless.

Looking back now, I think all these prudential calculations passed through my mind really in an attempt to justify a feeling of loyalty to what was after all my side. However I might hate and distrust Jakoub, I was yet pledged in a sense to abide by him.

So I resigned myself to the long wait, crouching there in the darkness of our stone vault.

"How long will these men stay?" I asked at length.

"When the khamsin ends they will go; unless the camel-men betray us."

"And can you trust them?"

"I trust no Arab. But they know it is death to betray me. But one can come in here at a time. Allah is very merciful and my knife is sharp. Many would die before Jakoub is taken. If the Excellency will agree now to make no light or sound, I go to wait by the entry. It will soon be day and a little light will come then. But to one from outside it will be dark in here. He would feel the knife of Jakoub before he saw it, and then he would see no more."

"Go, Jakoub," I said, "I will not move."

There was no sound but I somehow felt that Jakoub was withdrawn from close beside me.

For a long time, as it seemed to me, I crouched there, my hands clasped round my knees, wondering if I were destined to be the helpless witness of a murder or series of murders.

But gradually the strain on my mind, the heat and the close unchanged air numbed my spirits. I sank back thankfully on my rug, and slept as soundly as though I were back in my own vicarage.

I awoke unwillingly and unrested. There was a dim light by which I could just discern the graven rock that formed the walls and roof of our refuge—or our prison.

It was Jakoub's voice calling softly that had awakened me. I could see the outline of his figure squatting like a graven image by the entry, and a faint gleam from the blade of his knife. Untiring he had watched there motionless while I had slept.

"Well, Jakoub?" I questioned.

"It is day, effendi, and the storm has gone. The khamsin has spared us one day. The leader of the camels has come, and says my enemies have gone. But that may be a trap."

I rose wearily and went over to Jakoub. By the entry there was a freshness in the air that revived me, and I noticed there was no longer any humming of the wind.

"How shall we know if it is a trap, Jakoub?"

He fondled the knife in his hand, and then looked up at me with pleading in his eyes. It was the first time he had humbled himself to me, and I saw that a vision of the gaol at Tourah was very clear to him.

"I like not to ask it," he said at last; "but if the effendi had courage to go first they would not harm him, and Jakoub would at least be warned. If Jakoub must die, he will take some with him, to bear false witness against him before the Prophet. But the Prophet is not deceived. He will intercede with Allah, and Allah is merciful to the true believer."

Nothing could better have restored my self-esteem than this appeal. I had hitherto been entirely dependent on this abhorred protector; but now he needed my aid and appealed to my courage.

I said no more, but walked past him and climbed up the steep and narrow entry to the desert surface above, dazzled indeed by the glare of light, but thankful to breathe again the fresh pure air of morning that was wafted across by a faint sea-breeze. The terrible oppression of the hot wind had gone. The sand was at rest. My spirits rose as, looking around, I saw no trace of the enemy.

The sun was just rising and the desert lay once more sparkling and burnished beneath its level rays.

I saw before me the stately mass of the great Temple of Osiris.

The mighty wall, wherein I had spent the first night and morning, was revealed as part of a great quadrangle enclosing an *enceinte* of about 100 yards square.

The wall and the gateway, which I seemed to know as a blind man knows things by his sense of touch, were the only parts of the building which retained any semblance of its original design. The rest was a vast tumbled ruin, wrecked by man and his unruliness, by Nature and by Time.

I climbed again to the summit of the great wall where I had been the day before.

There was a cool refreshing breeze, and I could see around me the great ruin, and on the slope below it what I took to be the outlines of a Ptolemaic pleasure city that had once been busy and important under the shadow of the Temple's walls.

Now the desert lay utterly barren all round, and far in the distance I could just see the sea with that bewildering blue of the butterfly's wing.

Looking inland I could still make out on the horizon a dozen horsemen, and through my field-glasses could see the white uniforms, the red tarbooshes and slung carbines which I presumed were worn by mounted police or troopers of the Egyptian army. Jakoub's enemies had certainly gone. His cunning and foresight and the labours of those old worshippers of Mithras had saved him for the time being.

Below me the Arabs were busy reloading the camels, and I was eager to be on the road again, willing enough to leave behind me all these relics of ancient mystery and magnificence which for me were associated with that night of vigil and horror.

A few hours later the Temple had faded like a dream into the sand that surrounded us, as our party toiled across the last few miles to the railway.

We came to it at last, a wavy track following the contours of the desert, an iron link with civilisation.

There was a plain stone building for a station, and Jakoub was almost immediately in the midst of a wordy fracas with the station-master.

This functionary came out and inspected our camels and their loads. He immediately fell into a state of almost maniacal excitement. My smattering of Arabic was not sufficient to enable me to gather more than the merest fragment of his complaint, but he seemed to be calling Allah and the Prophet to witness that no freight-train ever could or would take such a load as ours was.

Jakoub let him rave; but the camel-boys joined in, whether on the station-master's side or against him I could not tell. Even the camels put in their word.

When they were all out of breath, Jakoub said a few sharp authoritative words which started the whole tornado of sound again.

This happened several times, and then Jakoub came up to me.

"He requires 150 piastres backshish, effendi. There is a train coming in half an hour. Had I more time I would make him to take less."

I was so relieved to know that the train was nearly due that I did not grudge the money.

The camels were unloaded, and their owners led them away in dignified gratitude for liberal backshish.

The train came up like a miracle out of the desert.

There was another scene with the guard; but now Jakoub had a firm supporter in the station-master, and for the consideration of a 100-piastre note the whole of our cargo was safely stowed on board.

A feeling of intense relief from responsibility came over me as I found myself back in the impossibly familiar surroundings of a first-class compartment, and four hours of heat and dust were the end of my physical discomfort.

Remembering Edmund's injunction I wiped my heated face and neck and donned my clerical collar as the train ran into the Gare de Caire at Alexandria.

CHAPTER 9

THE DOPE TRADE

I HAVE said that Jakoub had compelled my grudging respect as he faced the sand-storm. Now I had to recognise in him again a master of circumstance, as from a fiercely clamouring crowd of apparently hostile natives, and some over-excited railway officials, he mobilised a little force of porters, and conjured from somewhere a kind of wagon, or rather a long beam mounted on two pairs of wheels and drawn by a couple of under-sized ponies.

On this he had all our cargo stowed in the time an ordinary man would have taken to find a hat-box. He had a *gharry* ready for me, with my hold-all on the front seat. Our tickets were delivered up, and the crowd more or less pacified with backshish. We drove off, watched with haughty indifference by a couple of Egyptian policemen.

I was back in the world of men and wires, and my first care was to send a cable home.

I had decided on Bates as the recipient of the first news of my resurrection.

So we stopped at the office of the Eastern Telegraph Company.

I had thought out my message during the long weeks in which I had been tending to this ganglion in the nervous system of the world, and I cabled simply "Unable to communicate earlier. Returning next boat via Marseilles."

There was no need to say I was writing, as I would be home as soon as a letter, and in any case I felt that it would be utterly impossible ever to explain why I had been lost so long. I intended simply to say that the weather had tempted me to a longer cruise than I had contemplated, and that I had not had time to write.

Snape, I felt, would believe this; Bates and Mrs. Rattray would not care, so long as I returned at last in safety and health; and some day I would tell the whole story to the bishop. There was really no one else who would be either curious or concerned, though Marshall would doubtless be glad not to have to apply to a court of law to "presume my death," and some day

I would certainly swagger a little in my corner at the Athenæum about my adventure in the sand, and my exploration of the Temple of Osiris.

I had begun to think of myself as more in my element at the Savage or the Travellers'!

I posted Captain Welfare's letter to his agent and we arrived at Van Ermengen's Hotel, a pleasant spacious place facing the sea, from which it was only separated by the wide tram-girt road and the sea-wall.

Van Ermengen, the proprietor, met us in the hall. He was a thin, grave man, with a hard face so narrow that his profile seemed to be cut out of the edge of it. He had a cramped mouth and restless, rather anxious eyes, as colourless as his face and hair.

He received me very graciously, and made no difficulty about my wagon-load of packing-cases. He instructed Jakoub, who arranged with the hall-porter about their disposal. He seemed very anxious to explain to me that he was of English "nationality," and that his establishment was run on "English lines." He did not seem to know Jakoub, and apparently had no curiosity about me, not even asking my name, or expecting me to write it in a book.

I suppose it is impossible to take me for anything but a British parson, for he had assumed my nationality before I spoke, and addressed me in English.

It was my first experience of a European hotel in the Near East, and I was a little astonished at the vast size and the bareness of my bedroom. But it was delightfully cool. The sun was just setting over the sea on which three tall windows of my chamber looked, and the sea-breeze blew freshly into the room. I looked out longingly with the desire to see the sails of the *Astarte* coming into port; but there was nothing in sight but a couple of feluccas and a distant steamer.

A window at the side opened on a narrow street, and I looked down curiously at the busy Oriental scene in the violet transparency that fills the streets of Alexandria at sunset.

Then I went and wallowed long and luxuriously in a great bath, and shaved myself decently and respectably again.

After my scorching in the desert the evening seemed cool enough for ordinary clothes, and it was with a curious sense of luxury that I put on the dark clerical suit that had last been folded by Bates in my dressing-room at home.

There were still some minutes before the vaunted "English dinner" would be served at eight o'clock. I lit a cigarette and sat down by an open window watching the rapid onset of night and the assembling of the stars.

Hungry as I was I realised that I was very tired. I could have slept where I was; but I did not wish to sleep. There was on me that feeling of excitement, almost of elation, that comes with physical fatigue after a long strain is relaxed.

I was glad to be rid of my queer and rather doubtful responsibility, and to have succeeded in my first commercial mission, but I regretted the end of what had seemed a momentous interlude in my uneventful life.

It seemed stupid to go straight home, but home called me. This was not the season for travel in Egypt, and anyhow, the experiences of a tourist would seem insipid after my journey over sea and land. I decided to revisit the country in the orthodox way, perhaps the following winter, and meantime I must go home.

Then into my mind rushed all those mundane details inevitable in what we call civilisation, which had been banished since I first put foot on the deck of the *Astarte*.

I had sent word that I would sail by the next boat, but now it occurred to me that I might not have money enough for the journey. If Edmund did not come in time how was I to get it? I knew nobody in this city, and even if my bankers cabled money, I was not sure how I could draw it without any means of identification.

I could no doubt find an English banker, or consul, or official of some kind, but he would ask questions. He would naturally want to know why an English clergyman, claiming to have ample means, found himself suddenly without resources in Alexandria? He would ask had I not arranged a letter of credit? He would want to know what boat I had come out by, and where I had stopped while in Egypt?

The blood rushed to my face as I thought of it. Who on earth would believe my tale of the *Astarte* and Jakoub, and my camel ride, even if I dared to tell it?

I *might* make what was left of my money do, but I reflected that Jakoub had earned something handsome in the way of a tip. He had not only refrained from taking my life; he might almost be said to have saved it.

I went down to the big dining-room with my mind full of these grovelling details; as certain that my connection with the episode of the merchandise was at an end, as I was convinced that my muscles ached with fatigue.

But if we deny the existence of Chance or of the Fates we shall have to include a sense of humour among the attributes of the Deity. It was what men call Chance that now prolonged the game of cup-and-ball the gods were playing with me.

The head-waiter was indicating my solitary table with the extraordinary gesticulations and grimaces of his kind, when I heard my name called out in a shout of surprise.

A tall man in the uniform of the Egyptian army rose from an adjoining table and came across to me, with a beaming smile and outstretched hand.

"You don't know me from Adam," he exclaimed. "It's this bally uniform."

"Brogden!" I cried, in a flash of recognition.

"Good shot!" he said. "It's jolly to find one's not quite forgotten after all these years. What on earth are you doing here? But you must come to my table, and we'll tell each other all about ourselves."

He had me by the arm and walked me across the room to his table.

Again my will had nothing to do with events.

I watched the waiters doing conjuring tricks with knives and forks and napkins, as they rearranged the table, and gaped in astonishment at my old friend.

For he was an old friend, once almost my dearest friend, although I had forgotten his existence.

"I had no idea you were in Egypt," I said. "You went into the Civil Service. I have heard nothing of you since."

"No, you old devil! I wrote you two letters and didn't get an answer. And then—you know the way, one loses touch."

I knew. We went on for a time each making the futile excuses and offering the explanations that men do for lapsed friendships when they are renewed by chance. We had been dear friends at Oxford for several terms, and had normally, and without unpleasantness, been separated by circumstance. There was nothing to apologise for.

The great majority of our friendships are determined by propinquity. Time and space have dominion over more of them than death can claim.

"I heard of your coming into the Irish estate," Brogden was saying. "I must congratulate you. But I see you are still a Padré. Do you know, I have only seen you once before since you were ordained? You're down from Cairo, I suppose? It's a bit hot there now but I suppose you have finished the usual beat. You got to Assuan, of course?"

This was just the kind of cross-examination I wanted to avoid.

"No," I said, "I couldn't manage Assuan this trip. I hope to come next winter; I must keep your address. But my tourist experiences won't be very interesting to an old resident. But tell me about yourself. How long have you been in the army?"

"Oh, I'm not a pukka soldier," he explained with a laugh, "though I wear this kit and am known as 'Brogden Bey'! We Egyptian officials sometimes trickle in and out of uniform as a matter of expediency. I'm really a rather superlative kind of policeman at present."

"I don't understand at all. Let's hear your story right from the beginning."

"Well, you remember I passed rather decently into the Civil Service? Eighth or ninth, I think."

"I remember it very well. We rejoiced together in town. It was just before I took Orders."

"Yes. I remember that dinner! I had taken a pretty good degree, and after that I had to go to an expensive crammer for three months to be sure of a decent place in that exam. I was nearly at the top in classics, history and law, but my higher maths let me down. Good God! the things one knew then! The Civil Service candidate has to do a lot of mental vomiting after his exam before he is quite human again. However, having demonstrated my amazing acquirements as a scholar, they gave me a job in the Printed Book Department of the British Museum. I had to lick the labels for the backs of new volumes of the Supplementary Catalogue.

"No, I'm not joking," he broke off in answer to my glance, "that is literally what I had to do. There was a man there who had been doing it for twelve years. He had been crammed even tighter than me for the exam., and he was quite unfit for anything else, poor chap! I didn't see my way to become Chief Librarian either, and I was frightened of getting cancer of the tongue. I wrote to an uncle of mine who was then one of Cromer's men out here, and he got me a billet in the Ministry of the Interior. I rather took to the languages, and happened to make myself useful in the Criminal Investigation Department, and—here I am."

"But what about the army? What are you doing now?"

"Let's go and have our coffee in the lounge," he said. "It's a bit public here for chatting."

We found a retired sofa at the end of the wide cool lounge, and a white-gowned Arab with crimson sash brought us coffee.

"What liqueur will you have?" asked Brogden. "Don't drink before sunset in the hot weather, but don't go to bed teetotal if you want to keep fit. Their cognac is not fit to drink without some curaçoa in it."

He had evidently taken charge of me; apparently someone always did, so I let him order the liqueurs.

"You haven't told me yet what you are doing now," I reminded him.

He bent forward mysteriously and whispered one word, "*hashish*."

I was about to repeat it aloud when he stopped me with a gesture.

"Don't shout about it," he said. "I'm not supposed to talk, and I don't want even the English people here to know what I'm about. But it can't matter telling you, and you'd be surprised what a relief it is to talk to some-one!"

I was thankful to have started him on a topic that would keep him from questioning me till bedtime.

"That's some kind of drug, isn't it? I remember it in the *Arabian Nights*."

"Good Lord! Where have you put yourself in Egypt? Yes, it's a 'kind of drug,' as you say." He whispered again, "It's *Cannabis indica, Indian hemp*, in the medical books. We call it the other thing. It's meat and drink, wife and family, lunacy and lingering death to the Oriental when he gets fond of it. Drink's a boon and a blessing, and opium is mother's milk to it. We've stopped it being cultivated, and we've prohibited its importation. We're still trying to stop its being smuggled. That's my job at present. I've been given a semi-military appointment with the temporary rank of colonel, Egyptian colonel of course, but that's a blind."

Any story of smuggling has always had a certain fascination for me. I became interested at once, and forgot my fatigue and my longing for bed. I thought it seemed a whimsical thing that I should live over a reputed smuggler's passage, and now find in an old friend a modern "preventive man."

"That must be an interesting job," I said. "Tell me as much as you can. I needn't tell you I have sense enough to keep my mouth shut."

"I know you will. You see, the natives, especially the wealthy ones, *will* have the stuff, and they simply don't care what they pay. Naturally, the value of it has become enormous—incredible. These damned Arabs and Levantines are always slipping it in. But there's a bigger trade going on. They grow it regularly now in Greece, and the Greek Government won't lift a finger to stop it. There's too much backshish about. It will be a big thing for me if I succeed. At present I'm sorry to say I'm on the track of two renegade Englishmen."

"Englishmen?" I repeated. "That's bad."

"It's damnable," he said. "You can't imagine how we depend on prestige out here. If I could get evidence against them, we should have to keep it quiet here and have them dealt with at home. At present I've only suspicions to go on; but they're in tow with a rascally native. The biggest blackguard in the trade. He was in the police and got to know all the ropes. Some years ago he made a big coup, collared two feluccas full of the stuff near the Western Frontier. There was thousands of pounds' worth of the drug in them, and he had risked his life a dozen times to bring it off, to say nothing of the brains he showed. Of course, he was entitled to a reward, and what do you think they offered him?"

"I've no idea."

"*Five pounds,*" he groaned.

"Think of it!" he continued a moment later. "Five pounds to a man like that! He put the money back on the desk, smiled, saluted and disappeared. The fellow who had to offer him the money told me his smile as he saluted keeps him awake at night still—the memory of it, I mean. He's had to take a long sick-leave on account of insomnia. Of course, the man went straight into the trade, and I fancy he really organises the whole business. I've all the evidence I want against him, and when I get him, he'll give away his English pals all right."

"What's his name?" I asked to fill another pause.

"Oh, names don't count with a fellow like that. He'll answer to anything—Osman, Ali, Jakoub—'anything that comes to 'and,' as the old lady said of her goat."

"Jakoub?" I asked, startled.

"Yes. Why?"

A blur of impressions and calculations mingled in my tired mind. It suddenly occurred to me that the description was like our Jakoub. But he had been on the *Astarte* all this time. Nothing fitted in. Still, some instinct made me disinclined to give any particulars about my enemy, if such I could still consider him.

"Jakoub is my dragoman's name," I replied.

"It's a common enough name," said Brogden with a laugh. "They've only got about a dozen names among them."

"But what have these Englishmen got to do with it?"

"They run the damned ship. A wretched little Greek schooner they picked up here, interned during the Balkan war, and sold for a song. They profess to be making money out of the fruit trade, which of course is rot."

I was aware only of the effort to keep any revealing emotion from my face. Suddenly and quite clearly I had seen who were the two "renegade Englishmen." I had only one idea—that they were in danger of betrayal by Jakoub. How he had managed to deceive them, or how far they might be compromised, I did not try to guess. My only thought was that Brogden was now an enemy, a skilful, questing enemy on the track of a frightful misapprehension. I felt my skin grow cold as I thought what a mere chance it was that I had not told him my story, enough of it anyhow to lead him straight to Jakoub—and Edmund's disgrace. People would never understand that Edmund was innocent. Suddenly the question occurred to me— "Would they understand that I was?"

Brogden was talking all the time, and now I listened again.

"I was making things so hot for them that they left the Mediterranean in the beginning of this year. They're experts at dodging signal stations, and I lost track of them till they got to London. Ship's papers, manifest, cargo and everything all right, but the police got warrants out for the Arab in the name of Osman Hamouda. Then they disappeared again. We hoped to pick them up at Jersey, where we found they had relations with some very shady customers. I don't know what their game was, but there's sporadic smuggling going on there still in the old commodities whenever a chance offers. However, we missed them again. They got warned somehow and disappeared. I shouldn't be surprised if they're back in the Mediterranean. We'll find them with a perfectly innocent cargo of bananas or something!"

Brogden laughed, and then I heard him exclaim, "Hallo! What's the matter? You're ill!"

A great darkness had come on me through which I seemed to hear his voice as a teasing sound at a distance.

I saw it all now. *Edmund had known all along!*

"No. I'm all right now; a bit fagged, and the heat."

"Let me help you to your room."

"No, no thanks. I can walk all right."

I stood up to show him that I could, and to my surprise I was really dizzy. I swayed and sat down awkwardly on the couch. But my mind was clearing.

"Stop there a bit," he said authoritatively, and rang the bell.

"Here, Esmah," he called to the Arab, "get a whisky, get two, large ones, and some soda."

I swallowed the whisky, longing only to be left alone.

"That's better," I said, and this time I managed to rise quite steadily; "I'll turn in, I think, if you don't mind. Many thanks. Good-night."

"Well, I'll look you up tomorrow."

He came to the foot of the staircase with me, and I felt he was watching me as I went up. I turned at the landing and smiled, I think quite naturally. He waved a hand, and I was rid of him at last and alone in my room.

I wanted to think everything out and understand as far as I could. But thought was blotted out by emotion. My mind seemed blackened by the sense of Edmund's degradation. Less worthily, but I suppose not unnaturally, there simmered the sense of personal humiliation and affront.

Edmund had associated with Welfare and Jakoub in making of me their tool and dupe. In my bitterness I accused them of laughing at my innocence. But I knew at once I wronged them in that. I knew enough of the good in both of them to realise the wretchedness for them of our association during those weeks on the *Astarte*. Then I began dimly to perceive the hold that Jakoub had obtained over them. I tried to put away all these profitless ponderings and think out what was now to be done, how some shreds of honour were to be saved, or at least depravity concealed. I remembered the cargo of "curios" brought into my house, and realised it must be contraband, and the shop in Brighton only an agency for its sale.

But my mind refused to think it out then. I went disconsolate to bed, and was mercifully surprised by sleep.

I slept heavily until the Arab came with my tea and opened the lowered shutters that closed my windows.

I awoke with my body refreshed and mind alert.

As though I had thought it out in the night, I saw that I must at once get control of that abominable stuff. Whatever happened it should not be released to poison the souls and bodies of men. I would be a passenger no longer, but must act now.

I hated and feared the timidity and indolence that I had made a sort of petted habit.

As soon as I was dressed I went downstairs and sent for Van Ermengen.

He came, smiling and urbane, and wished me good morning.

"Good morning. Those packing-cases of mine?"

"Yes?"

"I want them brought up to my bedroom."

There was a sudden hardening of his face, and I remembered Edmund saying, "Van Ermengen knows all about the consignment." I was certain now that he did know all, that he was "in the trade." It was evident too that he had assumed—how rightly!—that I knew nothing.

"But it is impossible," he said; "they will be called for this afternoon."

"Who says so?"

"Your dragoman told me." He sucked in his lips with annoyance at being forced to this admission.

"My dragoman takes my orders."

"He referred to your partners," said Van Ermengen with a touch of insolence.

"I am waiting for my partners."

Now that I had started, it seemed much easier than I had expected to assert myself. I had feared Van Ermengen. Now I saw that he began to fear me. I saw too that he was utterly puzzled by my demeanour.

"But your bedroom, sir? It is impossible. It will take a couple of Arabs all morning."

"I will pay them."

"If you will come, I will show you where your cases are. They are quite safe."

"I want them in my bedroom."

"But think of the weight! They are too heavy for the floor."

"If that's so, I will ask the English Consulate to take charge of them. Will you be good enough to ring them up?"

He darted at me the malevolent glance of a beaten man, and gave some orders in Arabic to a porter.

"I will have my breakfast in my room, if you please, so that I may count the packages."

He bowed, and we parted.

In spite of the misery that still afflicted my soul, I had a new feeling of self-esteem as I regained my room. I had come well out of this encounter, and felt I could depend on myself in the struggle that must lie before me.

Before I had finished my breakfast Jakoub was shown in, polite as ever.

"You have slept well, effendi? You seem no longer fatigued?"

"I'm quite well, thank you."

"The praise to Allah. You would have the packing-cases up here, effendi?"

I nodded.

"But it is against the orders of the Captain and the other effendi. Nasr Hussein calls for them today. I must obey my orders, effendi."

"You must obey *my* orders."

"It is not in my agreement. It is impossible, this."

He was evidently prepared to defy my authority.

I stood up and looked at him.

"Jakoub, if those cases are not all here in one hour, I shall send for the police to take charge of them."

I suppose he saw in my eyes that I knew all that was involved in this decision, to Edmund and myself as well as him, and realised that I was determined to take the consequences.

He smiled as he had smiled at the official who offered him the five pounds.

"Very well, effendi," he said, and departed with a salaam.

There was deadly fear of him in my heart as the Arabs piled the cases on the floor.

Shortly after they had deposited the last one a message came that Brogden Bey was waiting for me below. I had forgotten his promised call. It was another embarrassment.

I locked my door and went down to meet him.

CHAPTER 10

I HANDLE A REVOLVER

IT was somehow a relief to me to find Brogden in a suit of civilian linen. His exotic uniform, and the tarboosh which etiquette compelled him to keep on his head throughout the evening, had increased his effect of a figure in a bad dream. Now I could realise him as my old friend—and keep him at arm's length.

I answered his anxious enquiries by assuring him I was well. But I intended, however, to remain on guard over the abomination hidden in my room, and I made use of my supposed indisposition as an excuse for not leaving the hotel.

He, of course, wanted me to lunch or dine at his club, to meet his friends of the English Colony.

I knew that Edmund and Welfare might arrive at any moment, and the sweat broke out on me as I thought of their walking in and finding me with this man. And it was impossible to get rid of him!

Through all the gloom of my misery I saw, like a golden thread, the humour of our being there together, of my having in my hands the treasure for which he would have ransacked Egypt. Of all men he was one I would most gladly have helped; up to last night. But now I must use all my wits to foil him in his endeavour. I said the word to myself, to "betray" him! Yet I too was on the side of righteousness. I too would stop the issue of this poison. But the achievement of his ambition would destroy my brother, and drag my own name in the mire of disgrace. To deal uprightly was beyond my power now, and there were things I must learn from him.

We agreed that my indisposition must have been a "touch of the sun," a diagnosis which in Egypt fulfils the same function that the familiar "chill" does at home, and I decided that if I could not shake Brogden off otherwise, I would have a relapse.

He wanted to talk about people and things at home, and anxiety began to make me feel genuinely unwell.

"Tell me," I said suddenly, "do you know these two Englishmen you are after?"

He looked round uneasily, evidently disinclined to renew his confidences of the night before.

"No," he said, "I've never seen them myself. Not yet."

"Do you know their names?"

"Oh, I expect they've a different name in every port! They're known to us as Montgomery and Ringrose. Don't for God's sake talk about them."

"I won't utter a word to a soul. But I'm deeply interested."

"It is a queer business. Montgomery is said to have the manners of a gentleman. The other one is a regular old shell-back, I believe. Professes to be some kind of sea-captain. They're both slim, though! By Jove, they'll want handling."

"What's this drug worth? How much a pound?"

"Well, one can't say exactly. The actual buyer would give ten pounds, perhaps, for a pound of it, if he could get it. But of course the fellows who bring it in don't get all that. It has to go through the Lord knows how many hands. If they can dispose of it well, and in fairly big lots, they might clear a fiver on every pound of it. They wouldn't take the risk for much less."

Ten thousand pounds, I thought with horror, was represented by the load in my bedroom!

"But don't let's talk about the business," Brogden continued, "it's never safe. You never know. I'm going to have a cock-tail—the one exception to the rule of 'no drinks before sun-down!' Do you mind coming in the American bar?"

I went with him and sat on a high stool by the end of a marble counter on which were vast blocks of ice with soda-water bottles sticking out of them like spines.

Brogden went and busied himself in superintending the concoction of some mysterious drink which he averred was the only one suitable and wholesome for the time and place.

Behind the bar and opposite where I sat was a door which I knew opened into Van Ermengen's private office. It was slightly open, and through the crack I heard Jakoub's voice and Van Ermengen's, speaking in Arabic.

If they had spoken in English I could not have heard all they said. As it was I could distinguish only a few isolated words of which I knew the meaning. I had no qualm of conscience in listening, and only envied Brogden's knowledge of the language.

It sounded as though Jakoub were urging something and the other were demurring.

I heard the words "el moftah" (the key) repeated several times, and then I recognised "a part of it," "our share," and "tonight."

I trembled lest Jakoub should come out and be recognised by Brogden, but instead there was an exclamation of annoyance or alarm, as someone hastily shut the door.

"Here you are," cried Brogden, bringing a wine-glass filled with an amber liquor with an olive at the bottom of it. "That will do you more good than all the medicine in the chemists' shops! Good health!"

"Good health," I answered, tasting the liquor, which was certainly very agreeable.

"I hate leaving you alone, old man. But I can't cut lunch at the club—or dinner today, and tomorrow I have to go to Cairo for a day. When does your boat sail?"

"I've not decided yet. I may rest here a day or two in any case."

"Then we shall meet again, and I'll be able to trot you round a bit when I get back."

"Yes, I hope so. But remember if we miss each other we must not 'lose touch' again. We will write, and I'll hope to come out next winter. And you must spend part of your next leave with me."

His going to Cairo was an unspeakable relief; but I longed for an opportunity to make him some amends. So we parted very cordially.

I got wearily back to my room and counted over again the cases of hashish! They were undisturbed, but I felt more nervous of my trust than if they had been solid gold or dynamite.

I ordered my meals to be sent up to my room, sent for some papers and books which I knew I should be unable to read, and sat down once more trying to plan out my immediate future.

One thing only was certain. I must remain where I was until the *Astarte* came into harbour. Then I must face Edmund. I felt how much easier it would be to be the guilty one. What was I to say to him? How were we to adjust our new relationship? I was determined to insist on his coming out of this life in which he had lost his honour and his caste. I did not shrink from the notion of impoverishing myself if necessary. But even if I succeeded in restoring Edmund to his caste, how could he take his place in it?

I knew that, as a matter of practical experience, there really is no absolution without penance. Knowing Edmund as I did, I knew that he would impose the penance on himself, and refuse the absolution. How was I to persuade him that all the best of his life, which lay before him, must be lived vigorously and honourably if only to make reparation?

I feared the weakness and petulance in his character, which I knew might drive him to shirk the issue in a cowardly suicide. I determined that I would hold him by the immediate plain duty of getting rid of this present cargo of potential infamy. I began to see in the hated packing-cases the means of Edmund's deliverance from himself.

About their destination I was clear and determined, but as to how to get them there, how even to move them from this room without exposure and disgrace, I had no idea whatever.

Of Captain Welfare I thought little. In other circumstances he would no doubt have prosperously added sand to sugar like my churchwarden at home, or have made an "honest living" out of poverty as a pawnbroker. He belonged to the class whose ideal is "respectability." It would be wrong to expect of such a higher ethical standard than their own.

No doubt he had expected to retire on his share of the profits of this infamy. Once I had seen the stuff destroyed I would give him his pieces of silver. He could just "put up the shutters" for the last time and appear no more in his shirt sleeves.

The long day wore itself away amid my fretting; but Edmund did not come. Once more I watched the sun set across the sea and, with the darkness, my fear of Jakoub revived.

I knew now that he was in league with Van Ermengen, that they both knew I was an enemy to their schemes. In my loneliness and sense of weakness I wished that even Brogden were back. I was in the enemy's camp and had no means of finding even one man whom I could trust. I wondered about the fragments of their conversation I had overheard. What key was it they spoke of?

"A part of it—our share—tonight!"

I had not thought much of the words when I heard them. I was not quite certain if I had their meaning right, caught as they were in isolated fragments of a conversation I could not understand. Besides, my mind had been concentrated on the fear of Jakoub's appearing and being recognised. But now, at the end of my day of solitary pondering, they came back into my mind, and it seemed their meaning was obvious.

The key must be the key of my own door. Jakoub must intend to steal the poison from my room, or at least as much of it as he regarded as his share—his and Van Ermengen's.

From what I knew of its value I realised that a few cases of it would recompense him.

And the attempt was to be made tonight.

My dread of the man almost overcame me. I longed to leave the place, to escape, and let him do as he would. I do not think it was fear of any violence he might attempt against myself.

I have not tried to tell what the loss of my faith in Edmund meant to me. But I do know that I would have surrendered my life then without regret. Yet I shrank from the idea of conflict with this man. I mistrusted myself and my own will. It was exactly the same feeling I had had before my first fight at school. I was then not frightened of being hurt. But I was sick with the terror of finding myself a coward and showing it.

However, I determined I would not desert my trust.

I got out Edmund's revolver, laid it on the table, and sat down by it to wait.

The night was hot and it was late before I heard the voices and the closing doors of other occupants of the hotel retiring. Had there been an Englishman among them I believe I should have appealed to him to share my vigil.

But they were all foreigners. I had heard nothing spoken but Italian and a language I took to be Greek. I could speak neither. To explain would be impossible.

A clock somewhere struck one, and suddenly the strain became intolerable. I reflected that they would not come at all while my light was on, and like a kind of vertigo came the desire to get the encounter over. It was the same longing that one has to throw one's self down from a height. But could I endure the waiting in the dark?

I decided that I must.

There was a switch attached to a long cord over my bed. I placed it under my pillow. I turned the key and took it purposely from the key-hole, took the pistol in my hand, and putting out the light lay down on the bed.

I listened to my heart like a muffled drum within me, "beating its funeral march to the grave."

And then the one thing I had not contemplated happened. I slept.

I awoke dumb with horror and the certainty that someone was in the room with me; but I had heard nothing, and there was no sound but the "funeral march" within me, beating time.

I do not know how long I listened, but at last came the unmistakable gentle sound of fingers sweeping along the wall. It is a sound that would wake no sleeper. But I can imagine no sound more terrifying to one listening in the dark.

In a spasm of terror I pressed the switch and sat up, covering Jakoub with the revolver. He stood by the wall near the end of my bed. One hand was in the bosom of his galabieh. He was not smiling, but his lips were drawn back and his teeth bared in a kind of snarl, the reaction of a man startled and disconcerted by sudden fright. Fear was like a third party between us.

"Put your weapon on the table or I'll fire."

I had not meant to speak, and my own words startled me.

Jakoub hesitated. The revolver was not cocked and I began to pull the trigger.

Jakoub could see the hammer rise. He laid a knife on the table.

"It was but to cut the strings, effendi," he said with a return of his smile. I slowly relaxed my pressure on the trigger, the hammer sank again, and I cocked the thing with my thumb as Edmund had shown me how to do. Jakoub watched me.

"You know what will happen if I pull the trigger again?"

"I have used a revolver," he sneered.

"Sit down on that chair at the end of the table."

He obeyed, and I took a chair at the near end. I propped the pistol on a pile of books, so that it was impossible to miss him if he moved.

"Why do you threaten me, effendi? I mean you no harm."

"Why have you stolen into my room at night?"

"I have but come for my property. You have taken it from me unjustly. I knew you would not give it to me. I wished for peace to be between us. I am a very good, very peaceful Arab."

In spite of myself I smiled at his remark, and at my smiling I saw to my surprise a new respect and fear of me awaken in Jakoub's eyes.

It was as though he knew our Irish proverb, "Beware of the front of a bull, the heels of a horse, the teeth of a dog, *and the smile of an Englishman.*"

An immense relief swept over me as I realised that fear had changed places across that table. I no longer dreaded my own cowardice.

"Let me go now, effendi, and I will await my share till the Captain come. It is now morning, he will be here today."

"If you move, I will fire."

I was aware of an extraordinary feeling within me. It was an intense desire to pull that trigger and kill him. It was blood-lust. It had never visited me before, and I felt it now as an intolerable temptation.

Jakoub saw it in my face. I saw it reflected by the terror in his eyes.

"Do not, effendi," he moaned, and I pitied him. The desire for his life faded out.

"In an hour it will be day," he argued. "The people will awake. If I am found here there will be plenty questions. It is not wise, effendi!"

I reached out with my left hand and took his knife from the table.

"To cut strings only," he repeated.

It was true that if he were found there, questions might be asked, and talk might arise that would ruin everything. I was at a loss how to end the situation.

"Jakoub," I said, "I know now what is in those cases."

"Of course the effendi knows. Are they not his?"

"No they are not mine. I did not know what was in them until I came here the other night."

Jakoub's face told me what I wanted to know. He understood it was a time for truth between us, and I saw that he was surprised. He had evidently believed that I was all along privy to the conspiracy. I suppose his manifest contempt for me was due to some idea that I was willing to accept less than my proper share of the profits.

"I did not know what was in those cases," I repeated. "I did not understand that this was a scheme to poison your own people and make money out of their misery. I knew nothing about your accursed trade. Now, I tell you, I know; and as long as I live not one ounce of that stuff shall be sold. I will pay you for your services to me, but you shall not get one piastre of profit from your drug."

The man's avarice almost overcame his self-control. He started forward in his chair.

I raised the revolver an inch or two, and he sank back.

"It is my property, my share of it. Even the poor Arab cannot be robbed always. I have paid for what I have there. I will see the Captain. Who are you to take from me my goods?"

"I know the man who is hunting you, Jakoub. He is very close on your heels. If I speak to him today, you will be in prison tonight."

"If I am, *I* speak! What then for you and the others? We're all in one ship."

"I am not. I knew nothing of the business, and I can prove it to my friend who is looking for you—*only for you*, mind. The others can take care of themselves. They have deceived me."

I watched him closely to see if he believed my last statement. I gathered from his look of discouragement that he did. I suppose from his point of view, there was nothing surprising in it.

"If you wish to see Captain Welfare again, you may see him here, in my presence, when he comes. I will let you live till then. I will not answer for Montgomery Effendi." He showed no surprise at my mention of this name, and I hoped that perhaps he knew no other.

"Have you complaint of me for him? Have I not served you?"

"You served me well on the journey. I shall not forget to say so. But he will be angry when he learns what I know. You will not understand, perhaps, but he will not be just. This is his pistol. If he were here holding it now, you would be dead, Jakoub."

"I do not fear him or any man."

"All right. You can go now. I shall not lock my door. But I think you will not try again to take your property. See, there is the daylight."

I rose and opened the shutters. I had to risk the movement because my forearm ached so with holding the revolver that I knew I could bear it no longer.

The amber light of morning filled the large bare room, revealing the feebleness of the electric lights which before had seemed so brilliant. They glowed now as points of light without power to illuminate anything.

Jakoub looked yellow-skinned and old. I saw points of grey in his black hair that I had not noticed before. I felt as if I looked a hundred years old, and knew that whether he went or not I must sleep.

He was standing with his hands folded before him looking at the ugly pile of packing-cases.

"Effendi," he said, "it is many thousands of pounds. We have worked hard and suffered much. We have paid much money to bring it here."

"Go away," I answered petulantly. I was rocking on my feet with the desire to sleep. The man simply bored me now, like a guest that will not depart.

"It is no good," I added. "You cannot have it. You cannot have any of it."

"All my life I have dreamed of such a chance, and now you rob me. Why?"

"If you don't get out of this I'll—I'll ring the bell."

I was conscious of bathos in this threat, but somehow the ordinariness of daylight made it impossible to threaten him with the revolver. I was a clergyman again, longing to get into my pyjamas.

Jakoub went sorrowfully out of the room.

I undressed and lay down, leaving the door ajar.

I knew there was something more potent than gunpowder protecting me and my charge, and I slept secure under the ægis of my own will.

I had overcome Jakoub and I was proud of it.

CHAPTER 11

CAPTAIN WELFARE EXPLAINS

I HAD finished a late breakfast and sat trying to forget my trouble and take an intelligent interest in *The Egyptian Gazette* and an eloquent indictment in its columns of the "Ministry of Wakfs."

I was still at a loss as to the nature and functions of this institution when Edmund came in, very debonair in his white linen suit.

"By Jove!" he cried. "I'm glad to see you here safe. We were terribly worried about you when we saw the sand blowing—what is it? What's the matter?"

I had tried to keep all signals out of my face and aspect, but I could not command myself. I knew I looked a crushed and guilty man.

I saw the youthful joyousness fade out of Edmund's eyes as he turned and saw the pile of boxes on the floor, and more than ever then I knew how dear to me he was; how much dearer than I suppose most sons are to their fathers.

He had wronged me deeply. How would it be possible for him to forgive me? We pray to be forgiven as we forgive them that trespass against us. We dare not profess to forgive those against whom we have trespassed.

He faced me again, but now with a grave, stern face.

"Why have you brought all that up here?"

"I could not trust it anywhere else."

"I see. You know what it is?"

I nodded.

"You understand, of course, that I knew all along?"

"Yes, now. From what I have learned I am bound to suppose that. I want you to tell me all about it, to explain——"

"Explain? There's nothing to explain. I did want to keep you out of it. I tried, faintly. I loathed the idea of your being humbugged—oh! yes, that's what it comes to. But I was too feeble to prevent it. But I won't insult you further with my regrets. The other things are bad enough, but I wish to God you could know how I mind about you. Good-bye!"

He went to the door, and it was no mere melodramatic movement. I knew well that if he went it would be the end between us.

Very quietly I said, "Wait a moment. You have no right to leave me in the lurch now. You have got me into this hole. Even at the cost of a few days' unpleasantness for yourself, you must get me out of it. Then you can go on with your own plans for yourself."

It stopped him like an expanding bullet.

"I beg your pardon. If there is anything I can do 'at the cost of a few days' unpleasantness' I shall certainly not grudge them."

"I'm glad to hear it," I said. "There's a devil of a lot to be done. You'd better sit while we discuss it."

"Well?" he asked as he took the chair in which Jakoub had last faced me.

I felt I had a much harder, much more important contest before me now, one in which I should have no aid from revolvers or other mechanical weapons.

"Under the circumstances," I said, "I cannot consent to your calmly clearing out and leaving me with all this very incriminating stuff on my hands."

"You'll have no difficulty in getting rid of it. That was all arranged. If you had left it to Jakoub and Van Ermengen——"

"I know that. It would have been distributed by sneaks in spite of all we English are doing to prevent it."

"We English are fools to try to prevent it. If you knew the people that take it!"

This remark depressed me almost more than anything that had yet occurred. It gave me the measure of Edmund's deterioration. I was again reminded of the bishop's remark about becoming *déclassé*. But I had not thought the process could have led to this.

"We may be fools, as you say," I replied, "but it is our habit to be decent fools. That is cricket. You and I cannot start playing pitch-and-toss like street boys and obstructing the field."

Edmund flushed a deeper red. "Why bracket yourself and me?" he asked.

"Because we are brothers. We are both Davorens."

"I'm not. I gave it up ages ago. I've kept the name out of it all right. Welfare won't give it away, and he learned my name before we—before we both——"

"I know. I'm very glad you have kept our name out. But that's not the point at present. I called you back to know how we are to get rid of this stuff, to destroy it? I quite understand there would be all sorts of unpleasantness if I called in the police. What are we to do?"

"I don't know. Unless you burn the hotel down."

"I can't afford that."

"There are so many people interested. They would all be out to stop you."

"You must find a way. You and Welfare. It's the only way you can get clean again."

"I can't get clean again, except in one way. I'm afraid Welfare won't see it. He's used to being soiled. And, apart from the profit he was going to get, nearly the whole of his savings are there. There are plenty of pious Englishmen whose money is just as foul."

"I don't doubt it, but I can't help your savings."

"Mine? There's no money of mine in it! I don't own an ounce of the muck. Practically all that was left of my money went into the *Astarte*. But of course that makes no difference. It makes me feel all the more a worm. I was in at it, and it's they who lose."

I suppose it was in a sense not a very essential point, and yet I rejoiced exceedingly to know that Edmund was not financially interested in this wretched enterprise; not directly, that is, for of course he was privy to it, and it was obviously part of the business of the *Astarte*. I recollected with a twinge that I owned more of the *Astarte* than Edmund did. But then I was not privy to the business.

"Who are the other people concerned?"

"There's Jakoub, of course, and Van Ermengen, and the other scoundrelly native who was coming for the stuff today."

"Well, there's no use any of these people trying to prevent our having the stuff removed and destroyed quietly. As a matter of fact, the situation is that I offer to permit its destruction. The alternative is handing it—and them—over to the police. You have got to act for me in the matter. You must see them and explain. Then you must help me to get it destroyed. And I must see it destroyed myself."

"That can't be done in Egypt."

"Then it must be got out of Egypt."

"If it wasn't for old Welfare, I'd rather you did tell the police. But it would be terribly hard on him. It was a fearful temptation, and I know he tried to keep out of it. Better men than he is might have given in."

"I quite agree. It's just because we've got to consider Welfare that I propose this plan. You and he must carry it out."

"Yes; I see that. I don't know if it's possible, but, by God, I'm glad to have the chance of trying!"

"Is Welfare here?"

"He's in Alexandria, yes."

"Well, you must see him. Tell him what has happened and explain what he has got to do. And, look here, tell him when it's done I won't see him stuck. I suppose there will be some honest money over when all your joint business is wound up and the *Astarte* sold? Tell him that will all be his and he can rely on me to help him in any straight business he may take on. I know he's an honest man by nature."

"It's generous of you to say that."

"No. It's simply my belief. Try and explain to him. Could you bring him here this afternoon?"

"I could, of course."

"Very well. Then we'll thrash the whole thing out."

"Do you mind telling me how you got to know about the infernal business?"

"Not a bit. I met the man who is hunting you all down. He is an old Oxford friend of mine."

"My God! What an extraordinary thing!"

"It is. An almost incredible circumstance. But it's the way things happen."

"And you told him nothing?"

"He began telling me things, and I saw it all before I let anything out. Even now I think I could give him all this, and Jakoub, and keep you and Welfare out, but I prefer the other way."

"You couldn't muzzle Jakoub once he knew his own game was up. We are compromised utterly. They would bring you in as a witness. They might even arrest you! No, for God's sake, let's do it our own way."

A flash almost of fun came into his eyes.

"Do you know," he asked, "that we'll have to steal it from Jakoub and the others?"

"I don't care a hang about that."

There was healing in our laugh, and I was filled with a great thankfulness as Edmund went away. I knew that for the time being he was saved from himself. He had at last a clear, clean duty, and an enormously difficult task before him. I could not tell how he would accomplish it; but in the trying there would be reparation. After all he had not sunk so deep as I feared. He had tolerated depravity in order to live the life he desired, but he had not yet actually traded in it.

I was much more hopeful as I dozed through the stifling heat of the afternoon, waiting for Captain Welfare. They came at last about five o'clock. Captain Welfare hesitated, or professed to hesitate, about taking my hand.

"It's good of you to offer it, sir," he said. "I hope you'll believe as I'd never have allowed you to leave us when you did if I'd known such a storm as that were blowing up. It's the worst I've seen, and I've seen plenty. When we got sand coming on deck five mile from the land, I knew what it were like ashore. I thought you were lost, sir. I did, indeed. I didn't think as you would have stood it. Your brother will tell you how I carried on about it."

He paused, appealing with a look to Edmund, who grunted as he generally did when Welfare became eloquent.

"That's all right. We had a rough time, but now that it's over I'm glad to have had the experience."

"I wouldn't have had you come to harm, not for a million."

It was evident that Captain Welfare was perfectly sincere in his solicitude. I had no reason to doubt it, for in spite of the deception he had put on me, I believed him to have a regard and respect for me that was none the less real because of his very English pleasure in knowing one whom he persisted in regarding as a "swell."

Unfortunately he had the failing, so common in his class, of believing it to be necessary to put all the fine shades of his feelings into words. He would leave nothing to the imagination if he could help it. I feared he would drive Edmund quite mad.

"We had better have some tea," I said, and rang the bell.

"If you'll excuse me, sir, I think I could say what I have to say better if I had a glass of brandy."

"Then for God's sake don't give him any," said Edmund.

"Bring some tea and a bottle of brandy and some sodas," I said to the Arab. I was determined to be just to Welfare.

"Now, Captain Welfare, I have asked you to come here simply to discuss how we are to get rid of all this poisonous cargo. I take it that my brother has explained my views on the matter, and what I have decided must be done."

"I don't know how to tell you what I feel about it, sir. I'm a broken-down man. I've run straight, or pretty nearly straight, till I let myself go into this here. If you'll believe me, sir, it's not just the money, though I reckoned there would be pretty near enough for me to retire on. But I was never easy about that. I wouldn't have been if I'd had it in the bank at home. I'd have known the Lord's blessing wasn't on it."

Edmund got up and went to the window. He remained there, looking out across the sea. But there was not a tinge of hypocrisy in Captain Welfare. His God was horribly unjust in most things, so unjust that, as I already knew, he thought it necessary to fear him in the literal sense of the word. But he would adjust his rewards and punishments with a nice sense of commercial probity.

"No," he continued; "what gets me is the way I've treated you, sir, after all you'd done for us. I can do no less than take it all on myself. Your brother was against it from the start. I only wish I hadn't overbore him.

But I never planned it out beforehand. It came on bit by bit. I honestly thought, sir, as we'd go to Guernsey and back as arranged. Then when we got warned off there was nothing for it but to carry on. You'll understand now it wasn't only Jakoub was in danger. Well, there's times a man *can't* tell the truth, and we couldn't then. I think you'll see that yourself?"

"Quite," I said.

"Well, we deceived you then. It wasn't the first time, I admit. I suppose we'd been deceiving you all the time. I was nervous at first, but if you'll excuse me, sir, it seemed to come natural to you to be took in."

"Yes, I'm afraid it did. I assure you I blame myself very much."

"Don't do that, sir. For God's sake, don't do that! All the blame there is is wanted. Don't you waste it where it ain't wanted. Well, we had this job on, though we didn't mean to do it so soon. But it come over me that if we could work you in, it would make all plain-sailing. There didn't seem any harm in it. I didn't see what harm could come to you. But what I can't forgive myself is them books. Them books I showed you was false."

This seemed to me a curiously minor point to rankle so in his queer crooked conscience.

"I do wish now I hadn't done that," he added.

"It seems unnecessary to me," I said. "It's almost the only inartistic thing in the whole process."

It was an unkind remark, but it only brought a puzzled look into his pathetic green eyes. It made Edmund writhe, however, but then Edmund deserved it.

"Between you and I, sir, I thought I was giving you a fair chance to find us out. I thought you *must* see through them books. You would have if you'd have looked through them. But you never did."

"Captain Welfare, I might just as well give you a Greek testament to read. I told you so."

"Well, I don't know!"

"I know you don't," I snapped, for this meaningless exclamation always irritated me.

Captain Welfare looked so pained that I was sorry I had snapped. There was a real innocence about the man that made it almost impossible to keep him focussed in the mind as the old schemer he undoubtedly was. I was able to believe that in showing me his abominable faked accounts, he had actually been offering me a sporting opportunity of finding him out!

"Well, sir, I've told you the story now. I've acted bad and mean. I've not had the chance to know many real gentlemen in my life until I come to know your brother, and afterwards yourself. When I was a younger man, and come to understand what a gentleman was, and that I wasn't one, and never could be, it was a distress to me. I always wanted to be with gentlemen, to work with them and for them. Well, I got my chance, and this is what I've made of it. I've brought your brother into all this here. I've brought him down, and I've treated you—well, the way I've told you. I know now I'm not fit to have dealings with gentlemen. I don't mind admitting, sir, it's a disappointment."

There was a depth of sincerity in his crude confession that I think touched even Edmund. He continued to stare moodily out to sea. But it was evident he had been listening, and he made no gesture or sound of impatience.

"Captain Welfare," I said, "I told my brother this morning I believed you were an honest man."

"Sir, I thank you for it, though if you'll pardon my saying so, I think you'd believe any mortal thing, as long as it wasn't in the line of ordinary religion. Well, you know now I'm not an honest man, leastways I haven't been, but since you have said that, sir, by God, I am! and will be, if I end my days in the fo'c'sle."

"Have you thought how we can get rid of all this?" I asked.

Captain Welfare's theories were rather embarrassing.

"I haven't, sir. Not yet."

"It's got to be done."

"Van Ermengen and Jakoub won't let it go without a struggle."

"There are the police if they try to prevent it," I said grimly.

"They can easy square the police, sir. Backshish!"

"They cannot square my friend," I replied sternly.

"No; they couldn't square him," he agreed. "But we're not too well fixed for going to him either."

"I would much rather do it without him."

"Even if we got it away from here I don't know where we'd put it. If we had it on board, I could manage. But the *Astarte* will be watched every minute she's in harbour. They searched us for Jakoub, sir, and for this little lot. Your friend will have heard of it by now."

Captain Welfare smiled, a regrettably unrepentant smile. But many a man who has changed sides has a temporary hankering for the old colours.

"You say you could manage if you had it on the *Astarte*?" Edmund asked suddenly.

"Yes, if she were clear of the harbour."

"Well, I see how it can be done."

We both waited for his plan. He turned and came back to the table.

"This street is perfectly quiet from three o'clock in the morning until after sunrise. If there are any police about, a little backshish will keep them away. There's deep water right up to the sea-wall. I've often seen feluccas tie up there. All we've to do is to bring up a big fishing felucca, lower the beastly stuff out of this window, load the felucca and send her out of the way till the *Astarte* picks her up at sea."

It was a daring scheme, and its risks were abominable.

Captain Welfare pointed them out.

"You've got to take the risks because there's no other way," Edmund said. "I've been thinking while you've been talking. When you mentioned the *Astarte*, I saw the whole thing in a flash. We cheat Van Ermengen & Co. instead of buying them off, we hoodwink the police and get away, and we can sink the stuff in as many fathoms as we like."

"For that matter we could drop it overboard from the felucca without bothering about the *Astarte* at all."

"No," Edmund argued, "some of the crew would talk. Jakoub will know what we've done within forty-eight hours of their coming back. He would get it up again if he had any clue to its position."

"Besides," I said, "I stipulated that I was to see it destroyed."

"So you did, sir," Captain Welfare admitted, "and that will be done as per agreement. So we'll have to get it on the *Astarte*."

"Are you going to bring it all the way home, then?" I asked.

"That is impossible, of course," Edmund put in impatiently, "we'll have to get rid of the *Astarte* at Marseilles, and then disappear ourselves."

"Get rid of the *Astarte*?" I repeated. "Is that necessary?"

"I'm afraid it is, sir," said Captain Welfare. "You see they won't search us on the way because they will think we are going to pick up a fresh cargo. But we dare not leave the port in her again. This friend of yours knows too much, and he might get Jakoub while we are away."

"I see," I said, regretfully, "but I don't see how you will keep your promise about letting me see this stuff destroyed—not that it really matters. I'm quite willing to trust you."

"I'll not ask you to do that again, sir," said Welfare very solemnly, "you are bound for Marseilles too. We shall have a day or two's start of you, but you will get there first. I promise you faithfully you will see the last of the cargo."

"Very well. But, by the way," I asked, "what was that cargo you landed at home? Was it curios?"

"Of course it wasn't," Edmund said, contemptuously.

"I hope it was not more of this wretched stuff?"

"No, sir," said Welfare, "there would have been no use leaving that in England. That was ordinary old-fashioned smuggling. Brandy and cigars as a matter of fact. It's done still from the Channel Islands when a chance occurs, and of course the *Astarte* was a chance. We had meant to get the stuff through the Customs along with our straight cargo somehow, but we had difficulties at Tilbury. Then this tunnel of yours cropped up, sir. It made the whole thing so easy we were going back to Guernsey for more. Only this hashish business got in the way, and we learned there was a warrant out for Jakoub. Well, if they'd got the *Astarte* then, the whole thing would have come out. That was why our agents sent to warn us. Getting the *Astarte* back here without arrest was a fair masterpiece! But, by the Lord Harry! it was anxious work. You've little idea what I went through, sir. And the course we steered—oh, my Lord!"

"Life was worth living for the time," said Edmund. "I often felt sorry you were missing all the fun of the gamble!"

"Of course you knew all about this smuggling at home, Edmund?"

"Of course! Don't make any mistake about that. I was in it for all the money I could put up at the time."

I sighed. The whole business was so very sordid. But after all, brandy and cigars were not going to poison anybody. The whole thing was stopped now, and in face of the horrible traffic I had circumvented, I was not going to break my heart over his Majesty's Customs Duties.

"Well, gentlemen," I said, "our business now is to get this load back on the *Astarte*. The sooner it's done the better. I suppose we're all agreed to get it away as suggested?"

"I agree as there ain't any other way."

"How long will it take you to provision the ship?" Edmund asked of Welfare.

"I could do that tomorrow at a pinch."

"Very well, tomorrow night we'll shift this lot. Let me see. All we want is a few fathoms of rope. I'll bring that up in a suit-case. You and I will have to man-handle it out of this when Welfare brings up the felucca. Half a dozen good niggers will have it aboard as quick as we can lower it. Welfare, you'll have plenty of fishing nets aboard to cover it up with. Then I'll take the *Astarte* out first thing in the morning, and pick you up when we're well out of sight."

So it was settled, and the scheme began at last to look quite feasible to me.

"I wish," I said, "we could dine together, but I cannot leave this stuff unguarded, and it would be awkward here if my friend Brogden turned up. But, Edmund, I want you to sleep here tonight. I was disturbed last night, and I'm tired and sleepy. Anyhow, I'm a rotten shot with a revolver."

I had to tell them of Jakoub's visit and my vigil with him, though I knew the knowledge of my danger would hurt both of them very sore.

The things they said made me realise that I was not insensible to flattery.

Brogden, to my relief, did not return that evening.

When Edmund came back to my room we talked long together. But what we said I think concerns no one but ourselves.

It left me happy in a new confidence that he would be restored at last to begin an honourable career.

The night was comparatively cool and I slept for twelve hours.

CHAPTER 12

A MIDNIGHT ADVENTURE

EDMUND had gone when I awoke, but he had left a note saying that he would be back early with what he called "the fixings for tonight." He would remain all day, he said, and I was to go out and leave all to him.

I was glad to be at liberty, for I felt as though I had been imprisoned for weeks in the hotel, and I detested the sight and the thought of the place.

The Arab brought up a message that Brogden was waiting to see me. I went down, feeling for the first time prepared to enjoy his society, so I agreed at once to lunch with him. He had a car outside and wanted to take me for a run round the more interesting parts of the city. I readily accepted the offer; but I could not leave until I knew Edmund was in charge, and so I invented pretexts to detain him.

I took his advice as to the best boat to return home in, and asked for an introduction to his banker so that I might cash a cheque. Then I insisted that he should again procure his patent cock-tail. During this performance Edmund came into the hall with his bag. He saw me with a stranger and of course went upstairs without noticing me; so I was free at last to leave.

We drove at first among the narrow flagged streets of the native quarter, which I specially desired to see, and all the brilliantly coloured but squalid scene, which seemed so commonplace to my friend, had for me a wonder and a charm which kept me silent.

It was too soon for me when Brogden said, "I guess you've seen enough of this now—and smelt enough. Now we'll have a spin."

We came back through the central parts of the city, through squares and streets that might have belonged to Europe, along the wide, smooth surface of the Rue de la Porte Rosette, between rows of acacias with flaming blossoms, and stately tamarisks, past villas drenched in the purple of bougainvillia, dotted with the scarlet of the hibiscus, gardens with lawns kept green with infinite toil, and blazing geranium beds, and so out into the country among cotton-fields, orchards of figs and vines and plantations of dwarf bananas.

Everything was new and delightful to me, and the rush through the air completely conquered the heat.

I had forgotten my companion and all my anxieties in surrendering myself to the delight of unaccustomed colours, when suddenly Brogden said:

"Those two fellows are back with their damned boat."

"The two Englishmen you told me about?"

"Yes, bad cess to them. They've done me again—for the time being. Only for the time being. I'm bound to have them. For one thing they haven't a notion who's on their track."

I felt meaner than ever before. The whole squalor of the business in which I was involved came back on me, and seemed to take the colour out of the sunshine. Yet I felt I must play the hand through, however dirty my cards might be.

I was committed now to Edmund's and Welfare's side, and I must learn what I could, even though I should feel spotted with treachery all my life.

"What happened?" I asked.

"They got ahead of their time-table, or rather my time-table. One of my picket-boats picked them up only a few miles outside. The native rascal I was after was not with them, and there wasn't a thing aboard that shouldn't have been there. I'm practically certain they had a big lot of hashish with them, but they'd got rid of it. Unfortunately there was only a native officer in charge of my crowd, and naturally he got nothing out of them."

"And what are you going to do now?"

"Oh, of course they've landed their rascal somewhere between this and the western frontier, and he is pretty sure to have the real cargo with him. He's bound to make for Alexandria, and he'll bring the stuff on camels to some hiding-place in the neighbourhood. I have every possible track watched, so I'm bound to get him."

"What about the railway?" I asked with beating heart.

"Oh, no native dare put a load like that on the railway. It would be stopped and examined at once."

I saw clearly for the first time how essential I had been for the working out of Captain Welfare's plan, and I could not but admire the soundness of his dispositions. I thought they showed that combination of imaginative power and attention to detail which is said to distinguish great commanders. I remembered my first impressions of Welfare, and how I had instinctively thought of him as taking a lead in his line of life, whatever it might be. Yet he had come to seem small in his ways, and paltry in his aims. I wondered which was the real man, how much the Welfare I knew was but the product of untoward circumstance.

"What will you do about the *Ast*—the ship?"

I had almost called her the *Astarte*, and shuddered at the thought of the consequences of such a slip. To be found out now! unmasked as another "renegade Englishman," a member of the gang!

"I can't touch her at present. I've no evidence yet. I must wait till I get this damned Arab."

"Supposing she sails?"

"She won't sail at present. They're waiting till they get their stuff safely here. If they went it would only be to pick up another load at some place on the Greek coast, and I should take jolly good care to get them on the way back. Nothing would suit me better."

We were back in the city now, and presently we pulled up at Brogden's club.

Here we lunched very comfortably, and I met many of his friends and brother officials.

Everybody asked me if I had met so-and-so in Cairo. I felt with embarrassment that my social ignorance must seem almost uncanny. When I said my time in Egypt had been short and that I had spent it in sight-seeing, I knew I had utterly lost caste. To the official Englishman in a foreign country the only objects worthy of regard are other Englishmen and women.

One elderly and evidently important person informed me that he had been twenty-five years in Egypt and had never seen the Pyramids. "And I never mean to," he added with a glance of mingled pride and indignation. I had not seen the Pyramids myself, but I felt it would be presumption on my part to say so, a futile attempt to regain the place I had lost in his esteem.

He evidently regarded the Pyramids as bad form. I think he suspected Cheops and the other potentates who built them of having done so with a view to attracting the undesirable tourists of a dim future. He might have dined with Cheops himself, had that been possible, but he was not one of those who could be expected to be amused by the remains of a pyramid. Was he not high in the Ministry of Finance, and decorated by a grateful Sovereign with the Order of the Bath as a reward for that magnificent inaccessibility to ideas which makes the British Official so universally loved and respected.

"No, sir," he puffed, "no Pyramids for me, thank you."

I did not think highly of this particular person, but the rest were very pleasant fellows, and Brogden was one of them. I was an outsider to them, and I was careful and troubled about many things at the moment. I could not enjoy their society as I would have done had they been my guests in my own vicarage. I desired very ardently to get away from them.

From the instinct of ordinary politeness, I tried to conceal this desire, but I fear that I failed. Anyhow, Brogden got up and said we must go and see his banker and the shipping agents.

I know I left that club with the reputation of a bore and a bit of a nuisance, but I console myself by reflecting that I was quite forgotten in five minutes. All the same I felt I had inflicted a further injury on the much-wronged Brogden. He had paid me the compliment of introducing me to his own little coterie in his favourite club. When one does that for a friend, one likes that friend to be a success. Among middle-aged men this is rarely possible. No doubt this is why our clubs at home debar the introduction of strange guests into the rooms frequented by members. I had not been a success, and as we went down in the lift I appreciated for the first time the profound knowledge of human nature that would prevent my taking Brogden into any room in my own club except one that suggests the waiting-room of a long-deceased dentist.

The fact is that an old friend, however valued, is apt to be a nuisance when he suddenly emerges from the Past and bursts in on the routine of the Present. In spite of his cordiality, I could not help knowing that Brogden wanted to be back among his friends of today, and at his usual rubber of auction.

Accordingly when our business was finished, I made excuses for getting away, and he let me go with shame-faced willingness.

I found Edmund busy with a block and tackle arrangement he had slung to one of the bedposts, and watched him in some surprise.

"We can lower six cases at a time with this," he said. "I'm going to make a pair of shears out of a couple of these iron bedposts and make them fast over the bit of balcony outside the window. I reckon we shall be able to shift the lot in half an hour; quite as quickly as they will load it. I hope Welfare has got the felucca all right. Did you get rid of your pal?"

"I did. He's fixed up for the evening at his club."

"Good. He knows about the *Astarte* being in, I suppose?"

"Yes; he told me all about it, and about searching her. He guesses Jakoub was landed just about where we did land. He is having all the routes to Alexandria watched."

"Poor devil! Is he a decent chap?"

"He is, very."

"It's rotten having to let him down."

"Of course it is. But the whole thing is rotten," I said wearily.

"You still think this is the best scheme?"

"It is. Please don't let us discuss it again. The alternative is unthinkable."

"What is he doing about the *Astarte*?"

"Nothing. He has no evidence at present. I asked him what he would do if she sailed? He said, 'She won't sail. If she did it would be only to pick up another cargo, and he would have her then.'"

"I believe," said Edmund, "he would have had us all right in the end—only for you."

"Edmund," I said after a long pause, "what about Jakoub?"

"Jakoub is at present our only risk. Fortunately he doesn't know our name. Nobody knows that, but of course he could identify us. He can't give us away unless he's caught and done for himself, then of course he would. I don't think he will be caught, but if not he will try blackmail."

I shuddered at the thought of spending the rest of my life under the threats of this man. I remembered the impulse I had felt to shoot him, and dreaded the possibility of being subjected to such a temptation again.

"Couldn't you take him home with you?"

"He wouldn't come. And what could we do with him if he did? It would only make it easier for him to start his blackmailing. He'll probably want to get to England in any case, and there's no use our giving him a passage!"

A note came from Captain Welfare announcing that the *Astarte* would be ready to start in the morning, and that he would meet us with the felucca as arranged. He was too busy to join us then.

"He must have had a heavy day," I said.

"Yes," agreed Edmund. "It's not everyone could have done it. But I must say for Welfare he's a worker. Nothing will stop him when he's fairly on a job."

I am myself naturally very deficient in energy, and so perhaps have an exaggerated respect for it in other people. I detest the photographs one sometimes sees of raucous politicians declaiming with wide-open mouths, uplifted fists, and over-developed facial muscles. To many, I know, such men are the type of energy and what they call "efficiency." The men whom I have worshipped, whose names I have seldom known, are those who have made great roads and bridges in remote places, who have conceived ships and mighty engines, and the few god-like ones who have written the great books of the world.

Between such men and myself there is a great gulf fixed; but between me and the loud-voiced politician there is only my own fastidiousness.

Some of this nobler energy Captain Welfare possessed in his degree. His intelligence was of quite a high order; he had the face and aspect of a man intended for doing things on a large scale; he had the simplicity and lovableness of a great man, and he was unhampered by what we call "higher education."

Yet beyond escaping from the dry-salter's shop he had done nothing with his life. He had seen men and cities, but he had not known them; he had certainly not commanded them. Had he succeeded in his first primitive ambition of making money, it might have been replaced by a nobler one, and in that he would have succeeded too. But he had failed. Poking about amid adversity he had done "shady" things; he had done this one blindly dishonourable thing. But successful men, who have the choice of avoiding dishonour, have done far worse things, and I believed that as a successful, happy man, Welfare would have done nothing base.

What is the flaw in such men as this, these many men who ought to bequeath something to their race? Is it all the bishop's "want of opportunity"? Was Edmund also to become one of them? That was to me the most poignant question.

As there was no chance of Brogden's returning we ventured to lock the door of our room and dine together downstairs. But it was not a festive meal.

The cloud of anxiety for the enterprise in hand was dark over us, and beyond that the sky of the future looked gloomy enough. There was the threat of Jakoub's malevolence and, more serious to me, the question of Edmund's eventual future.

I tried to get him to talk of this, but it was as though he could not see himself apart from the associations of his past.

"How can I get rid of it?" he asked. "I am only avoiding exposure now for your sake—and the family name. Otherwise I believe I should feel better if I went through the mill and took what I have earned; prison for a bit, and then the fo'c'sle for the rest of my time. It would be a way of disappearing, and that's all I want now."

"Naturally; but you have no right to think only of what you want," I said, "you are wanted yourself."

"Yes, by the police!"

"Don't scoff just now, old boy. Your services are wanted. I know you have capacities that have never been used, never touched. The plain fact of the matter is that up to now you have lived and acted as a boy—amusing yourself. I don't want to rub it in, but now you have got to make up for it by giving a man's work to the world while you can."

"How can I? What can I do? I can do nothing but sail a ship. Ten thousand old duffers can do that better."

"There is just one thing you can do that everyone cannot do. You can command."

All men like to be told they are capable of command, and Edmund did not question my statement.

"Much chance I have now of commanding anything or anybody," was all he said.

"Remember you come of the officer class," I said. "We have ceased to be a ruling class. I know it's old-fashioned even to think we are a class. The vulgar call it 'snobbish.' But heredity remains a law of Nature, and democracy is only an invention of man."

"I don't see that social theories are going to help us much just now."

"Then I'll come down to hard facts. However wrong and corrupt it may be, we are still to some extent a privileged class. And owing to that fact you can still get a fresh start, which, to be perfectly frank, a plebeian could not get."

"How do you mean?" he asked with an eagerness that greatly encouraged me.

I told him then of the bishop's suggestion about the Colonial Service.

Edmund made no reply. He was leaning his elbows on the table, balancing a spoon on the edge of a knife. The spoon see-sawed dangerously, and I watched it in an agony lest it should fall. It seemed as though our fate somehow depended on its equilibrium.

It swung slowly to a balance and came to rest.

"Do you think," Edmund asked, watching the spoon, "that the bishop would still do that, or try to do it, if he knew all this business?"

"I don't know. He will have to be told first."

"Of course."

"I shall tell him the whole story. Would you refuse such an offer if it came to you?" I asked, fearful that my voice had betrayed my eagerness.

He laid the spoon carefully down on the table and withdrew the knife.

"No," he said, "I should not refuse it, after what you have said."

I had gained all that I wanted, and much more than I could have expected so soon. There was no more to be said and no excuse for our lingering at the table.

We went out into the lounge to drink our coffee, both looking at English illustrated papers a fortnight old. Their dullness seemed intolerable in this weary gap of inactivity that had to be lived through before the time came for our final risk.

"I can't stand this any longer," said Edmund suddenly, throwing down a sheet of snapshots of advertising peeresses at race-meetings, foolishly photographed in the awful ungainliness which the camera reveals in the act of walking.

"Let's go out and walk or drive somewhere."

"We can't both leave. It's not safe," I reminded him.

I persuaded him to go out alone, for I felt I could better endure the irksomeness without him.

I returned to my room and sat by the window looking out over the sea, and listening to the sound of its waves on the sea-wall. The sound of the sea is always soothing and always melancholy, but it is especially so in distant places, for the sea has but one voice, everywhere its murmur is the same that we hear at home.

Edmund came in about midnight, and we sat together in the dark by the window.

Next door to the hotel there was a café, and its chairs and tables were spread out over the wide footpath. We could see under its electric lights the tops and tassels of tarbooshes, and the white discs of straw hats whose owners sat sipping coffee or lager beer, and eating olives and strange sweets. Most of them were talking loudly, and a strange babel of Arabic, Greek, Italian and French came up to us from the pavement.

"I have seen the policeman on duty," said Edmund, "and put him all right with fifty piastres. The street will be as quiet as the grave when that infernal café shuts up."

"It closes at one," I said.

The moon, now some four days past the full, was but newly risen, but star-light is very real in Egypt, and presently we could just make out the pale pointed sail of a felucca going slowly close-hauled to windward.

"That will be Welfare," said Edmund.

"Isn't he too soon?"

"He's all right. He'll go up to windward till he sees the lights go out, then take the sail off her and drift down here. I arranged to switch the light on and off a bit to show him where we are."

All the windows on our side of the hotel were dark, as the building fortunately faced on to the side street. The company at the café was thinning, and the guests who remained were calling for their final drinks.

"It's about time to get to work," Edmund said, "but I'm going to have a whisky and soda brought up. It will look more natural to Van Ermengen if he has any suspicions; besides, I want it."

"No, there is nothing else tonight," he said to the Arab who brought up the tray, and then he started methodically to take one of the bedsteads to pieces.

He took the two long pieces that formed the sides of the bed and lashed the ends of them together, crossing each other. From this cross he slung the block he had been experimenting with, and rove an end of the long rope through it.

I held the rods for him as he worked, greatly admiring the sailor-like precision and neatness, the economy of rope and of knots, with which the implement was completed. He put out the light and brought the whole arrangement to the window, and in a few seconds he had all the essentials of a jib-crane projecting over the balcony and firmly lashed to it.

He knotted the end of the rope into a double bowline (a bowline on the bight, he called it) which just held six of our packing-cases securely.

"Now I think we've earned a drink," he said quite cheerfully, as he switched on the light again, and filled a couple of tumblers.

"We shall have to work in our socks and move about as little as possible," he explained. "As soon as Welfare is ready I want you to hand me the cases. I'll put them on the parapet and get them slung. You must hang on to the rope and take the strain when I get them over the side. Then lower slowly. Do you understand?"

"Perfectly."

"I'm sorry to give you so much of the hard work, but I must see to the slinging myself. If a case slipped and fell—well, that would about close the operation."

"I don't mind the work," I assured him, "I only wish we were at it."

"It won't be long now. The café is shutting up."

I looked out of the window. Tired waiters were dragging in chairs from the pavement, and whisking the stained cloths off the very tables at which a few guests lingered, reluctant to leave. Others were closing shutters with a rattle.

The moonlight was steadily increasing, and now lit up the pink and yellow plaster of the tall shabby houses that faced the sea between us and the native quarter. It lit the minarets of a couple of third-rate mosques behind the houses, giving them an hour of delicacy and beauty which the crude sun denied them. The lamps along the sea-front paled, and the lights in windows disappeared one by one. The last tram crashed by, and a belated *gharry* passed with some shouting youths in it. Then silence settled down on the city as the moon raised herself above the buildings east of us, and "with delight looked round her when the heavens were bare."

Edmund noiselessly nicked the switch up and down three or four times, and lighting a cigarette came back to the window where we waited together in silence.

Presently a dark spot appeared on the sea to windward, and soon we could see the felucca dropping down-wind towards us. The big lateen sail was stowed and she came slowly on. Not a word was spoken as she sidled up to the sea-wall, which hid all but the top of her swaying spar.

In another moment Captain Welfare with a couple of natives was looking up at us from the pavement.

"All right?" he asked in a whisper.

"All right."

"Lower away, then!"

The first load was ready and we lowered it as arranged. The rope ran noiselessly on the carefully oiled pully. While the natives carried the cases to the boat, we got another load ready. Nobody stirred in the hotel. A *gharry* came past at walking pace; but we heard it coming and put the light out. Captain Welfare stood close to the wall below us. The driver passed on without taking any notice. He delayed us about three minutes and made my heart beat unpleasantly. There were just nine loads for our derrick; but thanks to Edmund's arrangements the whole job was finished noiselessly and without a hitch in less than forty minutes.

As the last load reached the ground Captain Welfare whispered up, "Good-bye!"

"Good-bye and good luck!" I answered, and without another word he went across the road.

I saw him clamber clumsily over the sea-wall, and then the felucca was pulling out to sea. Just as she got out of sight I heard the creak of the halyard as they got the sail on her.

I came back into the room, exhausted and streaming with sweat but happy. It was hard to realise that this most difficult and dreaded part of our task was actually over and without the slightest mishap.

I thought of Pilgrim and his rejoicing when he at last got rid of his burden. Mine had indeed been grievous, and, like Pilgrim's, it had been a burden of sin, even if not my own.

"Thank God that's over!" I said.

"Yes, it's a good job it's gone so well. By Jove! how hot you are. Strip and have a sponge down and get into your pyjamas. I must put this bed to rights and pack the tackle."

I took his advice and made myself comfortable as he plainly needed no help.

"Now I think we'll have our final drink. Then I'll have a couple of hours' doss, and be off soon after dawn. I must not leave poor old Welfare too long in that beastly felucca. He won't be having a very comfortable time, I can tell you. If those natives guessed what they had aboard I wouldn't give much for his life."

"Good Heavens! I never thought of that!"

"I know you didn't. We didn't want you to. But he has all ready to blow up the boat and cargo if he's attacked. He would run no risk of the stuff getting back into circulation. Yes; on the whole old Welfare's part of this racket is one of the few really courageous things I have known a man do."

And I had never said a word to him! I had not known!

"He's as pleased as punch about it," continued Edmund. "He's a sentimental old boy, and he has a feeling that he's doing something to make up for the way he has treated you."

"I shall be miserable until I know he is safe," I said.

"Oh, the odds are on him! Even if he has to hold the crew off with his revolver! Those fellows are easily cowed, and they know the *Astarte* is coming up. The danger is that they may rush him in the dark. Well, here's luck to him!"

But I could not take it so lightly, and I was certain that Edmund did not in his heart. I understood that he had felt bound to tell me in justice to Welfare, and now this anxiety would overshadow all the others until the suspense were over.

"You're about done, anyhow," Edmund said; "do get to bed. You'll sleep all right."

"I think I will. I am tired, but wake me before you go, if I'm asleep."

"Shall I?"

"Of course. I want to say good-bye."

The dawn had come and it was daylight when I was awakened by hearing him moving about the room.

"I shouldn't have had the heart to wake you," he said. "Good-bye. I say, you've been a brick. I wish I could tell you. Good-bye."

And with this he left the room and went on his way.

CHAPTER 13

CAPTAIN WELFARE KEEPS HIS PROMISE

MY boat did not sail until the following day, and I now felt a degree of mental and bodily lassitude and exhaustion that prevented my having any pleasure in the prospect of my last day in Egypt. I suffered from a profound nostalgia and craved only to be home. I had the feeling that I should never see my experiences in perspective until I saw them from my own study. Much as I dreaded the sight of him, I yet longed to see Jakoub, to have a final reckoning with him, to find out at least his intentions and know the worst; but Jakoub did not appear, and I had not the faintest idea how to find him.

I was very lonely and depressed as I gave notice to the hotel people that I should leave the following morning.

Van Ermengen had kept out of my way since our last interview, but the news of my departure brought him at once to see me.

His manner was grave and courteous as he bade me good morning. "Excuse me," he said, "but I understand you sail tomorrow?"

"That is so."

"Have you any instructions about the—ah—the goods in your room?"

"No; I don't think I have, thank you."

"They cannot remain here, you know."

"Of course not." I fear I was spitefully enjoying his perplexity and deliberately prolonging it.

"But you cannot take them with you."

"I had not thought of doing so."

"But what am I to do? I must have the necessary authority to hand them over."

"You won't be bothered about it at all, Mr. Van Ermengen."

"But I will be, I must be! I will not hand over the goods to anybody without authority."

"You will not be asked to; it is all arranged."

I turned away, but he came after me and caught my arm.

"But this is my house," he said, getting more excited; "things like this cannot be arranged without my knowledge."

"It seems to me that they have been," I said coldly, shaking off his hand. "'The goods,' as you call them, are in the charge of my partner."

"But he cannot leave them here without consulting me."

"I suppose not," I agreed; "I suppose that is why they have taken them away."

"Taken them away?" he repeated.

I nodded. His look of perplexity changed to one of suspicion, and then suspicious fury.

"But they cannot do this without my knowledge. It is impossible!"

"Well, they have done it. You can go and see for yourself."

The man began to lose self-control and raised his voice.

"But it is not legal," he cried shrilly; "it is robbery!"

We were in the entrance hall of the hotel, and there were people standing and sitting about.

"Please don't make a scene here," I said. "It cannot do any good, and it is unpleasant."

He glared at me, but controlled his voice.

"Will you please to come into my office and discuss this matter?"

"I see nothing to discuss."

"But I demand an explanation. Some of this property is mine," he blustered. "It was in your charge. If it has been stolen——"

"Come, then," I said. "I will talk it over." I saw that if I refused to go with him there certainly would be a scene, with, possibly, disastrous consequences.

He led me into the office where I had heard him talking with Jakoub. There was a sort of sloping counter along the wall under the window with papers and big account books on it, and we both stood by this facing each other. Van Ermengen's thin, knife-like face was eager and malevolent. It would have frightened me once, I reflected, but I had faced him before and had the better of him. Now I felt a kind of queer pleasure in the idea of conflict with him.

"I will have this cleared up at once," he began.

"Certainly, that will be best," I assented.

"I will not be played fast and loose with."

"Not by me, Mr. Van Ermengen, certainly."

"It *is* by you!" he insisted. "You speak of your partners. They are my partners. But I do not know you. I have no arrangement with you."

"None at all, except that I am responsible for settling my bill. I think under the circumstances I had better settle it now and change my quarters."

"It is not of that I speak, and I do not appreciate to be mocked! I tell you I had an interest, a considerable interest, in the goods which you insisted to have in your room. You tell me the goods are gone. Very well, I hold you responsible to me. I will have my money, please, if I do not have the goods. I will not be robbed by any damned sham parson."

"You shall not," I said quietly. "I am rather at a loss here in your country, but at home if you wanted to charge me with theft you would only have to call a policeman and give me in charge, as they call it. I happen to know these things because I am a county magistrate, as well as being a perfectly genuine parson."

"Damn you," said Van Ermengen, whose temper seemed to have gone; but who was as much impressed by the word "magistrate" as the lower orders still are in England, in spite of the degradation which has overtaken the once respectable Commission of the Peace.

There was a lull in the storm.

"I do not want your police," he said at length. "I want my money."

"And I will pay nothing, beyond my hotel bill, except through police or lawyers."

"How did they get the stuff away?" he asked, his curiosity getting the better of his anger. "Damnation, they must have taken it through the window!"

"I don't think it matters," I said indifferently. "You must get any information you want from them. As you say, you and I have no business relations."

"But I will have my money," he spluttered. "You will not leave Alexandria till I get it."

This made me uneasy, because I did not know what the man might do, or could do. But I felt it was essential not to betray any uneasiness.

"I shall certainly sail tomorrow," I said, "and I do not consider it worth my while to change my quarters. If you attempt to interfere with me in any way, I shall simply report you to a friend of mine as an importer of hashish——"

"For God's sake, hush!" he exclaimed. "Do not shout that word."

"I have nothing to fear," I assured him. "I do not mind who hears me say it. When I came here I did not know what the vile stuff was. By a coincidence I learned all about it, and I determined to stop your vile trade. I have acted accordingly. You may believe that or not; it does not matter what you believe. I made my friends remove your poison and theirs—it was not mine. It will never be sold. I shall see it destroyed. If you are wronged you can take what action you please. But I warn you, Mr. Van Ermengen, you will not get a penny out of me except by process of law. Now, if I am incommoded in any way while I remain here, I know what to do. I have nothing more to say, and I shall be glad if you will have my bill ready for me in good time in the morning."

"You will hear more of this," said Van Ermengen as I left his office. I thought it was rather a feeble remark, but I feared greatly that I *should* hear more of it, and that Jakoub would be the medium through which I should hear.

It was a relief when Brogden rang me up and asked me to spend the afternoon and dine with him at the Yacht Club. I forgot all my troubles while I held the tiller of his two-and-a-half rater.

Although we spent the afternoon and evening together, there was no more said about the hashish business. I understood that he must be at a loss and would avoid reference to it, and I had no longer any reason to question him.

Brogden saw me off at the dock the next morning.

I greatly dislike being "seen off," but after all his kindness I could not tell him so. Thus it was that I, who had so strangely and unintentionally stumbled into Egypt, left the land of sunshine and mystery like any respectable and most commonplace traveller.

The low line of yellow sandhills we had been so long approaching a few days ago soon sank below the horizon as the great steamer rushed seawards, and in spite of the sorrow that had come upon me there, I felt a certain sadness at seeing the land fade from sight. I felt that there in these few days I had had more of a man's part in the world than in all the other days of my life. I knew that what I had done there would offend many consciences more conventional than mine. A legal phrase cropped up in my mind, and I believed that I had "compounded a misdemeanour." I had certainly sailed "close to the wind." But I believed that I had saved my brother from irretrievable disaster. I had done what I could to break up a nefarious conspiracy, and though I now saw things that might have been better done, I looked my conscience in the face and was not ashamed.

That evening just at sunset I saw a sail ahead of us. It looked small and insignificant in the distance, but a great hope came over me that it might be the *Astarte*. As we overhauled her she altered her course so that we should pass closer to her, and I saw the leg-o'-mutton sails, the long high bows and the bowsprit with its head-sails "like a skein of geese." I found myself close to one of the ship's officers as I leaned on the taffrail watching her.

"What the devil is that idiot doing?" he said; "she looks as if she wanted to cross our bows. There'll be some swearing on the bridge if she makes us alter course!"

"She won't," I remarked. The officer looked at me with surprise and some amusement. I suppose it did seem quaint in a clerical passenger to assume a knowledge of nautical matters. But in a minute or two the helmsman let her away again, and put her back on a course nearly parallel to our own. The officer glanced at me as though there were something uncanny about me. At the same moment I saw a string of flags mount to her peak. The officer got his glass on her.

"I beg your pardon. Can you tell me what that signal is?"

"Yes; it's 'All well.' I wonder who the deuce they think they're speaking, or what they're playing at, anyhow. She's one of those little Levantine fruit boats. But she looks cleaner than most of them."

A great weight was taken off my mind, for I knew that Captain Welfare was safe, and they had taken this chance of telling me so, no doubt guessing I would find someone to read the signal.

We were rapidly overhauling the *Astarte*, and I saw that our converging courses would soon bring us within a few cables' length of each other.

Already through my glasses I could recognise Edmund at the wheel, and Captain Welfare holding by the shrouds, directing the movements of some of the crew for'ard.

I raised my white helmet at arm's length above my head, but it was doubtful whether they saw the signal; for already I was surrounded by a group of curious passengers, all waving handkerchiefs in obedience to that strange instinct which creates a sense of excited fellowship between strangers who meet and pass each other in ships or railway trains.

However, my movement was immediately followed by a wave of Captain Welfare's hand, and something splashed into the sea and sank in the *Astarte's* wake.

The splash was repeated, and I could see that the crew were heaving overboard the precious, hateful cargo.

Captain Welfare was keeping his promise.

I watched the process, fascinated at first, infinitely thankful to feel that the load of iniquity which had so burdened my spirit was thus at last cast into the sea and the *Astarte* purged of sin. But very soon I was recalled to uneasiness.

The curiosity of the silly passengers around me was excited by the process, and I still scented danger in every trivial circumstance connected with the nefarious trade.

"Whatever are they doing?" was the question I heard repeated all around me.

The ship's officer beside me came unexpectedly to my relief.

"Chucking bad rations overboard," he replied to one of the more eager questioners.

"Those Levantine schooners," he added, in an oracular tone, as he turned round from the taffrail to explain to his audience. "Those Levantine schooners always load up with condemned bully and other blown tins to feed their dago crew on. Sometimes they drive it too far, and the stuff gets into such a condition that nobody can live aboard with it. Then it has got to be jettisoned. That is what they are doing. Those fellows drew across to us because they were frightened of a mutiny while they chucked the stuff away."

He closed his telescope with a snap and looked round impressively, receiving the homage which landsmen pay to the omniscience of the officers responsible for their lives.

Thus was one minor wrinkle of anxiety smoothed away for me.

The *Astarte* fell rapidly astern, and the setting sun turned her white sails to bronze. In spite of all that had happened I longed to be back aboard her.

"I hope," Edmund had said, "that you will always keep a warm place in your heart for her." I found I had, and that it would hurt me as much as him when she was sold.

My blunder about "scrap price" had been prophetic.

When I thought of the little familiar cabin of the *Astarte*, all the pomp of the saloons and state-rooms on the steamer seemed to me but vanity and vulgarity.

I was back in my vicarage. In my absence the tremulous passion of spring had passed into the suave splendour of early June. I grudged having missed the pageant of April and May, for at my age one begins to count the number of springs one can still hope to see. I had rather dreaded my arrival and the necessity of explaining things, but it was made much easier for me than I had dared to hope.

Travellers are often disappointed by the lack of interest in their experiences which they find among those they left at home. The fact that they have temporarily enlarged the orbit of their little swirl on this planet gives them a new sense of their own importance. They are apt to look upon events that have happened at home as trivial, merely because they happened at home and not in some other latitude. Until they settle down again, they think of the people around them as absurdly interested in very minor matters. They forget that in them too distance had once annihilated interest, and will do so again.

As always happens on such occasions, Bates and Mrs. Rattray were much more eager to impart information than to receive it, and for once the returned adventurer was sincerely thankful for this perfectly natural attitude of mind.

Mrs. Rattray had deemed the occasion of sufficient importance to emerge from her own precincts and welcome me in the hall.

"We were glad to get your wire, sir," she said as Bates took my coat and brought my scanty luggage in.

"I was afraid you would be very uneasy," I said, feeling like a guilty schoolboy. "But I simply hadn't a chance to send word, and I could not resist going on."

"No, sir. It would have been a pity as long as you were enjoying it. We didn't worry the first fortnight. But then we did expect to hear. I would have been very anxious, only the weather kept so fine I felt you couldn't come to any harm, only for them wild men on the ship, sir. Bates didn't like the looks of them at all."

"Oh, they were really most harmless fellows."

"How did you leave Mr. Edmund, sir?" asked Bates.

"Quite well, thank you. He is on his way home, but it will be a few weeks before he gets back. Where is Mr. Snape?"

"He is away for the day, sir. He told me to apologise to you, and tell you he had made an appointment with his Lordship. He thought it better not to put it off."

"Quite right. There's no trouble, I hope?"

"Well, sir," Mrs. Rattray explained, "they will be very glad to see you again in the parish. Oh no, not trouble exactly, but they don't seem to hold with some of his ways, I don't know why. I'm sure a quieter gentleman in the house I never knew."

The highest praise Mrs. Rattray ever gave to one of my sex was to describe him as "quiet." She seemed to suspect all men of a tendency to sudden outbursts of noise.

"Some of them don't like his ritualistic ways, sir," said Bates. "There were none of the regular sidesmen collecting last Sunday, and there has been trouble because he asked Miss Reynolds to be secretary of his new communicants' guild. She's only been a year in the parish, and they did not like the idea of a guild, anyhow."

"All right, Bates. No doubt Mr. Snape will tell me all about it. Now I must go and see the pigeons till lunch is ready. Then I'll have a walk round the village."

All was well in my pigeon-loft, and the young birds were promising. It was a peaceful little world. I sighed as I thought what a pity it was that Christians could not make more allowance for each other's fads. Most of us are so terribly anxious to close all avenues to the Kingdom of Heaven except our own crooked little path.

Among my parishioners in the afternoon I found that I had to protect poor Snape from a widespread suspicion of his being a secret emissary of the Vatican. The other mistake he had made was to start only three of his "organisations." There was thus much jealousy about the filling of official positions in connection with them. I saw at once that in a community as small as ours the only sane method would be to start sufficient "organisations" simultaneously to provide secretaryships and treasurerships for the whole of the adult Church population. I decided to do this, unless the existing ones first died a natural death. I hoped they would for so far they did not seem to have made people behave better, but had been the source of a good deal of envy, hatred, malice, and all uncharitableness.

However, all this turmoil saved me from enquiries about my own recent movements. They were much too preoccupied to take any interest in these, though they were, I believe, unfeignedly thankful to see me back among them. I decided to preach to them about Charity. I would tell them that though nobody knew exactly what St. Paul meant by "Charity," for all his list of attributes, yet we all knew exactly what was meant by "uncharitableness," and that the main thing was to avoid the latter.

On getting home I wrote to the bishop. I apologised, unnecessarily I knew, for my prolonged absence. I told him frankly it was impossible to explain this in a letter, but that I had many surprising and painful things to tell him, and was in great need of his counsel. I besought him to give me an opportunity of talking to him as soon as he could spare an hour or two, and added as in duty bound, that it was not in connection with the affairs of the parish that I wished to trouble him, but that my distresses were entirely personal.

His reply was delayed a day owing to his departure for London, but I will quote a part of it here. "I could give you a brief interview immediately on my return, but I feel sure from the tone of your letter that you have matters to discuss that demand more than this. If you could have me for a night next week we could talk things over as of old. It would be a great pleasure and rest to me too. For the time is a terribly harassing one. I think it is not at all generally known how fearfully anxious the European situation is becoming. There are many forces at work that appear to be intent on war, and I feel that Satan may be unchained among us almost any day. Do not, however, speak of this at present, and if you wish to see me earlier do not hesitate to come over to the Palace any day after tomorrow.

"Poor Snape was over the day you wrote, and told me of his troubles with your flock. I am arranging other, and I hope more suitable, duty for him. Dare I ask you to keep him with you for a few days? I know he has to consider expense, as he has got into debt, among other troubles, purely through financing some of his own attempts at 'organisation.' To paraphrase the Book of Common Prayer: 'He has left unpaid those bills he ought to have paid, and paid those bills he ought not to have paid, and there is no sense in him.'

"You will no doubt have perceived that he is one of those excellent, earnest idiots that are so hard to keep out of mischief. But he is a lovable soul too, and capable of great good if I could only find the right sphere for him. I know you will not mind helping me to help him."

The bishop's letter made me feel that, after all, I did know what St. Paul had meant by "Charity." It was the spirit that could see the worst in a man and believe the best of him, the love that could recognise folly and succour it without contempt.

After having mingled so much with what was base, and paltry, and mean, the thought of seeing the bishop again was to me like mountain air to one who had dwelt in a dungeon.

Snape returned in time for dinner, and after a few perfunctory enquiries about my "trip," as he called it, he told me of his interview with the bishop.

"I could see at once," he said, "that his Lordship was put out. He had a very worried look. Somebody must have told him about the attitude of the people here."

"Perhaps he has something else to worry about besides this parish."

"Oh no! He seemed full of it, of the parish, I mean. He spoke of nothing else all the time I was with him."

"And did he make any suggestions?"

"He was most kind, most kind; and very interested, but——"

"Yes?"

"I don't at all wish to be misunderstood, or to seem in any way wanting in respect for his Lordship, but I cannot honestly say that he was very helpful."

"I'm sorry to hear that."

"No, I really would not call his advice helpful. He seems to share your view that scientific organisation in parochial affairs is not universally applicable."

"Good heavens! I never said that!"

"Not perhaps in those words, but that is how I have formulated what I understood you to say."

"My dear fellow, I couldn't have thought of anything half so brainy. I was only afraid that those sort of things wouldn't work very well in this particular parish. As a matter of fact, they don't seem to be taking very kindly to them, do they?"

"They need educating," said Snape, quite complacently. "At the start there is bound to be friction. And, as you know, friction always generates heat!"

He evidently felt that he had said a neat thing, and laughed in the manner of a pious man making an innocent concession to frivolity. I felt as if he were beginning to hypnotise me.

"What we should do," he continued with a bland air of superior wisdom, "is just as in mechanics—to find the co-efficient of friction, that's what we want—the co-efficient of friction."

"What we want is lubricating oil, I should think."

"Quite, quite. Oh yes, we must have our lubricating oil too, but at a later stage. We must first find our co-efficient."

He had a morbid delight in the phrase, a bubble from the forgotten mathematics of his Little-go days that something had set dancing in his brain-pan. I knew it had no meaning in this connection, but like most of us, the man did not want meanings. I saw he would make a great hit at a clerical meeting with his "co-efficient of friction," and I felt certain he was making a mental note of it for some such purpose.

He surprised me, too, for although he had manifestly made a mess of things in the parish his manner had an assurance, and even an assumption, of superiority, very different from the timidity I remembered at first. No doubt that had been merely the result of the shyness which mere unfamiliarity produces in weak natures. It had worn off now, and I liked him even less.

"It seems to me," I said, rather brutally, "that the friction is mainly about who should be secretaries and so on."

"That is merely a superficial manifestation of a deeper spiritual unrest, I hope of spiritual hunger," he assured me. "It will be quite evanescent."

"It didn't strike me that there was anything evanescent about Mary Gregson's temper at not being asked to be secretary before Lizzie Reynolds."

"Of course," said Snape with dignity, "if we are to be turned aside by the vulgar jealousies of uneducated young women, we cannot make much progress on the road to spirituality, can we?"

I felt it was impossible to argue with the man, so I propounded my theory of multiplying guilds and brigades and things. But he did not approve of this either.

"No," he said. "That would be to jump from one extreme to another, which is always a mistake. Just as in the natural world, so in the spiritual, there must be a gradual organic evolution. We must be content with small beginnings."

"The thin end of the wedge, eh?"

"Oh no, pardon me!"

I chuckled. I had deliberately tried that wretched old phrase on him. And the hackneyed metaphor is so invariably used of something undesirable that I was certain he would shy away from the sound of it.

"Well, I suppose you told the bishop I had given you a free hand in the parish?" I enquired.

"Yes, I had already written to him to that effect very shortly after you left! I regret to say that his Lordship seemed to advocate what I can only describe as a policy of *laissez-faire*. That is why I venture to say that his Lordship did not strike me as very helpful."

If I had had the bishop's letter when he again used that word I am afraid I should have thrown something at him.

"And what about stopping on here for a bit?"

"Ah, yes. I fear that is now out of the question."

I manfully repressed a great sigh of relief.

"The fact is, his Lordship wants me very soon elsewhere. In any case, I hope I have started the engine, and it may be that you will find it easier to keep it going in my absence. I understand there will be some ten days' interval before I am required, but I should not feel justified in remaining here. I suppose I must return to lodgings for the time being."

There was a wistfulness about him as he said this that made me feel mean in my gladness at getting rid of him.

In spite of himself I feared that the comparative comfort of my house had softened his ascetic fibre a little. There was something fine, too, about his immediate acquiescence in the idea of leaving it as soon as he was no longer on duty.

"Why not stop on as my guest until you are wanted?"

The invitation was an impulse I could not resist.

"You are very kind, Mr. Davoren. I have not been used to very much kindness in my life," he said simply, "and I thank you very warmly. To be frank, what you suggest would be a very real help and convenience to me just at present. But I hardly like to accept——"

"I consider it settled," I said.

He went to his room early, and I was glad I had asked him, for I felt my soul was in need of some penance. Afterwards I was especially glad that I had done it before I got the bishop's letter.

I was at last alone in my familiar study with silence, with my shaded lamp, with the June twilight on the garden outside. I sat down, hoping to find the perspective I had lost. But instead I found only a new foreground; a foreground of Snape and his absurdities, of the passions and excitements of my parishioners. It was only as in a mirage that I caught disconnected visions: of the *Astarte* with her sails golden in the light of the setting sun, slowly pushing her way along with her cargo of iniquity; of the desert with its hot bright sand and lilac shadows; of the rushing terror of the sandstorm, and the pale back of a camel moving ahead of me in the dark; of the stupendous masonry of the half-buried temple of a dead worship; of a sherbet-seller in the native quarter of the Eastern city, with his flaming red tunic, his clashing brass trays, his huge water vessel and great lump of melting ice; of tall yellow buildings draped with purple flowers; of a great pile of packing-cases, a rope and pulley, and a fearful trepidation in a man's soul; of Welfare sailing out into the night with the crew who would certainly murder him if they guessed his secret. Through every scene in the panorama stole the sinister face and lithe figure of Jakoub. But amid all this, myself I could not see.

CHAPTER 14

BLACKMAIL

MY natural indolence prompted me to settle down again in my old familiar rut while I awaited the bishop's visit and Edmund's return.

Snape's presence in my home, however, effectually prevented this programme. He was a discomfort to me, constant and irritating as a piece of grit in one's eye, with the added annoyance that he was ostentatiously trying to be inoffensive.

When I went to my study to cope with arrears of correspondence he would follow me and sit in a wicker chair which he creaked until he drove me forth to my pigeon-loft. If he sat by the fire-place he kicked the fire-irons rhythmically, filling me with the dread of homicidal mania.

He could not read a book without saying "Just listen to this" and reading a passage aloud, when he would expect some intelligent comment from my exasperated mind. During meals he expounded the duties of a parish priest as conceived by himself, and twenty times a day he thanked me abjectly for my hospitality.

But I endured all patiently, for I felt that need of penance which comes to all of us at times, and felt that Snape had been sent to me to chasten me.

His chastening bore fruit too, for it stimulated me to perform one more task that my indolence would have postponed.

I shrank from returning to the shop in Brighton, though it was a duty I had undertaken. The shop was part of the iniquity, and the prospect of re-opening all that business struck a chill through me, like getting into a wet shirt.

To discuss the matter with Schultz was particularly revolting, for he alone, of them all, struck me as being completely abject and unclean. Jakoub was at least a courageous scoundrel and had a dignity of his own; even Van Ermengen was probably in some respects a man. But there was that about Schultz which made me think of him as an insult to humanity.

Nevertheless, stimulated by the presence of Snape in my house, I drove over to Brighton and visited the shop.

Schultz received me with an obsequious reproachfulness in his manner that covered a hint of possible impertinence. His smooth, pink, waxen face, his curls of the barber's block, and teeth of the dental showcase, all brought back upon me the feeling of nausea I had experienced on first seeing him.

But now there was added to this a nausea of the soul, for I knew that he regarded me, quite naturally, as a party to his foul intrigues.

Except for these sensations I was indifferent to him, for I knew that Welfare had power to keep him harmless.

I waited while he served, and doubtless swindled, a stray customer, and then went with him into the little office behind the shop.

"I have been most uneasy," he complained, "at hearing nothing, at receiving no more stock. For weeks I have expected the consignment from Guernsey, and I have had difficulty in explaining to our London agents. See, here are their letters."

He took a file from a shelf and pointed to letters from the people who I suppose were to have been the receivers of our contraband.

I closed the file, and pushed it back to him. "But they are indignant," he continued; "they have received only the first consignment; our contract with them——"

"I suppose," I said, interrupting him, "they can proceed against us for breach of contract, if they like?"

"Proceed against us?" he gasped; "at law? Holy Virgin! Do you not know——?"

"Never mind what I know," I replied; "at least, I know a good many things now which I did not know when we first met, Mr. Schultz. There will not be any more consignments for your 'London agents.' That business is at an end."

Schultz flashed at me a venomous look of surprise, distrust and fear. His pink complexion faded to an unwholesome yellow, as he sat down hurriedly on the office chair, from which he continued to glare up at me.

"At an end?" he queried. "But I do not understand!"

"I do not know how to make it any clearer," I told him. "Perhaps you will understand me if I say there is to be no more smuggling!"

"But I did not come here to sell what you call knick-knacks! Anybody can do that. There is nothing in it."

"No? Well, the business will be closed down as soon as you have sold up the present stock. If it's worth while you had better have an auction."

"But why is this?" he persisted; "I lose my job. Why am I dismissed?"

"Captain Welfare will explain all that when he returns—if you care to wait for him."

I added the last words in what I intended to be a very meaning tone. They had the desired effect, for any tendency to show fight immediately faded out of Mr. Schultz's countenance.

I then examined his bank-book and some other records which I found in this case quite intelligible.

Rather to my surprise Schultz appeared to have conducted the business quite honestly. He had credited himself with nothing but his wages, and not only was my deposit in the bank intact, but the bric-à-brac had been disposed of at a profit that seemed to me enormous. As the stock was so low I decided to close the shop at once and wait for Captain Welfare to dispose of what was left.

I felt justified in giving Schultz a little money over and above what was due to him. Then I watched him draw down the shutters and lock the door. I took the keys from him and he disappeared with the confidence of those who are always sure of finding some profitable form of minor dishonesty.

I went home to a hot bath with ammonia in it, for this renewed contact with Welfare's business methods had given me a desire for physical cleansing.

In a few days my penance ended, as Snape departed punctually, smothering me once more with his "earnest and sincere gratitude," and leaving in my hands his draft for the organisation of a unit of the Church Lads' Brigade.

And then at last the bishop paid his promised visit, and I looked forward to cleansing my soul by confession, even as I had cleansed my body after the interview with Schultz. When I met him at the station and grasped his hand again I felt as Pilgrim must have felt when Mr. Greatheart joined him. I was sure that the lions of fear and mistrust would be cleared from my path.

"It is a long story," I said, in answer to his enquiry about my adventures as we drove home.

"Then keep it until the afternoon, when we can have it in volume form. I dislike instalments."

"Very well. But you look rather haggard yourself. Have you been sleeping badly again?" I enquired anxiously.

"Not worse than usual, thanks. I am all right myself, but anxious, Davoren, as we all must be. Europe seems to be steadily and deliberately making for war and catastrophe, and at home we have want of unity, lack of discipline, loss of faith. For us Churchmen especially, the time is perplexing and distressing."

"I know," I said with the old feeling of humiliation at my own helplessness, my own failure to take my share in the battles of the world and of the Church, my own desire to settle back into my little rut in life.

"I wish I could help," I sighed.

"You do," said the bishop; "you help me more than you know."

There was a long silence, full of gratitude on my part, as I got my horse into his stride along a level stretch of the coast-road, while the bishop leaned back in his seat, enjoying the pleasing swing of the dog-cart, so much dearer to both of us than the fussy impetuosity of a motorcar, the true symbol of this age of blatant hurry.

"By the way," Parminter asked suddenly, "where is your brother now?"

"Somewhere between here and Marseilles, unless the *Astarte* has not reached port yet. I have not heard."

There was a constraint in my voice which the bishop must have noticed.

"But you expect him back?" he asked.

"Oh yes. He will come here as soon as he can."

"Well, you must let me know when he arrives. I have seen my friend at the Colonial Office, and I think your brother is the very man they are looking for."

I felt my face burning as I replied, "You must hear all my story first, before you recommend him for any post."

The bishop looked round sharply into my face.

"Oh? Very well," he said, as we drove up to the door and the conversation was cut short in the bustle of arrival.

It was not until we went for our favourite ramble over the Downs that I got my story told.

Since our last walk there the brilliance of the first new blades of grass had faded, and on the higher slopes there were already some of the browns and yellows of summer, but all the flowers of the field smiled up at us in the heyday of their reproduction, and there were sombre patches of the chocolate-coloured clover that grows there.

I started my narrative and gave the bare facts of the case right through to the end, the bishop asking a question now and then which helped to set things straight in his mind and my own.

Never in trying to think it over had I been able to go straight through like this. My mind had always been diverted into side issues of what might have been, what I ought to have done or said. But now as I told the story to my friend I began to see it straight myself, to appreciate the degrees of blame in all concerned.

Before I had come to the end of the story we were again sitting together looking down on the cool, still mystery of the dew-pond, and the footprints of the last generation of sheep around it.

When I had finished, the bishop said, "What a blessing it is you went!"

"I am very glad you think that," I said with a deep feeling of thankfulness for his words. "I feel that I was such an innocent ass."

"There are some worse things than innocence," he replied, then added very gravely, laying his hand on my knee, "My friend, I think that, as you would say yourself, you behaved very well."

I have never received any praise, even in boyhood days when one longs for praise, that so filled my heart with gratitude as this.

"I am very proud that you can approve," I said, and we left that subject by mutual consent.

We both sat thinking for a time, and then he said, "I can see no good reason why your brother should not serve the Government, if——"

"Thank God for that," I broke in.

"Yes, I think we ought to thank God for it. At the same time, badly as he has acted—he has acted badly you know?"

"I know it. So does he."

"I am glad he feels it. I was going to say," he continued, "that we must not take it all too seriously. I think his is simply a case of delayed development."

"I don't know that I quite understand."

"Some of the best of men take the longest time to grow up, like trees. There are oaks and cabbages among men—a terrible lot of cabbages! So a prolonged boyhood may be a good thing. It is far too short in most of us. But of course there are limits. Your brother has been so thwarted, punished no doubt in lots of ways that we know nothing of, for many things he perhaps knew were not his fault. I see in him an embittered schoolboy with the intellect and appetites of a man. He will know dirt now when he sees it afar off, better than his contemporaries, and he will hate it even more."

"But supposing, as I greatly fear, that there is more trouble, supposing this Jakoub is arrested and denounces him?"

"Then we must take Mr. Bumble's view of the law, and do all in our power to circumvent it."

"You would agree to that?"

"Of course I should. Any reasoning being must. Law is necessary, and in England it is generally just. But special circumstances may arise in which Law is inapplicable, in which it becomes an organised stupidity. Men of good conscience must have courage to recognise such circumstances and act righteously, whether they act legally or not. So this existing reprehensible person must disappear, and your brother must reappear."

"I see that," I assented. "By the way, what about Welfare?"

"I don't know yet. He is a much more difficult problem in psychology. But that was a splendid thing he did, going off alone in the felucca. You think he would have sunk it if necessary?"

"I'm certain of it. I trust him—now."

"Well, I think he has redeemed himself. Yes, we must help him too. I should like to see your brother again. Do you think he would dislike meeting me under the circumstances?"

"On the contrary, I know he desires, just as I did myself, to see you and tell you everything. In fact to confess, and, if it may be, to receive absolution."

"It is a natural and proper human need, that desire to be assured of 'the absolution and remission of sins.' But after all you are as well qualified as I am to pronounce it."

"Edmund will want to hear it from you," I insisted.

"Well, I shall be glad to see him. You must let me know when he comes. I should like a long evening with both of you. If Welfare can be there as well, so much the better. I shall want to explain to your brother about this Colonial Office job, which I hope he will accept. They want a man to organise and manage a small steamboat service on Lake Nyassa. It is a good climate, and much of the work will be congenial to your brother. They have at present nobody else especially qualified. I think if your brother asked for Welfare as an assistant there would be no difficulty about arranging that, and he would be useful on the commercial side."

"My dear bishop," I exclaimed, "it is ideal! How can I or Edmund thank you?"

"You know there is no need for that. It is an interesting country, and the pay is fair. It is a land full of opportunities for such a man as your brother. Above all he will be doing some real useful work for his country."

"And," I added, "he will be out of Jakoub's clutches once he gets there."

"Yes, Jakoub will only be able to threaten *you*. And as long as he is at liberty I cannot see that you need fear him."

By the time we reached home we had said all we needed to say about these matters. The bishop is not one of those who repeat the same thing over and over again, and call it "discussing the situation."

So we were able to spend a happy evening together in the sixth century, forgetting even the brief pyrexia of modern Europe.

It was with a clear feeling of well-being that I came down the next morning to meet the summer sun that shone in through the open window with a scent of wallflowers which mingled agreeably with the faint fragrances proper to an English breakfast.

It was above all pleasant to see the bishop coming up the red garden path, bare-headed, a towel round his neck, fresh from the morning swim he loved, still lithe and athletic-looking as in his undergraduate days.

While I waited for him to complete his toilet I took up the pile of letters lying on the sideboard, and saw with a painful start one in an unknown handwriting with an Egyptian stamp on it.

I knew instinctively that this must contain a declaration of war, yet Jakoub could not write English. Nervously speculating, I had guessed the authorship before I could bring myself to open the envelope and read as follows:—

"REVEREND SIR,—

"I have been surprised that I have not yet heard from you and am now bound to address you as to my claims against you.

"In my hotel while you were here you took possession of property belonging to myself and others, and while under your charge against my protests that property has disappeared. The cash value of my share in that property is £750 and my prospective profit in its sale was £1,250. This sum of £2,000 in all I now demand from you with £500 for other expenses and loss to which I am put and for my refraining to proceed against you at law as I might well. I shall look for your money in one month. If not, my agent, whom you know as Jakoub, will be in England and will call upon you to arrange for my share as well as his own. This will add expense and he informs me he will accept £500 his share, without charge for his services rendered to you. Your cheque for £3,000 will oblige and you will then receive discharge in full from both of us.

"Failing this, I must take action as above and my lawyer will advise as to proceeding in Egyptian or English Court.

"Your obedient Servant,

"E. VAN ERMENGEN."

I felt as if thrust back again into a world of mean anxieties and sordid men. My mood of content was shattered as a mirror by a stone, and all the pleasantness of my surroundings was gone as if it had been no more than the reflection in the mirror.

If three thousand pounds would end the matter, how gladly would I have made that sacrifice! But I knew that money would not end it. What had been done must still be expiated in other coin. I must still oppose courage to baseness. For me there could as yet be no settling back into my comfortable groove, for courage was not habitual to me; it had to be secreted, as it were, by a constant effort of will.

I was wondering if that were true of all courage when the bishop came in.

"I am afraid you have had bad news," he said, looking at me with concern as he took his place at the breakfast table; "nothing wrong with your brother, I hope?"

"I had not meant to tell you until after breakfast," I answered, sighing; "no, Edmund is all right still, as far as I know."

"Tell me the worst, then. No news should spoil a man's appetite when he has had a morning swim. In fact that is the time of all others to face anything that threatens."

I read Van Ermengen's letter to him. When I had finished he read and re-read it to himself as he finished a hearty breakfast.

"I do not regard this as bad news at all," he said at last, "but may I have a final cup of coffee outside? It is too lovely a morning to waste indoors."

We went out through the French window to a seat by the lime tree, which was already humming like an æolian harp with the wings of insects.

Bates followed with the coffee and cigars, but the bishop would not smoke.

"One can smoke all the year," he said, "but an atmosphere of wallflowers can only be enjoyed on such a day as this."

I thought of the strange contrast between my Sussex garden with its peace and tempered sunshine, and the fierce glare with which the same sun was even now smiting the streets of Alexandria. It seemed scarcely credible that a threat from evil men out there could penetrate even into my secluded vicarage. But there was the letter, and as I watched the bishop studying it again it occurred to me that the fighting spirit in him was glad at the prospect of taking part in a struggle against the manœuvres of the wicked.

"No," he said, laying down the letter on the seat between us, "on the whole it is good news. You must have known that some such attempt was inevitable. The man believes, of course, that you have somehow disposed of the drug for your own profit. To him that would doubtless seem a perfectly natural move on your part. He simply looks upon you as a hypocrite by whom he has been outwitted. Of course such a man will not easily be reconciled to the loss of his share of the plunder. It should be a relief to you to know how he means to open his game."

"I suppose it should," I admitted, "but the prospect of seeing Jakoub here is not agreeable."

"Of course it is disagreeable. But on the other hand, it is a great gain that Jakoub is at liberty. No doubt they are sending him here because they feel he is no longer safe in Egypt. Van Ermengen and his colleagues are as much interested in his remaining free as we are. No doubt Jakoub can convict them all and destroy the conspiracy should he be taken himself. By the way, do they suspect your relationship to your brother?"

"I don't think so. They have no reason to suppose we are more than partners, for they have never heard his real name."

"Then if we can once convince them that the hashish has been destroyed they will realise they have no real weapon against you."

"I wish," I said weakly, "that I could pay them off and be done with it."

"That would be absolutely fatal, and in my view immoral," said the bishop sternly. "Besides, you never would be done with it then."

"Should I reply to this letter?" I asked.

"I think not. At present I think not. But it requires consideration. It is better that Jakoub should come here. We must keep him under observation and safe from arrest. I hope your brother and Welfare will return first, for they will know better than we can how to handle the ruffian. It might even be well, if they go to Nyasaland, that they should take him with them. They could offer him safety at least, and he might look upon it as a new field for villainy."

"He would certainly make it that," I said.

"Yes. But no doubt Satan will see that he is employed wherever he may be. I have little hope of our power to save such as he is. There is my car," he continued as the sound of a motor-horn came to us from the road; "my chaplain is there to see I keep to his time-table. Well, I am sorry my little time here is up. Keep me fully informed of anything that may happen, and don't worry if I cannot answer your letters."

We went back sadly through the house, and as he was stepping into the car he paused and said: "Do not write to Van Ermengen. It would be a mistake. You can only wait now for things to happen. Believe me, I know how difficult that is."

With a heavy heart I watched his car drive off, for I knew that anxiety and perplexity would return to dwell with me in his absence.

CHAPTER 15

AWAITING DEVELOPMENTS

THE period of waiting for news of Edmund, of what was really the opening of a campaign against Jakoub, and the persons whom he so largely controlled, was necessarily for me a very irksome time.

I tried to thrust all these affairs into the background of my thoughts and to wait on events in a spirit of philosophic curiosity. In this laudable attempt I was much helped by my necessary preoccupation with parochial affairs.

I had left a peaceful community of Christian souls, most of them doing their duty in life more or less successfully, a few of them refusing or shirking their responsibilities, and some behaving really badly.

I returned to find a population of whom practically all were members of committees, all competing for chairmanships and secretaryships, and nearly all imbued with an acrid jealousy of each other. Bee-hives and even gardens were being neglected in this new enthusiasm for the redemption of everybody by the formation of committees, and envy, hatred, malice and all uncharitableness stalked the parish in the wake of poor Snape, just as though he had been some emissary of that Potentate of the Manicheans to whose destruction he had devoted his harmless, ineffectual life. Even in the public-house I found that the old academic discussions about prices in the local markets, and their influence on Imperial stability, had given place to acrimonious wrangles as to the personality and conduct of competitors for prominence in the new hierarchy of committees.

The publican said to me, "I'm selling less beer and more whisky, sir. I'm making a bit extra, but I don't like it. They'd be better on beer and the old-fashioned doctrines, and we'd all be more comfortable. Whisky makes them quarrelsome, and the new teetotallers as comes in for ginger is mostly *rancorous*, sir. They says things as I won't have said to me or my missus in my bar. And your reverence knows how my house has been conducted ever since you was here."

I departed, leaving my verbal certificate as to his conduct, and pondering over his word "rancorous." It was the just word. It described exactly the new spirit that I had to combat in my parish. It appeared to me that christianity had had a definite set-back in the village.

With a confidence newly born in me as the result of my recent victories over Jakoub and Van Ermengen, I asserted myself for the first time as vicar of the parish.

As though they had been wasps' nests, I stamped out every committee that had been inaugurated by Snape, and so restored to my parishioners their natural good feeling and loving-kindness.

These preoccupations helped to divert my mind from the more pressing anxieties of life while I waited for news of Edmund, and it was not until I had been home a month that I received a wire from London telling me to expect him on the same afternoon.

My first impulse when he arrived was to tell him of the bishop's offer and of his new prospects, but I felt I ought perhaps to leave that to the bishop himself.

In any case the announcement would perforce have been postponed, for Edmund arrived full of anxieties. He had an alert and vigorous air which I was glad to see, but it was clear that he was harassed and anxious. He cut my greetings rather short and asked me to come straight into the study.

"I must tell you the worst of it at once," he said, as he closed the door; "Van Ermengen and Jakoub are on the move already."

"I know that," I told him; "I have had a letter from Van Ermengen."

"You have? Confound his cheek! What does he say?"

I took Van Ermengen's letter from my desk and handed it to him. He read it carefully, standing on the hearthrug with one arm resting on the mantelpiece.

Watching him from my desk chair I noticed his face flush and the frown deepen on his forehead. He looked older than I had ever seen him look before, and it struck me that Edmund might be a very dangerous man to an enemy.

"Yes," he said as he replaced the letter in the envelope; "of course you have sent him no money?"

"Of course not. I have not answered the letter at all."

"Good. Well, it is not an idle threat about Jakoub. Jakoub is on board a tramp which is due in Southampton tomorrow. If he is not arrested he will make straight for here. Welfare has gone to Southampton to see what happens and to keep an eye on him. If necessary, he will follow him here. Then we shall have to decide on the best means of keeping him quiet."

"I do hope he won't be arrested," I said; "why do you think he may be? Tell me how you know all this."

"Welfare heard it all from Van Ermengen. But I had better tell you the story right through. Have you got any of those cigars left?"

I produced the cigar box, and as Edmund settled himself to smoke comfortably in an arm-chair, I could see that he was tired and short of sleep.

"Welfare and I only met in London yesterday," he said. "We met by appointment, after parting at Marseilles. We thought we could cover up our tracks better by taking different ways. I think you may take it that Montgomery and Ringrose have finally disappeared from the knowledge of mankind. We have evaporated, volatilised in fact. I ought first to tell you that we had to sell the poor little *Astarte* all standing for about a third of her value. It was a nasty jar parting with her to a Dago Jew anyhow, but of course it was a forced sale. There was no time to bargain. Apart from the loss, we both felt that our accepting such a price looked fishy. But that could not be helped, and in any case, as Montgomery and Ringrose, our number was up! We had to get rid of her quickly and clear out."

"Of course," I said as he paused in his narrative, "you know how sorry I am to have parted with the *Astarte*. The price cannot be helped. The loss does not matter as long as you do get clear in the end."

"Well, I hope to," Edmund replied dubiously, eyeing his cigar. "It all depends on Jakoub. As long as he is free we can manage him. Once arrested he would of course try to drag us all in. He would do that out of spite, anyhow; besides, it would be his last card, his only hope of pardon. And we are not sure how much he knows about us. But he knows you in your proper name."

I felt the perspiration break out all over my body as I thus saw clearly for the first time all the possible consequences of Jakoub's arrest, of his turning informer. I knew for the first time what it meant to have one's "heart sink," for it seemed as though my heart actually became a weight in my body of which I was conscious, and a horrible sensation of weakness spread downwards to my thighs. For a few moments I am sure I could not have risen from my chair as I realised that everything that social man holds dear was, in my case, in the keeping of a rascally Arab whom the Law was seeking to attack. And the Law was on the side for which I had sacrificed so much! I was as anxious as the Law to stop the atrocious conspiracy that was poisoning a race. And I had actually achieved my object—illegally. The bishop's phrase recurred to me. "Surely," I thought, "here was a case where the Law became an organised stupidity."

"I hate upsetting you like this," Edmund continued, "but you simply must be told."

"Of course," I said; "go on."

"Fortunately," he continued, "you have done nothing wrong. You will have no difficulty in clearing yourself. But obviously Welfare and I would become your essential witnesses, and nothing you could say, nothing in heaven or earth, would stop us giving evidence on your behalf. But I know,

I understand. Everything you have worked so hard for, would be, well—simply done in! You wanted to save me, to save the family name. You cannot save me if Jakoub is a prisoner, but surely you see, every straight man must see, that my disgrace, as far as the family honour goes, would be far more than balanced by your—your infernal decency."

I found myself out of my chair and tottering foolishly about the room.

"It can't happen! It must not happen!" I exclaimed.

"It may not happen," Edmund said, "but you and I must be ready for it if it does happen."

"Tell me," I said, calming myself with an effort, "tell me just what the risks are. How did Welfare hear? What did Van Ermengen say?"

"Welfare picked up his letters in London yesterday, and among them were two from Van Ermengen. You probably don't realise that Van Ermengen is convinced that you have collared the whole cargo in order to sell it yourself. What puzzles him is that there should have been anyone in the trade unknown to himself; especially anyone capable of controlling Welfare. He is not sure now where Welfare stands in the matter, and his first letter simply appeals to him to remain 'loyal' and assist in squeezing you. The second letter was to say that he had smuggled Jakoub on to this tramp as a stoker, partly to get him out of Egypt where he is no longer safe, and partly to help in blackmailing you. His fear is that the police may trace Jakoub to the ship and get him arrested at this end. You see Van Ermengen is naturally as anxious as we are to keep Jakoub out of the grip of the law. Van Ermengen is more hopelessly compromised than any of us, and he knows Jakoub."

Edmund's apparent imperturbability, his calm exposition of the situation, did a great deal to restore my nervous equilibrium. I sat down opposite to him, and for a time there was silence as we both thought out the probabilities. Edmund's meditations had evidently reached the same point as mine when he broke the silence.

"It is about five to one," he remarked, "that the police here will have been warned and will try to arrest him."

"Do you think there is any chance of their failing?" I asked.

"Lots of chances. Jakoub has been warned himself, and he is not an easy man to catch. He has spent most of his life dodging the police or somebody else. He will probably get away from them at Southampton, but there, in a strange country, he will be handicapped. Welfare may be able to help him. If he makes his way here we shall have to hide him—that is, if you are willing to."

This proposition startled me. It seemed somehow quite a different thing for me at home, as vicar of the parish and a county magistrate, to join in evading English law and English policemen, and for that other self of mine who had wandered across the high seas in a little sailing boat, and across the desert on the back of a camel, to take part in outwitting Egyptian laws and Egyptian police.

Edmund noticed my hesitation and took me up in the old quick way of his boyish sensitiveness.

"Of course I know it would be a horrible risk for you in your position. Personally I advise you to have nothing to do with the business."

He spoke in the hurt tone I remembered so well in old days when I had refused to countenance some wild cat scheme of his.

"I am not calculating the risk," I said; "I see and understand it clearly, and for myself I do not fear the consequences. To get us all out of this wretched tangle I am willing to do anything that is just and honourable. Would this be just and honourable? For myself I think it would; but then am I a competent judge of my own actions in a thing like this! I don't know. I don't know!"

I was thinking aloud, forgetful of Edmund.

"My dear old man!" he cried, getting up and taking my hands, "you are straining your conscience until you'll dislocate the poor old thing, just for my sake. Don't do it. I cannot stand it! Welfare and I can evaporate again. The world is round and one can go round it. Hand over Jakoub and let him get what he deserves. I shall be glad of it, and I will let you do anything else you like for my sake. And we shall find ways of seeing each other again. But don't do this. I hate myself for suggesting it. I simply had not thought."

"Thanks, dear lad," I said, returning the pressure of his hands, "but don't let us exaggerate things. I repeat that I think your proposal is the right one, right from every point of view. Even Jakoub was a straight man once, until he was defrauded by stupid official people. Why should he not have a chance to become straight again? I was thinking he might be worked into the bishop's scheme for you and Welfare. By the way, you have heard nothing about that. But I do feel that we both need guidance. I have sent word to the bishop that you are here. I promised him to do that, and I know he will join us as soon as he can."

"The bishop coming here?" Edmund asked, shying from the idea like a nervous horse. "But must he be told all this?"

"He has been told everything. That is, everything I knew up to now."

"And he would still meet me?"

"He is most anxious to meet you, and Welfare too for that matter. He has a project that he will tell you of himself. He knows that Jakoub is our one danger."

"But surely," Edmund exclaimed, "he would not approve of our sheltering Jakoub?"

"If he does not approve, I cannot consent to do it. I don't know, but I think he would approve. I am sure he would if he had any reason to think that so we might save Jakoub. 'Save' him I mean in the only true sense, which is to make a true man of him again."

"Nothing would make a true man of Jakoub," said Edmund.

"To refuse to believe that is the real meaning of what we call Faith," I answered.

There was another long pause between us, and then Edmund said very thoughtfully, "I cannot understand this bishop of yours."

"It is not to be expected that you should," I assured him. "I doubt if anyone understands him. Probably I understand more of him than anyone else, and I know only a little of him. But I know this, that he sees men as they are, not as 'trees walking.' He is not half-blinded like so many of us parsons. He knows the residuum of decency there is in all human nature, and how it is buried under the silt of mere majorities. But never mind all that. I hope he will be here tomorrow, and he will tell us what to do."

"I am in your hands, of course, and therefore it seems in the bishop's. I shall certainly do what you and he think right, only first I must tell him everything myself."

"That is exactly what I want you to do."

I had greatly dreaded the possibility of Edmund's refusing to meet the bishop at all. I knew how intensely his pride must be wounded by the prospect of such a meeting, of such a confession. But I knew, too, how necessary it was for the healing of his soul. I regarded it as his penance, and for him the way of salvation. I was accordingly careful to conceal my knowledge of his feelings and to treat the bishop's visit as a matter of course.

"With all your news," I said, "I have had no time to tell you that the bishop is coming mainly to offer you an appointment abroad under the Colonial Office. He will tell you the details, but I think it is one you would like."

"Like it!" he exclaimed, "I am sure I should 'like it.' I should like it better than going to prison as the accomplice of a set of particularly unclean Dagoes. But don't you see I am much more in the hands of Jakoub than of the bishop? I can decide nothing until Jakoub is muzzled or—dead. And if Jakoub is taken—well, the matter is settled as far as I am concerned."

I saw it very clearly, and there was nothing to reply.

We spent the evening under a cloud of anxiety trying to calculate the chances of Jakoub's evading the police at Southampton and the probable time of his arrival at the vicarage if he succeeded.

CHAPTER 16

IN WHICH CAPTAIN WELFARE MAKES A SIGNAL

BOTH Edmund's temper and my own were naturally worn a little thin under the tension of this uncertainty, and the friction of our futile calculations of chances. But neither of us could leave the subject alone or settle our minds to anything else. Each of us made guesses which to the other seemed more and more foolish and irritating. Edmund set himself to prove the inevitability of disaster, really, I suppose, in order to elicit my arguments in favour of optimism, which nevertheless he took a morbid pleasure in demolishing.

The bishop's arrival on the following afternoon was only just in time to dispel something like a positive mutual dislike which was being engendered between us by the strain.

But, as I knew he would, the bishop brought with him an atmosphere of sanity and hopefulness. He did not attempt to minimise the gravity of our position when it was explained to him, but helped us to look the hard facts in the face.

"If the man has been arrested," he said, "it seems to me that we are powerless. The whole of the facts are bound to come out. Your conduct," he added, turning to me, "has of course been blameless, even, I should imagine, from the legal point of view. At least I do not quite see in what form any charge could be made against you. The extreme difficulty of the circumstances in which you were placed would of course be appreciated. I do not see how your action could be described as abetting, since you did all in your power to break up the conspiracy and defeat its ends.

"Your brother's case is of course quite different. The fact that he had no direct financial interest in the sale of the drug is only an extenuating circumstance. You were aware of the whole transaction," he said, addressing Edmund; "you aided in it, if only by helping to navigate the boat. I do not think there is the least doubt that a judge would take a very grave view of your offence, and of its effect on the prestige of the English in Egypt. In your case discovery would of course mean irretrievable disgrace, a punishment utterly out of all proportion to the real sinfulness of your act, at least as I see it. It is because of the injustice involved in that, in what would be the real sentence, and because of the damage that would be done to our countrymen in the East, that I feel we are justified in circumventing the law, if that be still possible."

I could see the tide of humiliation pass across Edmund's face, as he sat with folded arms, listening to the bishop's calm judicial statement of the position, but when at last he looked up, I thought I saw in his eyes that it had been a cleansing tide.

"I am afraid," he said very slowly, "it would be impertinent in me, my lord, to thank you for what you are doing, for what you have proposed to do, even for speaking to me, after you have known all this about me. God knows I understand now the rottenness of my whole life so far. If I could only keep my brother's name out of it, I would rather that everything came out; I would rather take the punishment. I do not mind, since you and he think I might have made good still, if the chance had come. I can face everything but disgrace coming home to him. You know he has been more than any brother to me. I had forgotten what it was to be a gentleman. But if I have to make my new start in prison I shall act as one now. I can do it, since you believe I could. I wish I knew how to thank you."

Edmund's voice broke in a sob very painful to us to hear.

The bishop rose and went over to him. "My dear boy," he said, laying a hand on his shoulder with an instinctive pastoral gesture, "you are welcome to thank me. I know it is a natural, wholesome desire. But you must understand that I am only trying to interpret what I believe to be our Lord's attitude to sinners who repent. You have probably come to disbelieve in what is called prayer. Nevertheless prayer is a natural instinct implanted in all of us; a desire we cannot get rid of, whatever our beliefs or disbeliefs may be. I advise you to leave us now and go and yield to that instinct. Whatever may happen now we need say no more about this aspect of the case."

As Edmund rose to obey him, the bishop took his hand for a moment in silence, and there was a look in his face that made me think of Him who rose "with healing in his wings."

"Poor warped boy!" he exclaimed as the door closed; "there is a great capacity for goodness and nobility in him, all stunted by mere circumstance. Davoren, I feel that we must save him at almost any cost. Why should we desire the punishment even of this nefarious Arab? It will surely be better to make him 'cease to do evil and learn to do well.' Have you ever thought out the distinction between crime and sin?"

"I have never regarded them as necessarily related," I answered.

"No, they are not. If we could establish that essential relationship we should have achieved the ideal State. Probably that was what Plato really meant. But now we must come down to sordid details. Assuming that this Arab escapes the police and finds you here, have you any plan for dealing with him?"

"None. We have discussed it up and down since yesterday, but could come to no conclusion."

"I should be inclined to offer him a chance to accompany your brother and Captain Welfare, that is if they decided to go to Nyasaland. We could offer him congenial employment, fair pay, and above all a chance of escape from 'justice.' We must remember that the one strength of our position is that he is a hunted man. A desperate man is dangerous, therefore the proper treatment for him is to offer him hope."

We spent a long time discussing what our course should be if the worst came to pass, and how we were to make a future for Edmund when he should have purged his folly. The afternoon was fading into evening, when Bates came in with a perturbed expression.

"I beg your pardon, sir," he said, "there is a man at the door who refuses to go away until he has seen you."

"Well, Bates? Why should he not see me? What is his business?"

"He wouldn't say, sir. Excuse me, sir, but he is a foreign looking person, though not dressed as such. I think he is one of those Arabs that came in the yacht, sir."

The bishop and I looked at each other with a great relief. Here was Jakoub, and he was still at liberty, the worst had not yet come to pass.

"I'll go and see him, Bates," I said; "will you excuse me, bishop?"

"Don't mind me if you wish to bring him in here," the bishop answered in a perfectly natural manner.

I went out to meet Jakoub at the door, Bates following me like a dog bristling with distrust of some instinctive foe.

As soon as he opened the door a man stepped quickly inside, in spite of a protesting movement from Bates.

For a moment my heart misgave me, for in this cloth-capped stranger, clad in cheap but respectable brown tweed, I failed to recognise Jakoub. But a flash from his eyes reassured me, and there was no mistaking his greeting. "All raight, effendi!" he said in his old mocking tone, "it is I, Jakoub."

I think his quick intuition was disconcerted at my manifest pleasure in welcoming him! No doubt he had calculated on meeting fear or anger.

"Come in," I said cordially. "I am very glad to see you again, Jakoub. It is quite right, Bates, just go and tell Mr. Edmund he will find an old friend with us in the study."

Bates went upstairs distrustfully, and I led Jakoub into the study.

"Bishop, this is Jakoub," I said with a happy smile; "Jakoub, this is my sheikh."

The bishop nodded pleasantly and Jakoub instinctively salaamed, touching his forehead and breast.

He stood with his hands folded before him looking uneasily from one to the other of us. He was evidently nonplussed and suspicious, and doubtless felt at a disadvantage in the strange ugly clothes which vulgarised and robbed him of all his natural dignity.

"I came to speak with you private," he said sullenly.

"Sit down then. We are private. The sheikh knows all about our business, Jakoub. Mr. Montgomery is here too. He will be with us in a moment."

I used the false name purposely to try if Jakoub knew Edmund by any other, but he made no comment.

"If you think I am in a trap, you mistake. Very big mistake," he muttered viciously.

"None of us thinks so, Jakoub. If you are in trouble, we want to help you. Have a cigarette?" He took the cigarette greedily, as one who had fasted for some time. It seemed to restore a little of his confidence.

"Jakoub is in no trouble," he remarked, as he sat uneasily on the edge of a low chair.

Edmund came in at this moment, quite calm and collected, without a trace of his recent emotional crisis.

"Well, Jakoub," he said, "you have turned up?"

"Yes. I have come. I have come for my rights, for my money and for Van Ermengen, effendi's. We will not be robbed."

"No," said Edmund, "but you may be arrested, you know. The police——"

"Bah! Your police—I fear them not. We knew they would wait for me at your harbour. So I make myself to have the job to go away in the little boat with a line to the buoy. Last night before the steamer stop, before the gangway is out, I am away from her in the dark. I wrap my galabieh round a stone and drop her in the water. Then I put on these, these clothes, boots, hat; and I row to a good place on the shore, while your police are looking for me on the ship! Who will find Jakoub now? I am not a mouse to walk in a trap!"

"That was very clever," the bishop put in.

"It is my business to be clever!" said Jakoub, showing his teeth a little, as he looked round from one to the other of us, malignant and implacable.

I was at a loss as to how to continue the conversation. I felt as I have sometimes felt when trying to play chess for the entertainment of better players, uncertain even as to whose move it was next. It was therefore a great relief to me when Edmund spoke in a tone that suggested his intention of taking command of our side.

"You had better tell us," he said, "why you have come here, and what it is that you want."

"I have come for the money I am owed, I and Van Ermengen effendi. I have my papers, my account."

He sought in the unfamiliar pockets of what tailors call a "lounge suit," and produced a folded sheet of foolscap which Edmund took from him.

"We have already had all this by post from Van Ermengen," Edmund remarked as he looked over the paper. "Why did he send you here?"

"Because you did not answer. You sent no money," Jakoub answered doggedly.

"And suppose we send this money to Van Ermengen, how are you going to get your share from him? If we enable you to escape the police here, will you go back to Egypt? Don't take me for a fool, Jakoub. It won't help you."

"You pay me my share here. I care no more for Van Ermengen."

The bishop and I looked at each other. We began to see the drift of Edmund's diplomacy; to detach Jakoub from Van Ermengen was decidedly a gain.

"I don't suppose you do care for him," Edmund said, "and yet you are trying to play his game, knowing he will swindle you in the end."

"But without him I could not have come here," Jakoub pointed out with another smile of cool effrontery.

"I could stay no more in Egypt," he added, "so I use Van Ermengen to find you and Captain Ringrose, and the effendi here. It is you who have gone with my property—you are the thieves, and you will give back my share, or come with me to the prison."

"You might get us into prison, Jakoub, but you could not get us hanged. Do you know," he asked suddenly, taking a step towards Jakoub and standing over him in a threatening attitude, "do you know that we can have you hanged? Do you know that we found Achmed in Marseilles and he told us all that happened in that house at Damanhour where the merchant was murdered two years ago? We know where to find Achmed whenever we want him."

Jakoub's face was distorted with the spasm of sudden terror, like that of a man who suddenly sees some unsuspected object close by him in the dark. His right hand made a movement towards the unaccustomed breast pocket, but Edmund seized his wrist in a flash. His grasp brought a cry from Jakoub.

"Effendi! You break my arm! Let me go."

"Hand over your weapon first."

"I have none. I swear it. Search me, effendi!"

Edmund slowly relinquished his grasp. I thought of the knife I had seen in Jakoub's hand that night at Alexandria when I was awakened by the brushing of that hand along my bedroom wall. But I was paralysed by the sudden violence of this scene in my quiet study. I saw the bishop sitting tense, braced for sudden action. But Edmund did not trouble to search Jakoub; he lounged back to the mantelpiece and it seemed that a crisis had ended.

"It does not matter if you have a weapon, Jakoub, for you dare not use it. Now listen, we offer you safety, or at least to help you to safety if we can. You may not believe it, but it is a fact that the whole of the hashish is at the bottom of the sea. We threw it overboard and sank it for reasons of our own. We may help you to earn an honest living in safety, if you choose to. At least, that is what we meant to offer you. But these gentlemen did not know for certain until this minute that you were a murderer. When I tell them what the man was whom you killed, they may still help you. I do not know."

Edmund paused and looked enquiringly at the bishop.

"We ought to have known of this," the bishop said very gravely.

"I was going to tell you, my lord. If I may send Jakoub out of the room I will tell you the whole story. He had better think over our offer, in case it still holds good. But understand, Jakoub, that alone and unaided in England you can no more escape our police than a quail can escape your net when it lands in Egypt. This is not Egypt. If you choose to quarrel with us you know now what to expect."

I felt a kind of pity for Jakoub as I looked at him. He was changed from the masterful villain I had known, the man to whose skill and courage in the desert I probably owed my life.

He was now a huddled figure in his chair, and under Edmund's new threat he looked beaten, weak, and forlorn. It occurred to me that he might have had little or no food on his journey, and I always find something pathetic in the more primitive human needs. I was sure, too, that Jakoub would regard Edmund's last remark as a warning that the whole system of backshish would, in this country, be against him as a foreigner without money. It would seem to him quite natural that a person like myself should have the entire legislature in his pay, and this would of course be a depressing thought. My feelings as a host were aroused on his behalf, but I recognised the impossibility of suggesting that he should join us at dinner.

"Perhaps," I said, "Jakoub is ready for some food and a glass of wine? I am sorry not to have thought of it sooner. I am afraid you are tired, Jakoub."

I noticed a flicker of humorous appreciation of the situation pass between Edmund and Jakoub, and as the latter must have had murder in his heart but a moment before, and the other had used force to frustrate the intention, I suppose my conventional words were really somewhat absurd.

But Jakoub rose and salaamed with the ceremony demanded of an Oriental when hospitality is in question.

"Jakoub is never tired," he said, "but he has come far, fasting. The effendi is kind, and Jakoub gives thanks to Allah and to him. Jakoub needs food and remembers the red wine he drank in the Temple of Osiris. It is not yet Ramadan."

"That's all right," I said, "I'll ring for Bates."

Bates at the door, in response to my summons, gave us a wonderful piece of acting. He was representing the part of a servant unconscious of the existence of the foreign element in our conclave. The perfect correctness of his demeanour made all three of us feel abject in a way that no threat from Jakoub could have done.

"Bates," I said, "this gentleman will have some dinner in the morning-room. And tell Mrs. Rattray that we shall be ready in a quarter of an hour."

Bates's aspect relaxed its severity at once, and I perceived that I had acquired merit in his eyes. He knew that I never referred to my friends as "gentlemen," and my use of the term now was, in his eyes, opprobrious. I think he may have suspected me of an intention to have Jakoub in the dining-room, which would have involved his giving me notice, and wrecking his own life's happiness. As it was, he made an imperious gesture to Jakoub, who followed him out of the room quite meekly.

"I think we had better go and dress," I said, looking at my watch, "we can talk things over after dinner."

We said no more to each other then, but as we went upstairs in silence it occurred to me that Bates might handle Jakoub more successfully even than the bishop.

Dinner that night was a meal purposely abbreviated, for we could not resume our discussion until Bates had completed his functions and left us with the walnuts and a decanter of port for Edmund and myself.

The lingering twilight of summer reduced the shaded candles on the table to the level of an agreeable but adventitious ornament. There are few things more lovely than the ruby patch on white damask of candle-light focussed through cut glass containing some ancient vintage of the grape of sun-soaked Portugal. That crimson spot, with radiating lines and concentric curves of topaz light, has always given me, since childhood days, the thrill of joy that jewellery provides, and stained-glass windows, and distant rockets bursting inaudible in a summer sky.

I think we all three were conscious of the hedonistic influence of our surroundings, and found it difficult to bring our minds back to the sinister presence in the adjoining room, to the idea of Jakoub there, calculating his line of conduct from an ethical standpoint unintelligible to us.

I certainly felt an intense reluctance to return to the consideration of our clouded future, and I am sure the others shared it.

We might have sat there indefinitely as far as I was concerned. But the bishop with a sigh recalled us to the immediate necessities of our situation.

We had been discoursing pleasantly of many things interesting but remote from our immediate circumstances, when he broke in on our artificial calm.

"Well, we are keeping Jakoub waiting," he said; "had we not better know the facts about this new charge against him?"

"Yes. You must know the facts. I have been waiting to tell you," Edmund answered. "I can only give you the facts as I have heard them from a man who has no reason to love Jakoub. All I can say is that both Welfare and I have every reason to believe the story, for we both knew the man who was killed. Either of us would have killed him if we could. It is a disgusting story."

It was a story so loathsome in its details that I have tried to blot them from my mind. It concerned an elderly Egyptian who had made vast sums of money by land speculations at the time when the Egyptian cotton industry was embryonic. He had chosen one of his sons as his heir, and sent the youth to Europe to be "educated." The young man had absorbed all the villainy and corruption that can be found in the lowest classes of the great cities of England and the continent, and returned to inherit his father's wealth with his native Oriental brutality instructed and refined by Western cunning and Western niceties of debauchery and greed. As he lost his inherited wealth to more cunning rogues, he tried to recover it by becoming the principal organiser of the hashish trade. In this capacity he came to owe Jakoub the wages of subordinate villainy. Jakoub had taken him by surprise in his secret villa at Damanhour. He had found him torturing a woman who had been a girl in Jakoub's village in the Delta. Jakoub had slain him and escaped undetected. Edmund had now found a witness who could prove Jakoub to be the murderer.

"I have threatened Jakoub with this knowledge," Edmund concluded, "but sooner than use it against him really, I would have my tongue torn out."

Neither of us made any comment on the story, and Edmund remained silent during a considerable pause, nervously fidgeting with his napkin ring.

"I think we must have the man in, Davoren," the bishop said at last, "but first we must be quite assured as to what we are to say to him."

"Yes. We had better get it over," I agreed.

"Am I to understand definitely," the bishop asked Edmund, "that if all goes well you will accept this offer of the Colonial Secretary?"

"I will indeed, most thankfully," Edmund assured him.

"And you think it probable that Captain Welfare would join you?"

"I cannot imagine his refusing."

"Well, that's all right so far——"

He was interrupted by a metallic clang, twice repeated. It was the old sound of the hammer on the anvil in the forge, brought to us along the tunnel. But it was an unusual time to hear it, and to all of us there was something minatory in the sound of those three strokes.

The bishop broke off in his sentence, and we all three listened, silent and uneasy.

The three loud strokes were repeated.

"They are working late at the forge," the bishop remarked.

"That is not blacksmith's work," I answered with an apprehensive note in my voice.

There came a succession of blows, apparently from a lighter hammer, yet with a sound unusual and unfamiliar to me, making as it were a kind of tune.

Suddenly Edmund's face "sprang to attention" as it were. He took a pencil from his pocket, and seizing a menu card, began making rapid marks on it, as the tune on the anvil rang on.

The bishop and I watched him in amazement.

"It's Welfare," he said; "our private call in Morse. Here's his message coming. Excuse me."

For some minutes the noise went on, the bishop and I, elbows on table, watching Edmund as he jotted down dots and dashes on the cardboard. He put out his hand for a fresh card, and I had had the sense to have one ready for him, so there was no interruption in his recording of the message.

Presently the hammering ceased.

We listened for a moment, but no more sound came from the anvil. Edmund set himself to deciphering and transcribing the message.

Finally he read aloud: "Police traced Jakoub to vicarage. Doors watched. Will arrest at once. Send him down passage. I will meet him at end."

"We must act at once," the bishop observed, rising from his chair; "perhaps you had better get him away," he added to Edmund. Edmund nodded and moved towards the door.

"One moment," I said, "I must get Mrs. Rattray and the maid out of the kitchen. We shall have to take Bates into our confidence."

I left the room, and finding Mrs. Rattray sent her and her assistant to carry out some extraordinary rearrangement of the bishop's room. I told her that his Lordship had been unwell, and these arrangements were the doctor's orders. This silenced her protests of amazement, and having got rid of the women I spoke hurriedly to Bates in the hall.

"Bates," I said, "the police are coming here for this Arab. They will be here any moment now."

"Very good, sir." Bates answered with evident gratification.

"But he is not to be arrested here. Mr. Edmund has particular reasons for not wishing it."

"Oh, very well, sir."

"Mr. Edmund is going to let him out through the cellar, into the passage. When the police call you will show them into the dining-room. In the meantime you must make it appear that the man has gone through the morning-room window. Do you understand?"

"Yes, sir."

"I am afraid, Bates, it may not be possible for you to speak the precise truth about the business—to the police, I mean. Have you any objection?"

"Well, sir, as long as you and his Lordship say so, I have no doubt it is all correct."

"That's all right then."

As I spoke Edmund came out of the morning-room with Jakoub.

"The idiot swears it's a trap. He says he won't go unless the 'sheikh,' as he calls him, promises we are doing the straight thing."

"It is Ringrose," growled Jakoub; "I know him; this is his plan to trap me."

"I swear, Jakoub——" I began, but then the bishop, who had overheard the conversation, joined us.

"I promise you," he said, "in the name of the one God whom we both worship, that we are doing what we believe to be the best thing for you as well as for others. I promise that in this we are dealing faithfully with you. Now go quickly. It is your only chance of safety."

Jakoub followed Edmund down to the cellar without another word.

The bishop and I returned to the dining-room and resumed our seats at the table.

My heart was beating painfully as we heard through the floor the harsh grating of the door that led from the cellar to the passage. We heard it opened, and it seemed an age before it was dragged to, and the rusty bolts shot back. I think the bishop breathed a little rapidly too.

As Edmund rejoined us with an enquiring glance I shook my head.

"I wonder what is keeping them," he said as he sat down in his place.

I explained briefly what I had arranged with Bates.

"Don't you think, bishop," I asked, "that it would be better for you to leave us? If anything were to go wrong, it would be intolerable that your name should even be mentioned."

"It is certainly disagreeable," he replied; "it is intensely painful to deceive these men in the execution of their duty. We are unquestionably aiding a criminal to escape, in fact 'compounding a felony.' Nevertheless, my conscience is quite definite in the matter and approves of what we are doing. It is the old question, Davoren, of the difference between crime and sin. The crime for which the law would put this man to death was not a sin. It was manifestly a righteous action. It was an impulse which no decent man would have resisted. Of course, society could not exist if everyone were to be allowed to decide such questions. But I claim as much right to judge of wickedness as a judge has to decide questions of crime. But if I left you now it would be cowardice, and my conscience would not acquit me."

"But how terribly the world would misjudge you!"

"That is not a thing from which a Christian should shrink," the bishop observed quietly, and so closed the discussion.

Edmund helped himself to a glass of wine.

"It will look more natural when they come in," he said, "as if we were only just finishing dinner."

I was glad to follow his example, for in truth the sudden development of our perplexities, the strange manner of its announcement, and the necessity for sudden action had left me shaken in mind and body and, I fear, a little tremulous.

As Edmund lit a cigarette the hall-door bell was rung.

CHAPTER 17

HOW CAPTAIN WELFARE RETURNED

WE waited but a few moments in silence before Bates ushered in our local constable, an old friend of mine, and one who had a professional veneration for my position as a County Magistrate, who sat in judgment alike on vagrants and poachers, and those haughty contemners of the law who exceed the speed limit in expensive motorcars.

He was clearly very much embarrassed as he introduced his companion, an officer in plain clothes, whom he announced as Sergeant Moore, of Southampton.

All three of us looked keenly at the stranger whose personality might mean so much to the success of our plans and hopes. He was a thoroughly representative specimen of our admirable County police. A well-built man, in superb physical condition, good-looking and intelligent. I summed him up at once as a man who would be inflexible in the exercise of his duty, and alert in detecting any suspicious circumstance; in fact, a difficult man to hoodwink, and impossible to corrupt had anyone wished to do so.

Nevertheless, I was encouraged by something in his face that suggested the influence of routine. It was not the face of an imaginative man. This was not the detective of fiction, nor even one of those choicer spirits of Scotland Yard to whom no combination of circumstances is so improbable as to appear incredible. I trusted that it might be impossible to Sergeant Moore, confronted with a bishop and a magistrate, to suspect them of complicity in the vice of an obscure Oriental criminal.

When the introductions were completed, Sergeant Moore himself proceeded to explain.

"I am very sorry to intrude, my Lord and gentlemen," he began, "we would not have troubled you if we could have helped it. But the fact is I have a warrant to execute, and Constable Davis has seen a man answering the description coming here just before I arrived. To avoid troubling you, sir, I have had the house watched so as to take him when he came out. But as it was getting dark and he did not appear I became anxious, and thought you would excuse me coming in to arrest him here, though I know it must be unpleasant."

"I hope none of us are wanted, sergeant?" Edmund enquired jokingly.

"No, sir," replied the sergeant with a smile. "No, it is some kind of a foreigner from Egypt, name of Osman. He was one of the crew of a steamer that made Southampton last night. He managed to give us the slip there, but we had no difficulty in tracing him to Brighton, as he took the train there, and the young man in the ticket office remembered his way of speaking. I came on to Brighton with two men in a car and we lost the scent there, but we heard of a foreigner being seen on this road in the afternoon. Fortunately, Constable Davis here noticed him and followed him to this house. He naturally thought it was all right when he saw him let in. I hope he is still here, sir."

"I left him in the next room, having some food," I said. "He was my guide, or dragoman, during a recent trip in Egypt, and came here asking for money, as he said he was destitute and knew no one else in England."

Sergeant Moore looked much relieved.

"I think it will be best if we go and slip these on at once," he said, producing a pair of handcuffs. "Davis and I will just slip in quietly, and get him unawares. He is said to be a dangerous character, and I don't want any disturbance in the house."

"By all means," I said, "I will show you the room."

"I had better go and bear a hand, in case you want any help," Edmund said, rising.

The sergeant looked approvingly at his athletic form and thanked him.

"I suppose there is no doubt of this being the right man?" I hazarded.

"He is certainly the man referred to in my instructions. If you don't mind we'll go at once, and very quietly, please. I will go first and get on the far side of him; Davis, you follow and grip him, and look out for a knife. These fellows are handy with them."

We all rose, the bishop, who had not spoken, following us to the door.

We stepped noiselessly across the carpeted hall, and I pointed out the door of the morning-room, my heart beating almost as fast as though Jakoub had still been there in fact.

Sergeant Moore opened the door and slipped inside, followed closely by Davis. I heard an oath of extreme impropriety from the sergeant, followed by the shrill sound of his whistle.

We followed them into the room, and found both policemen leaning out of the open window. Sergeant Moore blew another blast on his whistle, and then turned round, his face flushed with vexation.

"He has done us again, sir. For the present, that is—bolted through the window! Halt there!" he cried, looking out of the window again as a constable came round from the front in response to the whistle. "Get your bull's-eye going, and come carefully up to the window, but don't pass it. Look for tracks of someone leaving the house this way."

Here was something I had not foreseen.

The turf of the lawn came right up to the house on this side, but to the trained eyes of these men the total absence of any vestige of a man's jumping out would be intensely suspicious. They would be bound to search the house. They would find the entrance to the passage, and traces there. How then could they avoid the conclusion that I had connived at the man's escape?

While these thoughts passed through my mind the constable had lighted his lamp and reconnoitred the ground.

"There's two heel-marks here," he now reported, still stooping with his lantern, "somebody has jumped down within the last few minutes. I can see a track across the lawn where the dew has been brushed off the grass."

"Follow it carefully," said the sergeant, "but keep off it. Don't foul it."

For a moment I was bewildered at this information. Who, I wondered, had made these tracks, since Jakoub had not? Then I caught a faint smile of understanding on Edmund's face, and I realised that Bates was a much cleverer man than myself, that he possessed what Ruskin calls "imagination penetrative."

"Somebody has been through the fence here," said the constable from the far side of the lawn.

"Wait for me, then," the sergeant replied, lowering himself out of the window. Beyond the fence was a private footpath, hard as iron in this weather, where Bates's footprints leading back to the kitchen entrance would be quite invisible. In the other direction the path led on to the high-road.

"Excuse me, gentlemen," said the sergeant as he reached the ground, "but I'd be obliged if you would be careful not to disturb anything in that room until I have a chance to examine it."

"Certainly," I said, "we are going to my study where you will find us if you have time to return, or if we can help you in any way."

I had a hasty look round the room. Jakoub's half-finished meal was there. Otherwise it was exactly as usual. I could conceive of nothing there that could suggest the truth to the most acute mind. Even if it were possible to leave traces on a carpet, these must all be obliterated since five of us had passed in and out.

I saw Edmund also looking round with a searching eye, and then we adjourned to the study.

The sense of guilt and even shame was stronger in me than I had anticipated, and I am sure the others felt likewise, for we all three sat silent and uneasy, as if we had suddenly become strangers to each other, as indeed in a sense we had.

The bishop was the first to break the silence which we all felt tightening round us like a cord, and I was thankful to him. There are situations in which people who allow themselves to drift into silence prolonged beyond a certain limit are powerless to regain the mutual confidence of normal speech. I am sure it was to prevent this happening in our case that he enquired of Edmund what he thought Welfare's present plan would be.

"I should think he will probably double back towards Brighton along the beach. Of course, he has no idea in which direction the police will search, and back towards Brighton is perhaps the least likely. It is bad going on the beach, but on the stones he would leave no track. Somewhere before reaching Brighton he would have to leave the coast, strike inland and find a hiding-place before morning. He is sure to make for London. Jakoub is too conspicuous in the country. They will have to travel at night and find a hiding-place for Jakoub during the day. It will take them the best part of three nights to reach London."

"Do you think they have much chance of eluding the police?" the bishop asked.

"I think they will, because Welfare can move about as he likes in the daytime. He can get provisions and reconnoitre. If they had any idea that Jakoub had a companion, and had a description of him, it would be almost impossible, as of course every village constable will be warned before morning."

"Welfare might find a boat," I suggested.

"Too risky," Edmund opined, "the boat would be missed, and even if they sank it and swam ashore the police would be able to concentrate their attention on the coast. Welfare will see that the police have a bigger job to cover the whole country."

This discussion of the possible plans and chances of the fugitives was quite an agreeable diversion and greatly relieved the tension of our feelings until Sergeant Moore rejoined us, looking irritated and crestfallen.

"I have just called to say we can find no trace of him beyond your hedge, not in this light, sir. I wonder if you have such a thing as a road map of these parts, sir?"

"Certainly, sergeant. Won't you sit down?"

"No, thank you, sir, I must get back to the station and spend the night on the telephone. It's all we can do until morning."

I spread a map on the desk, and we bent over it together, Edmund looking over my shoulder.

Sergeant Moore made a few hurried measurements of places within twenty miles of my house which I located for him on the map.

"Thank you, sir," he said, "I think it won't be difficult to put a ring round him before morning. I think you said he doesn't know the country at all, sir?"

"As far as I know he has never been in England before. But he seemed to find his way here all right."

"Of course he had your address?"

"Oh yes. He got that from the hotel I stopped at in Egypt."

"You would call him an intelligent man?"

"Very. He was an admirable guide in the desert."

"And he speaks English well?"

"Perfectly. Of course he expresses himself in a peculiar way, but he understands everything. I wish I could speak Arabic as well!" I added with a sigh.

"May I just read over the description I have of him? You could perhaps tell me if it corresponds with the man you know."

He read the description. Within its formal limits it was an accurate portrait of Jakoub, but I was able to add some details as to his present costume for which the sergeant thanked me.

"I think that's all," he said, pocketing his notebook; "I am exceedingly sorry for disturbing his lordship and you gentlemen."

I felt a sense of intense relief, for I had feared every moment that the man might ask some question which would embarrass me, and perhaps lead me to arouse suspicion. But it was clear that the whole story seemed perfectly natural and true to the sergeant. The idea of cross-examination had never occurred to him. The bishop rose and offered his hand with his peculiar winning grace.

"Good-night, sergeant," he said, "don't think you have disturbed us in the least. It is not often that we clergymen have an opportunity of seeing the actual work of such men as you. I have been intensely interested in the whole affair, and greatly impressed by your zeal and capacity. I fear we don't always realise how much we owe to our indefatigable defenders."

"Thank you, my lord," said the sergeant, flushing with pleasure at this unwonted praise from so high a quarter.

As he left the room with a final salute the bishop rather wearily resumed his seat.

"That," he said, passing a hand over his brow, "is the one man we have really wronged throughout this very painful transaction."

I thought of my poor friend Brogden, but I did not remind the bishop of him.

I had dreaded the interview with the police, but now that it was over, now that we seemed to have achieved our purpose, I felt none of the elation of complete relief. The sergeant's confidence in his ability "to make a ring round Jakoub" alarmed me, and I knew that I should have no sense of security until we heard from Welfare of his safety, until, in fact, Jakoub was out of the country, and I could believe that the hunt for him was at an end.

We formed a gloomy trio, disinclined to talk, yet unwilling to separate and retire to bed. I do not think my conscience was uneasy, but to the strongest mind I suppose there must be something strangely upsetting in finding oneself opposed to law and the commonly accepted standards of conduct.

I am sure I was not the only member of the party who felt this influence.

We continued for a long time in desultory talk with intervals of embarrassed silence.

It was after such a pause that my restlessness got the better of me, and going to the window I drew aside the curtains.

The full moon was high in the heavens approaching the meridian. It still rode in a clear sky, though to my surprise I saw a great bank of cloud towering swiftly upwards from the west, though the sun had set without any sign of an end to the long spell of summer drought we had experienced.

"It looks as if the weather is going to break," I remarked, still looking out.

I heard Edmund rise and tap the aneroid on the mantelpiece.

"The glass is coming down with a run," he said, then he and the bishop joined me at the window.

We stood there in silence, wrapt in contemplation of the splendour of the moonlight. Beneath it the channel appeared as a silver background to the black silhouette of trees. A faint flush was reflected from the red roofs of houses in the village. The lawn before us was a silver mystery woven of a myriad threads of dew-besprinkled gossamer, and flowers looked up with pallid, unfamiliar faces to the sky.

The lustre of the stars near the triumphant moon was dimmed, but low down in the south-east I could see the lovely constellation Scorpio, like a diamond pendant with a topaz heart.

Even the corncrakes were hushed, and nothing stirred on earth or in the air around us. The only movement was the majestic advance of the vast cloud spreading from the west, threatening an invasion of "the Peace of God which passeth all understanding." Standing thus with our backs to the room, we were all unaware of Bates's entrance until he was close behind us.

"I beg your pardon, sir," he said, almost in a whisper.

I turned to see his face, looking white in the moonlight, and with a perturbed expression very unusual in him.

"What is it, Bates?" I asked.

"There seems to be someone wanting to get into the cellar from the passage. I think it must be that native come back, sir. I thought I had better take your instructions before opening the door."

We turned back into the room at once, all three of us at a loss before this shock of the totally unexpected. The immediate return of Jakoub was something I had never contemplated. In the attempt to rearrange my ideas I was speechless.

"Why do you think he is there?" I heard Edmund asking, "tell us what has happened."

"Mrs. Rattray thought she heard a tapping in the cellar, sir. She has been very nervous about this man being in the house, and terribly upset at the police coming and the man's escape. She said she wouldn't sleep a wink all night. I thought it was her nerves when she said she heard something, so I went down and listened. I told her it was nothing and got her off to bed. But there was somebody there, sir, and he has just been tapping again, very gentle and careful like."

"We must let him in, of course," Edmund said, looking at me. I nodded.

"I will go," he added, "and, Bates, you had better come and bring a light. But keep well behind me. There is no saying what he will be up to this time."

"I shall go with you, too," the bishop said.

"Let us all go," I pleaded, "but we must make no noise. Mrs. Rattray must not hear us."

"One moment," said Edmund. He slipped out of the room and returned almost at once with a leather plaited "life preserver" which always accompanied him.

Without another word we crept down to the kitchen. Bates took an oil lamp from the table and lighted us down the cellar steps. As we descended I distinctly heard three gentle taps at the door.

Slowly and almost noiselessly Edmund worked back the bolts, then throwing the door open he stepped quickly backwards, and stood with his left foot forward, the life preserver in his hand poised ready for a blow.

But Jakoub made no rush.

A hoarse weak voice asked, "Are the police gone?"

Bates raised the lamp, and peering through the door I saw a figure sitting huddled on the step that led down into the underground passage.

"Welfare!" Edmund exclaimed.

I recognised Welfare's slab of a face, blanched and shrunken. A blood-soaked scarf was knotted round his head. One side of his face, his neck, and one shoulder, were plastered with blood congealed in jelly-like masses.

"Are they gone?" he asked again.

"Yes, long ago," said Edmund stooping down to raise him.

"That's all right then," Welfare answered. "Steady; I've been faint for a bit, losing blood from a cut in the head. Bleeding's stopped now I think, but I don't want to start it again. Let me get on my knees. That's it."

Slowly and painfully on hands and knees he crawled into the cellar, and managed to sit on the floor. I had not known a man could lose so much blood and live. I feared I should be sick, and I saw the bishop's face turn grey, but he did not speak.

"Let's have a look," said Edmund quietly, busying himself with the knot in the scarf.

"Three or four stitches," said Welfare, "will stop it breaking out again. You'll find a doctor's bent needle and some gut in the little case in my right-hand pocket. Then you can wash it, and cut away these clothes. I'll be all right in a few minutes."

"Hadn't he better have some brandy?" I asked.

"Not till I get the stitches in," Edmund said with decision. "It would only start the bleeding. I think, my lord, you and my brother had better leave us. Bates and I will get him upstairs in a bit."

We were evidently useless. As we turned to go we met Bates coming down the stairs with a basin and jug of water, a sponge, towels, cotton wool and bandages. I realised the hopelessness of my even giving directions to one so much more capable than myself.

For half an hour the bishop and I hovered uneasily in the smoking-room, listening to every sound that came from the cellar below. It had been impossible to question the sorely wounded man about Jakoub, but the same dread, the same horror, was in both our minds. Jakoub in his madness had wounded Welfare and escaped. Already I believed he must have run blindly into the trap prepared for him. Nothing now could explain my action in concealing him from the police, and the bishop himself could hardly escape aspersion.

At last we heard slow steps ascending the cellar stairs.

CHAPTER 18

HOW JAKOUB WAS NO MORE SEEN

CAPTAIN WELFARE came in leaning on Edmund, who helped him into an arm-chair.

His head was neatly bandaged, and he was clad in a dressing-gown. He was still evidently weak, although largely restored from the pitiable object that had crawled into the cellar.

The bishop and I hastened to commiserate him, and I suggested his going straight to bed.

"No, thank you, sir," he said, leaning back in the chair. "I'm better now. I shall be all right in a few minutes. Your man is getting me something to drink. Anyhow I *must* keep on my legs for a bit. There's a deal to be settled and done tonight."

"Where is Jakoub?" I ventured to ask at last.

"I don't think you will blame me, sir, or his lordship either, when I tell you about it. He came at me like a leopard. As you know, I meant him no harm."

"I know you did not, captain. We are so far from blaming you that we are only sorry you should have been so hurt. It was a dastardly attack."

"Aye. A proper dago's trick," said Welfare. He paused to sip a glass of hot milk and brandy which he had prescribed for himself, and which certainly seemed to revive him in a remarkable degree.

"It was quite dark in that passage," he continued. "I stood about half way up it, wondering would you have got my message. It seemed a long time waiting, but at last I heard the door open and shut, and then footsteps coming very quietly on. I flashed an electric torch to show I was there, and the footsteps stopped. I waited, and then as I heard no more I went up the passage searching it with the torch.

"Presently I saw someone crouching at the side. 'Is that Jakoub?' I asked, but there was no answer. 'It's all right,' I said, 'it's me, Captain Ringrose,' which was the name he knew me by. Then he seemed to take a little run, stooping like an animal; I saw the glint of a knife, and he was on me. I don't rightly know how things happened then. Them natives always strike at your neck. Either I ducked or I happened to knock his hand up, but I felt the knife ripping my scalp. 'You rob me, devil, I kill you,' he says in a kind of snarl, as I closed on him, and then by good luck I got his wrist in my left hand. He twisted round me like a snake, but I used my weight and crushed him against the side of the passage. I knew he was struggling to get the knife in his other hand. He gave another twist and was almost free, but I managed to hold his wrist, and I felt both bones of his arm snap, but that didn't quieten him, and then I got my right hand on his throat.

"I knew my strength would go in a minute with the blood I was losing, and if I didn't quiet him I was done for. I felt him stiffen like a steel spring as I gripped his throat. Then a buzzing came in my ears. He went limp like, and we fell together, me still holding him.

"I suppose the fainting stopped my bleeding for a bit. Anyhow I came to, and Jakoub was still there half under me. He wasn't breathing, and the blood started pumping out of my cut again, so I knotted my scarf as tight as I could over it and kept quiet to give it a chance of stopping. I felt about for the torch and found it, but it was broken. I was very giddy and sick, and I think I went over again. I seemed to be there a long while in the dark, and Jakoub never stirred. I put a hand on his face. His mouth was open, and his cheeks were dead cold."

Captain Welfare paused, exhausted by his long statement. Nobody spoke, or questioned him while he took another drink. The end of the story was already clear to us, and Edmund, of course, had already been told. The long intrigue of infamy had ended in battle, murder and sudden death.

Captain Welfare was evidently distressed at our silence, interpreting it as meaning condemnation.

"I think, gentlemen," he continued, "you will see it was self-defence. I didn't mean him no harm, I was there to help him. But he meant doing me in right enough, and very nearly did. I could do nothing for him myself, but I tried to get help for him in case there was a chance still. I started to crawl for the house, as I thought, but I had lost my bearings, and when I came round a bend I saw the moonlight at the other end of the passage. Then the bleeding broke out again and I had to wait. Half an hour I should think I waited, and when I got back to Jakoub there was no mistake about it any more. He was dead right enough. But I swear, my lord, if I never speak another word, it was self-defence. I didn't mean to kill him. I didn't want to kill him. What did he want to kill me for?"

"As far as I am concerned," said the bishop, "I accept your word absolutely. It is a heavy misfortune, especially for you, but there is certainly no blame attaching to you. If I remember rightly the wretched man said something about you just as he left us."

"Yes," said Edmund, "'this is a trap of Captain Ringrose,' or something of that sort."

"He always thought that I was against him. I had to watch him, and I often caught him out trying to cheat us."

"But all this must have happened hours ago, Welfare," I exclaimed, "why did you wait so long?"

"Why, you see, sir, it took me a long time to get to this end of the passage. When I got to the door I did not know whether the police would be in the house or not. I thought, if I try to get in while they are there we shall all be ruined. So I determined to wait until—well, until I was really afraid I could not afford to bleed any more. But I'll be all right now. The question is, what are we to do about it?"

"Unless we decide to own up to the whole thing," Edmund argued, "we shall have to carry him out and leave him under the cliff. They will think he has fallen over in the dark."

Welfare shook his head slowly.

"That would not do," he said, "I could not see him in the dark, but there will be no mistake about the marks I have left on his throat. It wouldn't take a doctor to tell he was strangled. They would be bound to trace back to the passage, and then ask how he got there and who killed him."

An idea came into my mind, but I forbore to utter it. It seemed to me to come in the guise of temptation; temptation to use this catastrophe to further our own ends.

"We might take a boat and bury him at sea," Welfare suggested.

This was so like my own idea, that I looked around to see how the others took it. The bishop had been sitting in silent meditation. He now rose, and stood with his hands clasped behind him looking down on us with an expression of great sadness.

"Why not bury him where he is?" he asked. It was my own idea, and I gasped to hear it propounded by him.

"This wretched man's life," he continued, "was forfeit to the law. Had the law taken him alive the law could only have slain him. That has been done as a result of his own wickedness and folly. Of what use is it to hand over his dead body to the law? He wrought enough mischief in his life. His dead body would but work more. It would involve some at least of us in utter ruin at the hands of the law. A ruin that none has deserved in such measure. I counsel you, Davoren, to let the wretched business end here. The man was not of our faith, so could not claim Christian burial or consecrated ground. But he was a human being and shall not be buried like a dog."

There was again silence among us, a silence quickened with apprehension. It became clear to me that the idea that had germinated in my own mind had only seemed to be tainted with guilt because my soul was not seated high enough for clear moral judgment. The intrinsic rightness of the thing was manifest now that Parminter had placed it in the clear light of an honest man's independent decision.

As it happened Welfare became our spokesman and his primitive outlook on life was the one thing needed to express the attitude of each one of us.

"If this seems the straight thing to your lordship," he said, "it's good enough for me. I would not have suggested it, because I seem to be coming out too cheap. It wasn't murder, because it was self-defence. But I'd be bound to own up to manslaughter."

"Don't you think, Captain Welfare, that you ought to get to bed?" I asked. I was really concerned about the man, but I wanted to get rid of him too.

"Thank you, sir. But there is no need. If you don't mind, I'd rather see the job through now."

It was impossible for me to protest. After all he was my guest. Nevertheless what I ought to have regarded as his indomitable courage appeared to me mere want of tact. His presence made any communion between the bishop and myself an utter impossibility. I wanted to talk to the bishop alone and Welfare's presence was something I resented in a great tragic moment of my life. I fear I suspected in him the love of the lower middle class for anything in the nature of a funeral.

Edmund said nothing, but rang the bell.

When Bates came in he whispered to him, and they left together. I knew they had gone to dig Jakoub's grave, and presently the thud of a pickaxe and the sound of shovelling were conveyed to us along the passage and through the floor.

It was weary waiting in that room, listening to those dismal sounds, with Captain Welfare endlessly repeating the same explanations, the same apologies.

Through the open window I heard a rustling in the trees, and then a sudden puff of wind blew the curtains inward and caused the lamp to flare. The long-delayed storm had reached us and the moon was blotted out. There was a sudden splash of rain hard driven by the west wind. I rose to shut the window, and looking out the thought came to me that this darkness and confused rushing of the wind was more natural for the passing of Jakoub's disordered soul than the serene tranquillity that had preceded it. It was as though the west wind had arisen to bear that soul back to the East where alone it could be at home.

One o'clock had struck when Edmund came back, soiled and perspiring, to tell us that all was ready.

Captain Welfare insisted on accompanying us, exhausted as he must have been, and he was helped down the stairs by Edmund.

By the light of a stable lantern we made our way for the last time along the fatal tunnel, and found Bates awaiting us.

The grave was dug close to the far end of the tunnel, and I marvelled at the immense amount of earth that had been removed in little more than an hour.

The body of Jakoub, shrouded in a white sheet, lay on a board beside the grave with ropes in place for lowering it.

The bishop took his place at the head of the grave, facing his congregation of four.

"My friends," he said, "this is a solemn moment which must ever be present in the memory of each of us. The wages of sin is death, and this our brother, who was not the only sinner among us, has paid the penalty. He has drawn his wages in this world. That he may be the only one to pay that penalty is a thought that should humble us who are left behind. We are committing an act for which we should certainly be condemned by the laws of our country, but it is an act for which I take full responsibility. I am sure that it is not only expedient from the worldly point of view, but that it is right. Because to act legally in this matter would cause injustice to be done in the name of justice. I therefore as a priest absolve you from responsibility in this matter, and I counsel you to pray for the forgiveness of God for the wrong that each of us may have done. Whether my judgment in this matter is right will be proved by the event. If this night's event should bring any of you to lead a better life and to serve God while you still have opportunity, I shall be sure that my action has God's blessing upon it. This man has died in his sin and without the faith that supports and consoles a Christian. But it is not for us to place limits on the mercy of Almighty God. Let us offer a silent prayer that that mercy may be extended to this our brother."

As we continued in reverent silence round the grave a pale gleam of moonlight faintly lit the scene, throwing dark shadows across the excavation and shining mournfully on the white wrapping of the corpse that lay beside us.

Looking out through the opening of the tunnel I saw as in a frame a portion of the sky. The main body of the great storm cloud had passed, and it was followed by a broken, hurrying rear-guard of ragged clouds through which the moon seemed to battle her way to the west, now submerged, now showing pale and dim, like the terrified face of a swimmer emerging between the waves of a heavy sea.

At a sign from the bishop the body of Jakoub was lowered into the grave. We threw a little soil upon it with the customary words, "Earth to earth, ashes to ashes, dust to dust."

Then as the grave was filled in the bishop repeated one verse from the funeral psalm: "For I am a stranger with thee and a sojourner, as all my fathers were," and then pronounced the benediction.

Thus with reverence and as much ceremony as is permitted by the rubric which prescribes that "the office ensuing shall not be used for any that die unbaptised or excommunicate," the body of Jakoub was committed to the earth, and his stormy passage through life ended almost within the precincts of my quiet Sussex vicarage.

As we parted for the night to get what rest we could, I felt that my tranquillity was at last restored. I could think almost kindly of Jakoub, for I believed that with him had gone the malign influence that had darkened Edmund's life and threatened to destroy his character.

CHAPTER 19

CONCLUSION

I HAVE done what I needed to do for my own satisfaction by putting in the form of a consecutive narrative the peculiar and perhaps sometimes unseemly transactions which have now been recorded.

I had only a fragmentary diary, occasional notes of conversations written while the spoken words were still fresh and vibrant in my memory, and my own recollection of events.

I dreaded lest the latter might fade as I grew older, and that loose leaves of manuscript might be lost or destroyed before I had even in my own mind a clear perspective of happenings that were often so bewildering to me while I dwelt in the midst of them.

I desire especially that Edmund's children may some day have an opportunity of appraising the truth about their father's youth, if it should happen that any aspersions should ever be cast upon his character. For I do believe in children knowing the truth about their parents. Filial love, without any opportunity for comparison and just criticism, seems to me but a hollow tradition, liable to collapse at the first whiff of truth.

I think no child of Edmund's need ever be ashamed of his father. His experience, his peculiar faculties and personality, have enabled him to render very signal and special services to his country in developing the waterways of Africa. In all his letters to me he apologises for the reputation he has gained, which he says is entirely due to the practical sagacity and knowledge of detail with which Welfare supplies him. Edmund has already been presented with a C.M.G., but Welfare's name is unknown.

Yet I happen to know that Welfare is an exceedingly contented man. In a recent letter he tells me, "I am able to save a third of my pay, and if I don't marry at the finish I shall have a few hundreds to leave where I shall die happy in leaving it. I have the work I am suited with, under the finest chief a man ever served. I have been baptised into the Church out here, but not until I was able to send a decent present to my father's and my old chapel. They tell me they have cut my name on one of the stones in the wall 'laid by Josiah Welfare.' Well, fancy!"

I reflected that I had never known Welfare's christian name before. But I was glad it was engraved on the old dry-salter's place of worship.

I have had a visit from Brogden, while he was on leave. He told me that Jakoub's disappearance from my house had become one of the mysteries not only of Egypt but of Scotland Yard. I had hard work to resist the desire to confess, but since that was impossible, I compounded by installing a motorcar on my premises during Brogden's stay. When he had gone I sold the atrocious thing at a heavy loss. But Brogden had enjoyed himself, and the financial loss was not enough to salve my conscience completely.

On the other hand, Bates resented the temporary chauffeur, and Mrs. Rattray disliked him. Between them they inflicted on me a penance which I think straightens my moral account with Brogden.

The penance might have been excessive only that Edmund's fiancée is the daughter of a fairly near neighbour, an ex-commissioner under whom Edmund had served. She is now constantly here awaiting Edmund's return. Bates and Mrs. Rattray are completely subjugated by her. She settled the matter of the chauffeur and got rid of him with a minimum of friction.

She makes me desperately jealous of Edmund, but I endeavour to realise that I belong to a bygone generation, that I am become, in fact, a "dear old thing."

Jakoub's bones are unlikely now to be disturbed. They are honoured by having a vault as well as a grave for their repose. For the smuggler's passage has been sealed up by solid masonry at either end. It will never be opened again in my lifetime, and I hope it is now closed for ever.

The bishop spent an evening with me recently, and I showed him parts of this manuscript.

"As far as I know the story," he said, "you have been very accurate. When I look back upon what has happened, especially on my own part in the affair, I am reminded of a phrase of yours—'I can look my conscience in the face.' What a waste it would have been if your brother had become a mere hanger-on to your charity, after undergoing 'prison discipline.' Whenever I think of him and of what might have happened to him, I think of those words of the psalmist, 'Though ye have lien among the pots, yet shall ye be as the wings of a dove, whose wings are covered with silver, and her feathers like gold.'"